OUR FAR FLUNG BATTLE LINE

OTHER BOOKS IN THE
H. BEDFORD-JONES UNIFORM
EDITION LIBRARY:

Abel Smith of Nantucket

Bellegarde

*The King Makers: The Complete
Adventures of Vincent Connor*

The Sphinx Strikes

Treasure Seekers

Will O' the Wisp

H. BEDFORD-JONES

OUR FAR FLUNG BATTLE LINE

H. BEDFORD-JONES

ALTUS PRESS • 2015

EDITED AND DESIGNED BY
Matthew Moring

PUBLISHING HISTORY

"Fast Work in Casablanca" originally appeared in the March 10, 1943 issue of *Short Stories* magazine (Vol. 182 No. 5).

"Loot of the Solomons" originally appeared in the March 25, 1943 issue of *Short Stories* magazine (Vol. 182 No. 6).

"All Quiet on the Tanker Front" originally appeared in the April 10, 1943 issue of *Short Stories* magazine (Vol. 183 No. 1).

"The Old Man of Iceland" originally appeared in the April 25, 1943 issue of *Short Stories* magazine (Vol. 183 No. 2).

"A Wolf in Wolf's Clothing" originally appeared in the May 10, 1943 issue of *Short Stories* magazine (Vol. 183 No. 3).

"Brazil Is in the War, Too" originally appeared in the May 25, 1943 issue of *Short Stories* magazine (Vol. 183 No. 4).

"A Toast in Water" originally appeared in the June 10, 1943 issue of *Short Stories* magazine (Vol. 183 No. 5).

"Nagasaki Scotch" originally appeared in the June 25, 1943 issue of *Short Stories* magazine (Vol. 183 No. 6).

"Second Generation" originally appeared in the July 10, 1943 issue of *Short Stories* magazine (Vol. 184 No. 1).

"Red Sea Boat Ride" originally appeared in the July 25, 1943 issue of *Short Stories* magazine (Vol. 184 No. 2).

"One Day in Trinidad" originally appeared in the August 10, 1943 issue of *Short Stories* magazine (Vol. 184 No. 3).

"Bombs and Olive Oil" originally appeared in the August 25, 1943 issue of *Short Stories* magazine (Vol. 184 No. 4).

THANKS TO
Everard P. Digges LaTouche and Gerd Pircher

TABLE OF CONTENTS

I

FAST WORK IN CASABLANCA

*…and Secret Agents, Particularly Nazi
Agents, Were a Dime a Dozen.*

TRIM, ERECT, aware that he was shadowed by Crepin's best men, Denis Burke strode across the Place de France. It was close to ten at night, but for Casablanca the evening had just opened up. A queer place, Casablanca, in those dying days of the dying Vichy regime; and by no means a safe place for an American agent.

The miserably aged city was neither old nor Moroccan, in the sense of the ancient barbaric beauty that makes other cities of this land heart-warming. A manufactured, synthetic city, it had grown up around the great port that served the whole West African coast. It was a hodge-podge of the worst of Rabat and Marseilles and Marrakech and Senegal, thrown together haphazard: it was no place to be fond of.

Of late it had grown sinister, as Burke was well aware; he himself was one of these sinister elements. Because Burke knew this country of old, because he could be of tenfold more use here than in khaki, and because the touch of gray at his temples told its own tale, here he was. Here, too, was the same crowd he had seen in Lisbon and Madrid and elsewhere. Casablanca swarmed with them. Twenty minutes after landing, he had seen von Grave, for instance. Secret agents, and particularly Nazi agents, were a dime a dozen here.

Tonight he was happy with work well done, and his debonair manner showed it. He had been dining with Arab friends. Crepin of the French Intelligence would have given his eye-teeth for the knowledge now in Burke's head; the news still had to be passed on—a minor detail. Two minutes would see it done.

The evening was beginning. This commercial city where eighty thousand Moors rubbed elbows with as many Europeans, where the Parisian shops maintained gay branches, where sailormen from the seven seas found diversion, was all astir. The little Place de France, so tiny as scarce to show on the map alongside the Parc Lyautey or the Murdoch Gardens, was in reality the pulsing heart of all western Morocco. In the cafés surrounding it were settled staggering business deals, politics, espionage affairs, and all sorts of private rascality. On one side opened the gates of the Old Medina, the vast rabbit-warren of the native city; and opposite was the Excelsior Hotel, not the newest hostelry but the one preferred by Burke.

The square itself hummed with pedestrians, automobiles, soldiers, Arabs, motor busses. Somewhere a Senegalese drum and fife corps was filling the night with squeals and thudding drumbeats. Burke turned in at the Excelsior entrance, and there stood Si' Dris, bulky and fat and ornately garbed, and very black.

This doorman, long years ago, had gone to America as a groom with circus horses, and had remained overseas a long time. Now he called himself an American; he was extremely capable, and was a link in the undercover chain Burke had forged.

He saluted impressively as Burke paused.

"There is a man here, sidi, who arrived by air from Algiers this evening," he said. "Twice he has telephoned Captain Crepin, but has been unable to reach him."

"So? Well, here's work, and fast work." Burke passed him a penciled message. "Have your brother send this at once on his short wave radio to the Algiers address."

Si' Dris pocketed the note. "Within the hour, sidi."

"Make it faster than that, if you can. It's urgent!"

"Within the half-hour, then. One thing more! A man and

his wife arrived and took a room; they came from Marrakech."
Si'Dris spoke the word in the manner of the country, "Marrak'sh,"
the word from which was derived the name of Morocco. This
was the ancient capital of the south, where the Pasha el Glaoui
ruled mountains and desert and seacoast under French aus-
pices. "The name is Dupont; nothing is known of them."

Burke nodded and passed on. Dupont from Marrakech; the
doorman thought the pair worth noting, or would not have
mentioned them. Another of the sinister elements centering
here, perhaps. Well, Marrakech was in the bag now, and the
hell with Nazi agents!

The writing room and parlors, which did duty as lobby, were
gay and noisy. Burke, in no haste to seek his room, made himself
comfortable at one end of a lounge and scribbled a note to the
U. S. consular agent in Algiers—just in case that short wave
message did not get through. It was hard to keep his brown,
aquiline features and glowing dark eyes from showing the wild
exultation that spurred his heart-beats.

At dinner this evening he had met a son of El Glaoui; the
bargain was concluded. They all thought Burke was acting in
British or Fighting French interests, of course. No one dreamed
that Americans might occupy this country. El Glaoui feared

and hated the Nazis, feared and hated Vichy. Yes, said he; provided the Allies occupied Casablanca and the little ports north and south, they could count on Marrakech. The French navy and the Foreign Legion might oppose; but he, the great Berber chieftain, could assure them a welcome—if first they took the seaports away from the French!

Burke chuckled to himself as he signed and sealed the code message, and stamped it.

"Lord, what a stroke to pull! And he doesn't dream how close the time's running. I'd better pull out of here before the blow falls, and get to Fez. Hm! I'll have to wangle it with Crepin, somehow. That fellow certainly keeps a sharp eye on me."

Denis Burke, in humorous vein, was taking orders for typewriters and Chicago pianos and harvesting machinery, for postwar delivery. He even had order books, printed order forms and so on. Captain Crepin knew better. Twice Burke had been interned, twice he had been set free. He knew that von Grave was working like a devil to have him put away for keeps.

Out of Casablanca—the thought was good. He hated this place, which was neither French nor Moorish. In the other Moroccan cities where each kept its individuality and the new French towns were distinct entities, by the plans of the wise Lyautey, things were different. There a man knew where he stood, especially if he had native friends. But Casablanca, alive with Nazis, was just a mess. Looking about the lobby, Burke could count four obvious squareheads in full sight. Half a dozen Nazi missions were in these parts, too.

He sighed, snuffed out his cigarette, and went to the elevator. As he ascended to the fourth floor, he resolved to see Crepin in the morning and try to get away to Fez if possible.

Even with his work done, he felt nervous here. Damn von Grave! That chap was too clever by half; he had the inhuman, soulless Nazi eyes, too. Perhaps he knew or guessed that Denis Burke was an American undercover agent.

As Burke inserted the key in his own room door, he paused.

It was ten o'clock, to the minute; he could hear the hour struck from the clock-tower in the square, just across from the hotel. Then he heard something else. He paused, listening, leaving the key unturned. It came again; his sharpened senses caught the direction. It came from the room directly opposite. A groan? Impossible; such a sound would not come through a closed door....

But the door opposite was not closed. He went to it and saw that it stood open an inch. It had slammed and bounded open, as did his own at times, and no key had been turned. As he stood there, he sniffed. Something burning; wool. Burke shoved at the door, and the odor became stronger. The groan came again.

BURKE SHOVED the door full open upon a dark room, across which pierced a shaft of light from a bathroom door, half open. He stepped inside, switched on the lights; and then, quickly, closed the door behind him.

Like all the rooms in this comfortable old hotel, this one was high-ceiled, the walls being tiled shoulder-high in gay patterns. Close to the bathroom door, Burke saw a man lying on his face, motionless, covered only by a dressing-gown. Between this figure and the bed, to the right of the bathroom door, was a curly-thick Berber rug. From this rug was ascending the smoke and the odor of smouldering wool.

Burke stepped swiftly to it. In the red, slowly widening patch showed a length of grayish ash, quite distinct to the eye. He left this untouched, as he stamped out the spreading circle of red that was eating through the mass of dyed wool; it was not by chance that he did so. Denis Burke was trained in the handling of tiny details.

Only now, when he turned to the prostrate figure and knelt, did he see the blood on the man's neck. He touched the shaven cheek, then felt the outflung right wrist; in that hand was still clenched a bath-towel. The pulse was fluttering. From the lips almost against the floor came another groan and a mutter of words.

"*Les Americans!* Tell Crepin—the Americans—it is the Americans—American general and staff came by—by submarine—Algiers—"

The pulse fluttered again under Burke's finger, and abruptly stilled. With the harsh sighing breath of that final word, the unknown man was dead. That he had been struck down as he left the bathroom, was obvious. Burke glanced around, and suddenly froze.

Lying on the floor close by was a heavy walking-stick, a knotted, loaded stick; it was his own stick, the silver plate upon it bore his own name, and blood was smeared over it. He had last seen it in his room before he went out; only by chance had he not taken it. He stared at it, incredulous, until a fit of coughing seized him. The fumes of the burning wool filled the place.

Rising, he went to the window. Even in Morocco, the French believe that it is certain death to sleep with a window open. Coughing again from the pungent odor, Burke opened the window and drank in the cold night air. From a café came a lilt of music—the waltz movement from Tchaikovsky's string serenade. It filled his ears, as sharper thoughts filled his brain.

The Americans! This was the man who had arrived by plane, who had tried and failed to telephone Crepin. The Americans! Was the secret out, then? But how had his own stick come here, as damning accusation of brutal murder?

Burke fairly jumped. A rap was at the door; then a voice, brisk, imperative.

"Gaspard! Gaspard!" It was Captain Crepin's voice. "Open!"

In a flash, Burke realized what it meant for him to be found here—but there was no evasion. Before he could think or move, the unlocked door was flung open. Crepin appeared on the threshold, staring at the scene.

Even in mufti, Crepin looked the soldier—stiff, erect, grayish mustache clipped close above his thin lips. A capable man, vividly intelligent, with eyes wholly alive.

"So, M. Burke!" he said quietly. "In the very act, eh?"

"I was only a moment ahead of you," Burke observed, "as you no doubt learned down below. This man died as I knelt beside him, murmuring your name. You know him?"

His assumption of perfect calm was masterly. Crepin stepped forward, produced a pistol, knelt, touched the outflung wrist. His eyes went to the knotted stick, the name on the silver plate, flicked back to Burke as he stood up. Burke shook his head.

"Careful, now! I am here, blood on my hands, and my loaded stick, which is an illegal weapon, beside the body—it's a good thing you're not an impetuous man, Crepin. You know him, I presume?"

"Certainly," said Crepin. "Your nerve is excellent, m'sieu. This is Gaspard Boulhaut, of the Intelligence, a member of the staff of Admiral Darlan, now in Algiers. He is a friend of mine. Learning of his arrival, I came to find him—and I find you. It is unfortunate for you, Mr. Burke."

"I'd not say that," rejoined Burke cheerfully. "Rather, it may prove fortunate for you that I'm here." His gaze drove about the room. "Hello! Some odd details here—look at his clothes! Half on the bed, half on the floor, jumbled up every which way, not as a man puts them down on taking them off!"

Crepin stepped to the bed and eyed the mad jumble of garments. He put out a hand and began to search them; he picked up a belt to which was attached a small pouch, empty and with the flap dangling.

"Where is it?" he snapped at Burke. "Hand it over at once—"

"Easy, my dear Captain," said Burke, his eyes alight. He knelt and swiftly examined Boulhaut's wound and the tiled floor around, then came erect. "Now it begins to come clear, Crepin! Give me five minutes, I beg of you. Five minutes will matter little to your friend here, but much to us. First, listen to me."

He briefly told how he had come to be in the room, while Crepin regarded him steadily. Then the Frenchman spoke.

"It is hard to think of you as a liar, M. Burke, but—"

"Look at this lamp." Burke pointed to a tabouret with an unlighted lamp on it, just to the left of the bathroom door. "Here's what happened in this room! Your Gaspard was taking a bath; rather, a shower, because the drip can still be heard. On this floor of the hotel it continues for a long time after the water is turned off. He dried himself, got into his gown, and lit a cigarette. He then caught up a towel with which to dry his hair, which is still soaking wet—and started into the bedroom. As he crossed the threshold, he was struck down in the act of reaching for this light-switch by the bathroom door. He was struck by the stand of this lamp on the tabouret here. Now give me a minute longer—"

Ignoring the puzzled, suspicious Crepin, he went toward the room door and caught up a key he had seen lying on the tiles. He gave it a swift examination, sniffed the air, pulled open the closet door close by, and looked in. It was empty except for a suitcase partly unpacked and in great disorder.

Burke stepped into the closet, nearly closed the door, and an exclamation broke from him. He came out again, rubbing his cheek and smelling his fingers.

"Crepin, you seem to know what is missing; I don't. However, let me reconstruct the scene for you. While Gaspard was bathing—in fact, as soon as he turned on his shower, which can be heard running by anyone out in the hall—two people entered his room by means of a skeleton key. These are old-fashioned French locks in which the key must turn twice."

"Oh!" said Crepin. "They used a skeleton—while this door key was in the lock?"

Burke extended the key he had picked up.

"Here's your friend's doorkey; examine it closely. Those tiny scratches at the end show a pocket-knife was used to turn it in the lock and push it clear; it dropped inside. The two entered with their skeleton. The man was full six feet, wearing a dark suit; he was a tall, powerful man, who wore pince-nez and was left-handed. The woman was shorter; a brunette about five feet eight, young, handsomely dressed, and a cool hand at this sort of thing. Both were professional hotel rats—or else adepts at crime. They did not intend to kill Gaspard, and when they left did not know he was mortally hurt."

"I am only too well acquainted with your audacity, M. Burke," said Crepin with sardonic mien, "and therefore I must doubt your fairy story—"

Burke smiled. "Oh, my surprises aren't finished! But one thing at a time. First, the woman. If you'll step into that closet, you'll notice a distinct odor of Beaujolais, one of the most expensive of perfumes; only a young and handsome woman would indulge in it, and certainly not your friend Gaspard.

"Upon entering, she slipped into the closet to examine his suitcase. Later she pulled the door nearly shut, watching through the crack, pressing her cheek against the door—look at my hand! Do you see the smear of fresh rouge? She must have put it on thickly, thus has dark hair and a natural pallor; a blonde would use a lighter rouge, and sparingly. All this would indicate that the couple had just finished dressing for the evening."

Crepin went to the closet door and investigated it.

"Name of a name!" he exclaimed. "Go on, by all means. You interest me, m'sieu."

"Thank you." Burke was working for his life now, and knew it. With every sense on the alert, he plunged ahead. "The man went over to the bed, searching the clothes there; when, unexpectedly, Gaspard finished his shower and lit his cigarette. The woman stuck close in the closet. The man darted to the side of the bathroom door—to the right side. The cord of that brass lamp on the tabouret is disconnected; he pulled it loose, grasping the little lamp as a weapon, in his left hand. Gaspard came into the room, reaching with one hand for the light switch, holding the cigarette in his left hand. Our left-handed man hit him with the lamp, whose base struck him at the base of the skull. At the shock, the cigarette flew from his fingers and fell on the Berber rug, to the left of the doorway. It was not noticed."

Crepin, his alert eyes showing interest, shook his head slightly.

"No, no, my American friend; that is sheer fantasy!"

"Devil a bit. Look where I stamped out the smoulder; in the center of the burned patch you'll see the ash of the cigarette where it burned out. Wool is very slow to catch from such a source; the intruders were gone before the smell became noticeable."

CREPIN EXAMINED the burned patch in the rug.

"Hm! Decidedly, you are doing well," he observed. "You say your stick was not used?"

"Definitely not," went on Burke, who was now actually enjoying himself. "To strike such a blow, the assassin was tall and powerful. Seeing the blood, the woman slipped out and went into my room; perhaps she had previously been there. I was evidently known to them. She brought my stick.

"You will observe that it was merely smeared with Gaspard's blood; it does not fit the wound and the lamp-base does."

Crepin, putting his pistol away, was already at work testing this theory. He spent some time at it, thoroughly satisfying himself.

"*Tiens, tiens!*" he exclaimed. "The base of the lamp—ha! Hairs upon it; and it fits the wound." He looked up at Burke. "Monsieur, I must apologize!"

"Oh, I'm not through!" said Burke. "When I first heard the groans, I had just put my key into my door; it is still there, unturned. When I left this evening, I first meant to take this stick of mine, then tossed it on the bed and left it. There should still be the mark of it on the bed, which was freshly made. Come along and convince yourself."

He led the way across the hall. Crepin unlocked his door. They entered; Burke switched on the lights, and the impression of the weighted stick was clearly seen on the bed.

"Right," said Crepin. "Well, I am amazed! Also, delighted, by your shrewdness!"

"Spoken like a gentleman," said Burke, smiling. "What is missing from Gaspard's belt? Money?"

"No. I presume, dispatches," said Crepin thoughtfully. "Orders. I cannot tell. You say he spoke my name? Nothing else?"

"A few disconnected words. Something about 'Les Americains' and Algiers," Burke replied carelessly. He was satisfied that the words meant nothing to Crepin, and breathed more freely.

"Hm! You say the assassin wore pince-nez. Your reason for this?"

Burke grinned. "Go look under the edge of Gaspard's bed, by his clothes. A pair of glasses fell there and broke on the tiles. Some of the glass remains."

With an exclamation, Crepin darted off.

Left alone, Burke wiped his forehead and relaxed, smoking thoughtfully. He was well out of a jam; but it had taken concentration. What was this about an American general in Algiers? And this dead Gaspard must have come with some word from Admiral Darlan. The devil! Then the great push must be close, close! And there was work in Fez that must be done. The huge new aerodrome was there—

Crepin came back, beaming.

"My friend, you are uncanny!" he exclaimed. "But who knew that Gaspard was here?"

"Plenty of Nazis around," said Burke. "By the way, a couple from Marrakech arrived here this evening, strangers at the hotel. Not necessarily strangers in Casablanca. The name is Dupont. It's only a long shot but might bear investigation. I guessed that this pair in Gaspard's room had just dressed for the evening. Where does von Grave live in town?"

Crepin gave him a slow, hard look and dropped into a chair.

"The devil! Von Grave has an apartment on Boulevard Emile Zola."

"Would this precious pair go there, to him?"

"Not likely," mused Crepin. "Hm! This thing would be done carefully. Von Grave is a smart man. Hm! They arrive this evening, eh? They would have an appointment with him, say, for midnight. Neither they nor he would know exactly when their chance to get at Gaspard would come. So a safe hour would be set."

"Good thinking," approved Burke. "And where would the meeting take place? Ten to one at the most prominent place in the city—"

"Ha! Of course! The Roi de la Biere, on the square below!" broke out the Frenchman. "The best restaurant in town—they would go there, dine, dance—ha, let us put all this to the proof! Will you accompany me?"

"As a friend or as a suspect?" inquired Burke quizzically.

"As an American, m'sieu. Me, I have no love for Vichy, but I obey orders, and always I have liked Americans."

"Agreed."

Ten minutes later, they were sitting in the office of the hotel manager. Jean G. and Madame Dupont, of Marrakech, answered the description of the couple in question; Dupont had worn glasses, at least upon his arrival. They were not in their room. They had gone out, in fact; Dupont had made inquiries at the desk about the New Medina. Yes, they were dressed for the evening.

The New Medina or native city lay over behind the Sultan's palace, and was a very modern place of amusement for visitors, not unlike Chinatown in New York only worse. Sleuh dancers, brothels, huge tearooms, offered entertainment to man and beast, chiefly the latter; visitors with low tastes went slumming there at every opportunity, for it was a place where life in the raw abounded.

They went over to chairs in a corner of the writing room, and smoked.

"It is humiliating to confess," said Crepin, now extremely friendly, "but this von Grave has powerful influence; you understand."

Burke nodded. "Yes. You must be sure before you grab him. Or can you grab him at all?"

"Since this is a case of murder, yes. Even so, he'll slip out of our hands."

"Are you going to make this a police case?"

"No," said Crepin. "No. It is purely military. Let us see, first, whether we can find the assassins, No use bothering at the New Medina. Von Grave would not meet them there; they have gone to kill time before their appointment, I believe. Suppose we meet here in an hour, then drop around to the Roi de la Biere? I have some arrangements to make."

"Right. Here, in an hour."

CREPIN DEPARTED. Burke looked up the doorman, only to find that Si' Dris had been replaced by another man, so he went back to his room and wrote out a carefully phrased radiogram addressed to Chicago. If it got through the censor here, it would ultimately reach American headquarters in England; nothing was certain. Probably the only thing to get through would be the short-wave message via the brother of Si' Dris.

Despite careful scrutiny, Burke had found no evidence of visitors to his room; they had been skillful, certainly, in searching his effects. They had been clever, too, in seizing the opportunity to get rid of him. Von Grave must assuredly want him out of the way!

Burke fell into musing retrospect. Behind him were roving years, aimless wandering, odd jobs and placements; all sheer and utter waste of life, he had so often thought. And then, in a flash, this work for which the past might well have been pointed preparation. His friendships with these natives, who

so proudly called themselves Arabs yet were often of the darkest
Moorish strain; his knowledge of them and their country and
their language. Already he had accomplished marvelous things,
looking toward that amazing occupation of which as yet he
scarcely dared dream. Life, no longer wasted, beckoned warmly
to him now. He was ten years younger than he had been a year
ago. He was not a drifter, an idler, now.

But Casablanca—ugh! This was different, this ugly city that
lacked all the finest values either French or native. From his
hotel window he could look out across the native cemetery to
the Douane and the plage, to the port inside the two breakwa-
ters, and the wide Atlantic beyond. The massive Jean Bart lay
there, and other lesser vessels of the hapless Vichy navy.

He glanced suddenly at his watch and sprang up. Time had
come!

Crepin was waiting for him downstairs and, unhurried, motioned him to a chair. He realized now that he was a full partner;
this Intelligence man like him, trusted him. The knowledge
gave him a thrill.

"Our friend Dupont," said Crepin, "has a small garage business in Marrakech. His wife is an alert young woman of German
parentage. He is, in short, one of those parasites that have caused
us so much ill; both of them. She apparently has the brains."

"So our theory looks sound, eh?"

Crepin nodded, not hopefully. "I have men watching other
places; we'll look after the Roi de la Biere. We had better be
separate, not together. I think we'll both be watched; the devil
fly away with this town! It is full of human fleas. I'll go ahead.
You come."

Crepin departed. And Gaspard Boulhaut, thought Burke,
still lay dead and untended in his upstairs room.

The King of Beer, despite its gay murals picturing a jolly
Gambrinus, was eloquent of the forced and false jollity these
sad days had brought to Vichy France. When Burke passed
through the outer café where soldiers and Arabs sat sipping

and talking at the tables, and then on into the sacred precincts of the beery king himself, Morocco fell behind him. Here was poor tawdry France—smoke and music, shrill voices, dim lights, cocottes, shabby gaity, fewer Frenchmen than foreigners.

He found a table. Of Crepin he could see nothing. A pinch-faced waiter with angry eyes took his order and he settled back to survey the scene, ignoring the inviting eyes and smiles of half-caste girls. Almost at once he saw von Grave; the Nazi was dancing with a willowy and overdressed charmer to whom he paid assiduous attention. He was a man of forty, quietly attired, tall, with bony features and direct, challenging gaze.

Von Grave was the host, it appeared, at a large table seating a number of naval officers and several men in the midnight blue of the aviation. Burke watched them idly; he was worried over his own problem—that message from Algiers. Something about *les Americains.* He had no objection to seeing it reach Crepin, but to see it pass into Nazi hands was very different. What action he might take, what Crepin intended, was all hazy to him.

The table adjoining his was vacated by a maudlin seaman in tow of a frizzy-haired cocotte. It was cleared and rearranged; a "reserved" placard was placed on it. Still no sign of Crepin anywhere. Von Grave's willowy charmer, amid tremendous ovations, sang a song with the orchestra; from the comments it appeared that she was some well-known actress or cantatrice. Von Grave ordered champagne for his entire table and the noise redoubled.

Then they came.

Burke suddenly saw them coming to the adjoining table—a grubby, powerful man with reddish mustache, and a woman beautiful as the dawn in this shoddy assemblage. She was small, exquisite, daringly attired in flame and white, with an aigrette and turban. The two paused at the table, then went on to the dancing square. Burke, who never said no to the appeal of beauty, watched her with open admiration. She had the grace of a nymph in every movement and gesture; her petite, radiant face was that of a child.

"She watched while Gaspard was murdered!" lifted a sudden voice in his brain, startling and abrupt. Like an icy douche, it chilled him. "She is Crepin's affair—leave her alone! Your business lies elsewhere."

He sighed and drank his wine. Intrigue and beauty, wits pitted against sharp wits, with death the table stakes—he loved such a game and was fitted for it. But this night the game had run its course; in that room with the dead man, he had met her and whipped her. It was over.

They came back to their table, oblivious of him. Yet he knew they must know him by sight and must be aware of him. His gaze lingered down the room. Von Grave had risen and was coming, a moth to the flame. He approached, he saw Burke and smiled, nodding amiably in greeting, and came to the adjoining table.

He bowed over the woman's hand, and very correctly—not kissing it like a boor, but touching it to his lips. A tiny detail only Burke would have appreciated. Burke was looking away from them, his senses focused upon them, as one watches a star by looking aside from it. Suddenly he inched his chair back from the table; his muscles gathered, he sat taut and ready.

Von Grave, at Dupont's urging, took a chair and sat down; his back was to Burke, and the woman was on his left. Beside her plate was a small gold mesh-bag. She had laid it there, open, its mouth gaping. She was not a woman who did things by accident.

No sign of Crepin. Eyes will be watching, Crepin had said; no sign of watching eyes. The devil! And Gaspard dead for nothing, his message lost?

THE RADIANT little woman was talking. As she finished her story and leaned back, her arm brushed the gold mesh-beg and it fell from the table edge to the floor. Von Grave leaned over to retrieve it.

But Burke dove like a sparrow-hawk. He was on it, his foot knocked the Nazi's arm aside, he had it! And in that flashing instant, his fingers scooped out the sole contents—a small, thick, padded little envelope, just such a one as might have fitted the belt-pouch of Gaspard. He palmed it, came erect, and with a smiling bow handed the bag to the radiant woman.

Radiant no longer, but pale, startled, wide-eyed. Von Grave was on his feet. His voice burst in fury. He reached out and caught Burke's arm.

"Empty!" cried the woman—in German. "It is gone!"

"You rascally American!" broke forth von Grave. He had detected the motion, the truth. "Thief! Here, someone—police! A thief, a thief!"

Burke's fingers were still curling about the tiny packet. Von Grave, clutching him with one hand, was fumbling under his coat with the other.

Burke's free hand was already in action, sliding out, catching up a plate from the table and with the same continuity of motion slamming up the edge of it, hard—slamming it slap against the Nazi's face. Von Grave staggered. His pistol was out, the shot roared, but the bullet went wild.

Denis Burke hit him twice—plunging short-arm blows, hardly visible but low and deadly. Screams and oaths and shouts filled the air. Von Grave gasped and doubled forward; Burke's knee caught him under the chin, straightened him terribly, and he went down. The woman was shrieking, her husband was up and on his feet, others were darting in upon the scene.

Those hurtling figures struck Burke and sent him sprawling; but his fingers were tightly curled on that little packet. Above him pandemonium broke loose—officers, waiters, men in mufti, all striving to get at his prostrate figure. One did, and smashed him over the head with a bottle, and he sank back to the floor.

Then, as by magic, everything cleared. Army uniforms smothered the group. Dupont was seized and held, his wife was a prisoner; von Grave was helped to his feet and handcuffs clicked on his wrists. Crepin, cool, imperturbable and in full charge, was the central figure now. The orchestra had fallen silent; the crowd was brushed away.

Burke dizzily gained his feet, two men gripping him. He extended his hand to Crepin and opened his clenched fingers. Crepin took the little packet, glanced at it, and one exultant flash passed across his face.

"Out!" he ordered. "Everyone. Out! Bring them to military headquarters at the Caserne. M. Burke, come with me. A car is waiting."

Not one car but several waited at the café steps. Burke followed Crepin into a car; the officer spoke to the soldier who was under the wheel.

"Drive to the Caserne by way of the Boulevard du 2me Tirailleurs and Boulevard Ballande; and do not hurry."

The car started off in this long roundabout course. Switching on the overhead light, Crepin examined the little packet. Then Crepin turned off the light.

"My friend, I saw it all; you have the devil's own luck!" he observed. "Yes, this is it. But—*mon Dieu!* It can become public. It must go no farther. Dupont we can pinch; von Grave, perhaps, must go free, and the woman. At least, for a little while. I wish you were out of Casablanca."

"So do I," agreed Burke. He heard the other tearing up paper. "Here! Are you tearing up that message?"

"Precisely. And eating it. If this news is true—if it is true— ah, the imagination reels! Me, I do not love Vichy, but I have my duty. And at Casablanca, you understand, Vichy is powerful. Casablanca will fight any intrusion; the navy will fight."

He was breathing hard, speaking with stifled, muffled words; he was eating the message. Burke asked no questions, for he could guess something of its import. Crepin wanted it to go no farther, and this suited Burke perfectly. He could guess at the startled alarm, the frightful conflict of emotions, sweeping through the soul of this Frenchman.

"If you're going to keep this thing quiet," he asked, "then what can you do?"

"Hold Dupont for murder—until later. Much later. Until, perhaps, things have changed—who knows? You do not fool me, M. Burke. You are no typewriter salesman as you pretend. But me, I ask no questions. I am frightened of the future; where my duty lies, I cannot see. If this news is true—"

HE FELL silent, breathing hard. The car passed the Arsenal and circled around into the Boulevard Ballande that girded the waterfront.

"My job is finished here," Burke said, picking his words. "Where your duty lies, I don't know either. But there's a train at one-thirty for Rabat and Fez—and I wish to hell I was on it!"

Crepin lit a cigarette; his lighter-flame was unsteady. After a moment he leaned forward and drew back the sliding glass partition, speaking to the driver.

"En route to the Caserne, drive down the Avenue Pasteur and stop at the Gare."

He closed the partition and sighed.

"You've just time to make the train," he said. "I'll send your things from the hotel; also, your silver-mounted stick. Bon voyage, my friend!"

Their hands met in the darkness—a quick, understanding clasp eloquent of unuttered things. The Americans were coming, and both men knew it.

II

LOOT OF THE SOLOMONS

*Some Queer Characters Inhabit the Solomons;
and Not All Products of the War.*

BALANCING TO the thrust of the waves, Bill Stumler clung desperately to the wooden grating. It floated him, and no more; he was half-submerged all the time. Now, on every wave-crest, he twisted up his head and looked at the reef, and the land beyond. The current was setting dead for the reef, and it was close. If he took to the water at the right point, he could make it; he gathered his cramped, sodden, exhausted muscles for the effort.

It was a queerly curving reef, beginning a couple of miles away at the land in a high coral ridge that sloped gradually down to the water. There was a reason for this, as he was to learn. On to the left it curved in islets and reef-dots for miles. Where he was, Stumler had not the faintest notion. One of the Solomons northwest of Guadalcanal, was all he knew.

He had been afloat since midnight, washed off the destroyer like a fly in that pitching traverse. A lot of things had washed off, including the grating that had saved him. A lucky guy, he told himself. An admiral, earlier in the war, had washed off in just the same way. The admiral was still a total loss but Bill Stumler, chief pharmacist's mate, was alive and kicking.

"If the Nips are here, I'm dogmeat," he reflected. "If not, I'm old Robinson Crusoe himself. Well, now's the time; here's luck!"

He abandoned the grating with a curse; it had saved him, but before doing so it had knocked out a front tooth, and his lips were cut and puffed from the impact. He was only some thirty feet from shore, and made it neatly. A naked bit of coral and sand that glittered in the morning sunlight, stretching away toward the rising ground of the headland and the trees and mountains beyond.

CRAWLING OUT on the snowy coral sand, warm and alive with sand-fleas that jumped like white beans, he lay in blissful relaxation until he gathered enough strength to strip, and let clothes and pelt dry in the sun. He still wore his pumps because, balanced on the grating, he had been unable to get rid of them.

After a long while he yawned, sat up, then rose and dressed. He stared about in new astonishment. From the water surface, his horizon had been very limited; now, afoot, it had widened. He could see the line of reef curving away for miles, not a tree on the islets; to the east was visible another whopping island of mountains. Lucky he had landed here, where he could get ashore, and not on those islets to the south!

He started along the coral curve toward the headland; it was ebb tide and the wet sand gave firm footing. When he had covered a quarter-mile, the hummocks of coral unfolded and gave him sight of something ahead; it grew, it moved, and he stared at it with increasing amazement. Sure enough, it was a man; more, a white man bearded and naked to the waist. A boat of some sort was drawn up on the sand.

About this time, the other man perceived Stumler and ceased jabbing into the reef-pools with his spear. He mounted to a spur of coral and stared at Stumler, who waved and shouted. The other went to his boat, dropped his spear, caught up a rifle and came to meet the castaway. Stumbler caressed his sore lips and essayed a greeting.

"Hi, pardner! You talk English?"

"Well, blow me!" came the response. The man was brawny, sunburned, with black hair and eyes; he had a savage, hostile air. "Where in the devil's name did you come from?"

"Oh, the Navy dropped me off to look around," said Bill Stumler happily. "Any Japs?"

"Not now, thank the lord. What kind of a sailor are you? Aussie?"

"United States. Didn't you ever see a Navy fancy-dress costume before?"

The other man was still gaping in bewildered amazement.

"But how'd you get here? There wasn't any ship!"

"Durn it, I fell overboard last night and swum ashore. From a destroyer on reconnaissance cruise. Now you've got the dope, so tell me where I am."

"South tip of New Georgia; that island to the east'ard is Vangunu. See here, by heaven! This is amazing! American, you say?" The island man wakened to wild delight and comprehension. "Shake hands, shake hands! My name's Morris. Paddled out to fish the pools. Thought you were a ghost of some kind. How about a bite to eat?"

"I'm sure caved in." Stumler shook hands; Morris pumped his hand, slapped his back, showed yellow teeth in joyous laughter, and led him along to the dugout canoe. Laughing and talking excitedly, he produced some cold grub wrapped in taro leaves, and a gourd of water, then squatted down and watched his guest eat. Bill Stumler was conscious of something more than sinister in that fixed, unwavering gaze, but laid it to the man's unkempt condition. Morris pointed to the pile of speared fish in the canoe.

"We'll cook that ashore. Don't dare light a fire here for fear the smoke 'ud draw the Japs. Haven't seen a white man in ages, except for Jack Smith and that devil Grimm. This is great! Tell me about the war, about everything!"

"You tell me about where I am," said Stumler. They broke into mutual laughter. Morris was an Englishman; had been a trader up at Shortland Island, he said. When the war broke, the Japs caught them at that port of entry for the Solomons. A boatload of refugees got as far as New Georgia and were caught again. Morris and Jack Smith were all that now remained.

"This is Viru Harbor or it's close by around the point," said Morris. "The only good anchorage in these parts. The Japs came and played merry hell—shelled the two villages, landed and used machine-guns on the natives, then went away. The blacks took to the hills and stayed there; I imagine they put a tabu on the place here. We stuck around. It's been tough in the rainy season, but now the monsoon has changed and we're all right."

Morris had been marooned here for eight months past; there was a lot of war news to cover. His partner, Jack Smith, was down with fever at the moment. Stumler helped him run the canoe into the water, and got in with the fish. Morris paddled, and they started up past the headland for the harbor, while Morris listened to war news.

To Bill Stumler, the place was unreal and amazing, like all these places in the Solomons he had seen. Everywhere lay sharp cliffs; the island shore was a hundred feet and more above the sea, but flat. The harbor entrance, between fringing reefs, was a half-mile long and two hundred yards wide, and was flanked by vertical cliffs on either side; once through this entrance, a mile and a half of smooth ten-fathom water appeared, with the jungled shore beyond.

Jack Smith, said Morris, was a fine fellow and had been a missionary. The man's talk was interlarded with good-o and chum and other Aussie slang, but Stumler made out the gist of it. Three streams emptied into the bay, but fresh water was to be had only on the Viru, a couple of miles up, on account of the tidal influence. Traders and copra men had been here before the war; all gone now, like the blacks.

"And bloody lucky for us," said Morris with a chuckle. "Living like lords, we are. Wild pig no end, and fowl, taro and yams and so forth. Look out for crocs in the river, though."

"Who's the third man you spoke of?"

"Oh, Grimm." Morris became dark and savage. "German, a bloody damn Nazi who turned up and tried to do us in. Lives in the woods like a native. Lucky he hasn't any gun; as it is, he damned near murdered us both. Got to stick together, or we'd get our throats cut. We've hunted him, but he's no end clever. Well, here's our river."

A LOVELY vista it was—a river eighty yards across at the mouth but rapidly narrowing, and overhung with arching cocoanut palms from either bank. Stumler looked back at the harbor; he could appreciate the marvel of this hidden anchorage, deep enough for any craft, and so landlocked that surf or even swell never reached it. Not even the trade wind ruffled that smooth glassy surface.

The river became heavy and moist and hot. Not a native for miles and miles now, said Morris; that Jap visitation had sent them all scampering back to the Karu Mahimba range, the mountain peaks that scarred the northern horizon.

The trees retreated suddenly. Here had been the cultivated lands of the village, now an expanse stretching along the stream knee-high with new growths. Beyond showed what had been the village—a blackened ruin, the trees around fire-scarred and burned. Ruins of large war-canoes showed on the banks, and half a dozen small dugouts like this one. And, on a point of land over the water, stood a huge brown canvas tent with a thatched roof above.

"There's home," said Morris. "And that's Jack Smith sunning his bones."

He sat on a mat in front of the house, as they called it, a rifle by his side. He stood up in astonishment to stare at them—a tall, skinny man with reddish long beard and hair, garbed in tattered whites. He stalked down to meet them as they landed. He had a broken nose and little deep-set blue eyes; they rested on Stumler with apprehension, even alarm, and a distinct hostility. Even when he shook hands, he did not look pleasant about it.

"Lucky thing for you—no Japs," he said. He spoke in jerks, as it were. "Might show up—we can skip out—mountains, lots of room. Welcome to New Georgia, Yank—nothing to smoke— no cinemas—no women—rains over now, lots of sunlight. Leeches in jungle."

This said, he loaded up with the fresh fish, went back to his mat, and began to clean them, merely throwing the refuse to one side and leaving it. Morris proved to have about the same idea of sanitation. This was enough to leave any Navy man appalled; when he realized that his two hosts were just plain dirty and enjoying it, Bill Stumler began to regard them with a different eye.

But those fish did make one grand fry, after which Mr. Stumler just loafed around and got acquainted and talked war. The big tent was well supplied with mosquito-bar and all other essentials of jungle comfort, including brass bedsteads; this loot, he gathered, had come from the houses of the traders here before they were burned. There was even an old tinny phonograph with half a dozen scratchy records.

By evening, Stumler had come to the conclusion that there was something cockeyed about the setup; he could not tell what it was, and did not care particularly. Jack Smith, who was much yellowed and ravaged by fever, was perpetually talking about how much good it would do him to spend a day in the sunlight and sea-wind of the reef. After supper that evening the three had a game with a pack of greasy old cards, and when Smith harped on the same subject, Morris petulantly gave in.

"All right, all right! I'll take you out tomorrow and you can bloody well roast in the sun till you get your fill! Stumler, we'll leave one of the rifles with you; if Grimm shows his nose, shoot first and talk later. Don't trust his gab—he's a shifty devil. He may not be close by, but until now we haven't been able to leave camp at the same time. He'd like nothing better than to raid the place."

"Okay," said Stumler. To himself he thought that, for a missionary, Jack Smith had a remarkable vocabulary of cuss-words, and knew a lot about cards. With some liquor and some tobacco, these two gentry might form a bad combination, he reflected.

There were plenty of half-wild pigs about, and fresh roast pork would be just the ticket, he promised himself as he tucked in the mosquito-bar later and took his ease on a real, if dirty, mattress. He was asleep before he could enlarge on the thought, however.

Morning found him well shaken down. After breakfast Morris gave him one of their two rifles, an old Springfield, and six cartridges; not to be wasted, since they were getting low. Then the two set forth downriver in one of the dugout canoes; Stumler, who would have much preferred the open reef to this steaming jungle, waved them farewell with promises of fresh meat for supper. He had been raised on an Arkansas farm, and slaughtering held no terrors for him.

He waded in and for an hour worked hard and fast giving the camp a badly needed clean-up. Funny, he thought, that neither of his two hosts had opened up, as men do, about themselves, with talk of home and family and ambitions and so forth. He had mentioned his girl back home and they had let it go at that. Strange! They sure were two odd ducks and no mistake.

A smoke! What would he give for one! Well, no use grous-
ing about it; he was lucky to be alive. He took a look at the old
Springfield; its rust and dirt astonished him, and he got to work
cleaning it. This done, he went down to the river and selected
a good spot to do his slaughtering, laid some mosquito-bar
handy, then took the rifle and went after his pig.

Plenty of the animals were rooting about in the overgrown
clearings. He plunged in, found the thorns too thick for comfort,
and skirted the fields toward the jungle, where the bright green
verdure left by the rains alternated with yellow patches of kunai
grass, higher than his head.

He marked down a likely young shoat, got as close as possible, and let fly. His bullet went home behind the fore-shoul-
der, but the pig jumped for cover, screaming and squealing.
Stumler went after him and found him downed and dying at
the edge of a grass-patch. He had fetched along a knife from
the house, and laying the rifle aside, cut the pig's throat as soon
as it was dead.

He rose and wiped the knife, and looked straight into the
eyes of a man.

For a moment, Stumler was absolutely paralyzed. The stranger had parted the grass and was staring at him—a gaunt fellow
clad in rags and tatters, with wild eyes in a cadaverous hairy
face. On the instant, he knew who this man must be, but he
could not move. The rifle was on the ground behind him, out
of reach.

Suddenly those wild, staring eyes closed; the man toppled
forward and lay inert, senseless. Stumler jumped back, then
examined the limp figure. Grimm, if this were his name, must
have collapsed from sheer depletion; he was all skin and bone,
was shaking with fever, and was covered with jungle sores. For
a moment Stumler stared down at him; then, in abrupt compassion, picked up the pig and rifle and went staggering back to
camp.

He had seen Jack Smith taking quinine, found the box, got

some water in a gourd and some food, and went back across the clearing. Holding Grimm's emaciated torso, he got some water down the man's throat. A shiver, and Grimm's eyes opened.

"Easy, now!" said Stumler, at a convulsive movement. "Here's some grub, and some quinine for your shakes. You may be a Heinie but you're in damned bad shape. You come along into camp and I'll find something for those sores, too. There's a medicine chest, and that's my chief business. You struck the right guy when you struck a chief pharmacist's mate. Able to sit up? Here goes for the powder, then. Wash it down and wade into the grub. There's plenty more."

The other put down the quinine, gabbled something, and seized the food. He was not old, as Stumler had first thought; the face under that mass of brown beard was young. His mouth full, he stared again at Stumler.

"Speak English, do you?" said the latter. "I've forgot my German; my folks came from the old country. You don't look like the hell-raiser Morris said you were—"

AT THE name of Morris, the wild man came erect and went into the high grass with one frightened dive. Stumler plunged after him, missed him completely, and emerged cursing. He called and shouted; no response. Grimm had not neglected to take the balance of the grub with him in his headlong flight, however.

"Come along into camp, you fool! I won't hurt you!" cried Stumler, to no effect. He turned away, angrily. "All right, then, be damned to you!"

He cursed anew, on finding the knife missing—a fine big carving-knife he had meant to use on the pig. Still, there was no lack of cutlery in camp. He must have dropped the knife in the grass. Or maybe Grimm had caught it up.

"That's a fine bit of thanks I get," he grumbled, turning homeward. "Most likely the poor devil didn't savvy a word I said, except the name of Morris! Well, I did my best for him, anyhow; more'n my two bearded friends would have done, looks like."

He got back to camp, hung up the pig, sharpened up a new knife, took an axe for a cleaver, and went to work. Noon came and passed, and found the fresh pork hanging in a neat bag of mosquito-netting. Stumler washed in the river, with an eye out for crocs, and then got himself something to eat, and a mug of tea. The cabin stores, he reflected, were good. All this while the wild man never appeared again.

Stumler had just finished his tea and was wishing heartily for a cigarette, when a hail startled him. Morris and Jack Smith were returning, bringing some fish and octopi.

"Jack got his bellyful of sunlight, so here we are," exclaimed Morris, coming up from the landing. "Hello! You did get a pig, eh?"

"All butchered and ready," said Stumler, complacently. "And—"

Smith, who had ducked into the tent, let out a yell and emerged like a raving maniac. He was waving his arms, spluttering curses, and came for Stumler in a wild fury. The American leaped up, and he halted.

"You blasted thief!" shrilled Smith. "What d'ye mean by it? Look at the tent, Morris! He's been searching, looking for 'em—"

"Pipe down!" broke out Stumler angrily. "I've been cleaning up this filthy shack, if that's what you're talking about!"

"Who asked you to do that?" Morris, to his surprise, faced around at him with a snarl of rage. "What were you after? What were you looking for?"

"You guys give me a pain," snapped Stumler. "I clean up your dirt-pile and you go off your heads about it! And don't be so loose with your name-calling, or I'll learn you a thing or two. It wouldn't hurt either of you birds to get ducked in the river and scrubbed a while, if you're getting personal—"

Morris strode into the tent and rummaged around. After a moment he came out and clapped Smith on the shoulder.

"Easy, now," he said. "Our friend hasn't touched it."

"Touched what?" jerked out Stumler. Morris gave him a black look.

"None of your business. Here, Jack, calm down! The new chum meant all right. Don't go off your chump for nothing. Forget it, Stumler, forget it; sorry we flew off the handle. Come on, Jack, apologize like a gentleman!"

The other apologized in a mumble, then went after the fish. Five minutes later the two were joking and laughing and Morris was in a boisterous good humor. But Stumler knew what was what; he knew murder when he saw it in a man's eyes, as he had seen it in those of Morris.

"Your friend Grimm was around," he said. The two whirled and stared at him.

"How'd you know? See him?"

"Caught a glimpse of him," said Stumler, amused by their startled air. "Didn't have the rifle handy, and he was gone when I got it."

Morris shook his head. "Lucky for you he didn't catch you from behind and spear you."

SO THIS was New Georgia! It was one hell of a place, thought the American, as he brooded over nothing that afternoon, watching the two men wrapping the pig for roasting in wet leaves and raking out ashes from a stone oven that served for cooking. They dug some yams from the fields, brought in plantains, fetched down some drinking nuts—and through all of it Stumler remained alert and watchful and unhappy. He had ceased to trust them; passions so suddenly loosed, so murderous, disturbed him.

However, the feast went off in grand style toward sunset, and the three stuffed themselves on roast fish and pork. Afterward, Morris turned up a native instrument like a cigar-box banjo, and they sat around singing until they ran out of material. It was a pleasant evening, until Stumler voiced the impatient thought that bothered him.

"How about loading up one of those boats with grub and water, and hitting out to find the world again?"

They stared at him in the firelight. The words seemed to startle them.

"The canoes are too small," said Morris. "Impossible."

"I don't know. I was looking 'em over today. One has an outrigger and a place for a mast; it was made for open water. Natives sail everywhere. Why can't we?"

"No!" broke out Jack Smith almost violently. "No, I tell you! We're satisfied here!"

"Well, I'm not," said Stumler. "If you think I'm going to rot here doing nothing, guess again! There's a war on. We can coast down the island chain, and hide up if we strike any Japs—"

"Not for one minute!" exclaimed Morris firmly. "Never! It would be stark madness!"

Stumler looked at them in disgust and said no more.

Next morning he began looking around; the opposition had crystallized his resolve. He was leaving, and he was leaving as soon as possible. If they would not go along, he would go alone. The dugout canoe he had in mind was stout and capacious. With a pole for mast, and one of the many mats for sail, and a couple of the spare paddles, she was all set. Stacks of gourds were on hand, and water in the river; but he needed more than this. By noon he had sized things up, and when they sat down to cold pork and fish, he broached the subject.

"Boys, I'm going; that's settled. If you can spare me a rifle and some of your general plunder such as drugs, that'll be fine. There's plenty of yams, and I can take along some smoked meat—well, what's the matter now?"

They were both eyeing him savagely. Morris spoke up.

"Forget it, Stumler. We've only got two guns; we need 'em. Don't think you can turn up here and walk off with anything you choose; you can't. It's a question of self-preservation here. You're welcome to share, as long as you're here—"

"There's plenty for all," said Stumler, giving him a cold look. "I'm leaving. I'm taking that dugout with the outrigger, and a mat for a sail, and you'll have a hell of a job stopping me. If you don't want to share the other stuff, keep it and rot and be damned to you."

Jack Smith snarled in his reddish beard. Morris said nothing. With the matter settled so far as he was concerned, Stumler at once fell to work with the dry gourds. These had been prepared by the natives, evidently, and varnished with some resinous substance; with the necks cut and stoppered, they held water perfectly.

That afternoon, working hard, he got a score of the gourds filled and stoppered and in the dugout, and a big pile of yams to boot, with paddles and a fish-spear of pronged wood, a pole for mast, and a mat with some tangled cordage to serve as sail. A good day's work. His two hosts were sullen and offish, content to laze around and do nothing.

They loosened up a trifle at supper, and Stumler affected not to notice their black looks. He was not worried about food; the next island, the one of high peaks, was only a few miles distant. All these waters were deserted now, even by native fishers, so there was little risk. But some medicinal supplies might come in handy, if he could get them amicably.

"I'll report about you guys being here," said Stumler, "so they may send after you in time. Might even send a plane to bring you back."

The words were innocent, even friendly; their reception stupefied him. Morris, under his tan, went white as a sheet. Jack Smith leaped to his feet, terror bulging his eyes.

"You damned sneak!" he cried shrilly. "So you found out! Report us, will you? By the lord Harry, you'll never do that!"

With the words, he scooped up a fist-sized bit of coral rock and hurled it. Stumler, struck over the ear, was knocked flat.

Before he could recover, Morris was on top of him like a wild beast. Another bit of rock slammed him over the head and smashed him cold.

When he woke up, he was tightly lashed hand and foot and looking up at the stars. After a time he made out where he was lying; in the dugout canoe on the shore, with the pile of yams under his aching head.

He could hear voices, and he sang out. Morris made response.

"Stow your bloody jaw, you fool, or you'll draw a croc! And good riddance."

There was truth in this. He began to sweat with fear of those river reptiles, and held his tongue. Anger and bewilderment swept him; he was powerless to move. Why the devil had they jumped him?

THE MURMUR of voices continued. Presently he heard the shrill tones of Jack Smith.

"We got to finish him, I tell you! He knows too much. Dump him out on the bank and a croc will get him—"

Morris objected; the voices were only a faint murmur again. Murder, then! In vain did Stumler try to get loose; he effected nothing. The bonds were numbing his hands and feet. He cursed the unlucky puzzle; it was past understanding, unreal, like a nightmare.

Suddenly he felt something slither and slide alongside the canoe. It raised up over the edge; water dripped on him. A panic of horror and fright seized him—a croc! He began to twist and squirm anew, cursing in blind terror.

"Quiet!" came a low voice. "Quiet! Lie still!"

He fell back on the yams, with a gasp of realization. Not a croc, but a man! A wet arm and hand reached over at him, felt him, found his lashings. Then came a knife.

"Paying my debts," the voice breathed. "Can't have you murdered by those two devils, after what you did for me yesterday. Hold still, now."

Utter amazement thrilled him. Grimm! And speaking good English! He felt the cold steel slice through the bonds about his wrists, then it moved to his ankles. A faint chuckle rose.

"Thanks to you, I got this bully knife; now it's doing good work."

From Grimm emanated a terrifically vile smell. What it was, Stumler had no idea, nor did he care. His feet freed, he lay trying to rub some circulation into his hands. The stars were blocked out as Grimm leaned over, above him, and spoke in a low breath.

"I'm painted with native juice that makes the crocs leave me alone. I'll shove this canoe out; let her float downstream. I'll be along after you, as soon as I make a try for one of those rifles. Are you all right?"

"Yes," murmured Stumler, too amazed and wondering to tell the truth. He could not yet move his hands, and his feet were dead.

The canoe with its load began to inch along in the mud. It moved gradually, slowly, and at last took the water. Stumler sat up. Above, by the tent back from the bank, was a flicker of firelight; then a palm-frond hid it. The dugout was afloat now and in the muddy current. The ruddy flicker vanished from sight.

He reached out and got one of the paddles. His numbed fingers lost it and it fell with a rattle. A startled voice, a yell, sounded faintly from behind; then a chorus of yells, and the hammering explosions of shot after shot as the rifles banged. A screaming and chattering burst from the trees and wakened jungle—and everything fell silent again. Had Grimm gone down to that shooting?

The answer came in the grunt of a swimmer behind. Stumler spoke and was answered; the other caught up, hung on, and finally swung himself inboard.

"Hurt?"

"No. Where's a paddle—thanks! Let's get out of this, down

to the harbor. I almost got a rifle, but missed; too bad. I'll get this stinking stuff washed off me at the harbor."

"Why not keep going and be away?" asked Stumler.

"Too dangerous; reefs in the harbor and outside. We need daylight and can't take the chance of losing this craft. Where do you want to get?"

"Anywhere. Work down the chain of islands till we strike the U. S. flag."

"Suits me. Talk it over later."

"Thought you were a Nazi bad-actor?"

"Nazi? Me? I'm Pennsylvania Dutch, you galoot. Mission secretary at Shortland."

"What? Then they lied like hell!"

"Sure. What d'you expect of ex-convicts and murderers?"

STUMLER FELL silent from sheer astonishment and growing comprehension. They rippled along the starlit darkness, beneath the bending cocoanut-palms, without further speech.

Ex-convicts! That explained a lot of things, and chiefly the furious blowoff when he had spoken of reporting them. And Jack Smith a missionary, eh? Not likely. Bill Stumler felt a hot wave steal up his cheeks at thought of how he had fallen for those shameless lies.

The river mouth opened before them, the starlit harbor calm and clear.

"Let's chance the reefs," spoke up Stumler. "Too dangerous to stop here; let's get on across, and outside the entrance."

"Well, all right," assented Grimm dubiously. "I guess it's flood tide anyhow; might as well. I got into their tent, trying for a rifle, before they knew it."

"Both the rifles were outside, by the fire."

"So I discovered. However, I grabbed what'll hurt them worst of all. Show you later. And I'm about all in—can't stand much action. Had it tough with fever during the rains. I'd sooner sleep than paddle, right now."

"Me too," said Stumler. "Another reason for getting safe before we lay up. You rest a spell and I'll paddle," he added, remembering the emaciated appearance of Grimm.

They stole out across the smooth waters, and Grimm talked by snatches. He told of how the Japs had caught them at Short-land Island, off to the northwest. A dozen men had got away in a boat, as Morris had said, making New Georgia safely; but by that time the Japs were flooding in everywhere. All was hardship, starvation, evasion—and here at Viru the Japs had caught up again.

That had been plain hell, with everything machine-gunned. Morris and Jack Smith, however, had been worse than the Japs. They had murdered two of the party, had murdered a trader here, and bulged with loot. Everyone else had been killed; the natives skipped out. Grimm stayed on, hanging about the precious pair, living from hand to mouth through the rainy season; they had done their best to wipe him out. Some natives had helped him, once. Yesterday he had been desperate, when Stumler encountered and fed him.

"That quinine saved my life," he said. "It did make me pretty dopey, though. I came back and hung around, across the river, till I saw what happened tonight."

The dark and savage land fell behind them; the harbor entrance neared. The tide had begun to ebb and this helped them. At last they were cutting through those dark walls of rock; the open sea and the big headland showed beyond.

"There's a bight under that headland," said Grim. "Good place to lie up."

To Stumler, it was more than ever like a bad dream, all behind him now. They landed under the coral cliff, pulled up the dugout, and stumbled out into the warm white sand. With a sigh, Stumler folded up.

"I'm about done. See you later," he said, and fell asleep despite his aching head, with the monotonous thunder of the surf on the long reefs lulling him. They had made it; they were safe, and nothing else mattered.

He wakened to daylight around, and sat up. The sun was still hidden by the enormous extinct crater of Vangunu, to the eastward. Grimm, who had wakened him, pointed to a little fire where fresh-caught fish were cooking. They were in a tiny crevice of the high coral headland, whose vertical cliff rose directly back of them. A quarter-mile to the right, but shut out from their view, was the entrance to the big harbor.

"Speared a couple of small fish in a pool," said Grimm. "What's your idea of getting away?"

Stumler stood up, yawning. "Well, we've got water and yams aboard. We might cook some fish, then pull out for the big island yonder."

"Shake on it, pardner!"

They gripped hands, grinning at each other. Grimm, after a sea-dip, was improved in looks and odor; but he was still a walking skeleton. He pointed to the vertical cliff behind them.

"Look up there, about twenty feet—see the marks of the old sea level? Ages ago this island, mountains and all, was uplifted by a volcanic eruption. That's why it slopes down to the reefs out beyond."

They settled down at the tiny driftwood fire, wolfing half-cooked fish and talking, getting acquainted. On either side and behind, against the base of the cliff, lay coral hummocks, as though huge jagged fragments had been riven away in that ancient convulsion of nature. Then, with a chuckle, Grimm produced a fat tobacco-pouch of leather.

"Here, look what I got last night. Haven't taken a look myself, but I know what's in it and who it belonged to. I'll turn it over to his heirs."

Stumler opened it up, untying a thong about its middle. He brought to light cotton, and nestled in the cotton tiny globules that shimmered in the sunlight. Suddenly he realized what they must be.

"Pearls! Is that right? Real ones?"

"Smack out of the reef oysters," said Grimm, laughing. "Looks like about half are gone. Our two friends no doubt divvied up their loot."

Stumler's gaze widened on the iridescent gems. "Pearls! Real pearls! Worth money?"

"Worth a lot, enough to murder for," said Grimm. "At that, the pearl market is dead with the war and all. No wonder those devils were content to sit out the war! Funny, isn't it? With what's going on in the world, the value of these things to us is that of pretty toys; to those two men, it's boundless!"

Stumler packed them in the cotton again and handed over the pouch.

"I'd swap the lot for that many cigarettes," said he, and Grimm broke into a laugh.

"Right! Well, let's go. We'll never starve if we stick by the islands; we'll find fish in every reef pool. Our main job will be to evade any Japs. Ready?"

Stumler nodded and rose. They went to the dugout, which had been drawn up above high-water mark. And here, unexpectedly, they were faced with a tremendous job.

THE HEAVILY loaded canoe had to be moved to low water. It was too weighty for one man, and Grimm had no more strength than a cat. However, they bent to it and at last got it free of the sand-clutch. There was no mud for it to slide on, as there had been at the riverbank, but they heaved away and got it moving.

They were too intent at this task to regard anything else. Suddenly Bill Stumler jumped as something whined and buzzed past his head. At the same instant Grimm uttered a yell, and then came the crack of a rifle.

There, standing out from the harbor entrance and not two hundred yards away, was a canoe bearing Morris and Jack Smith, and heading toward them. Another rifle spoke; the bullet chipped the heavy gunnel of the dugout between Grimm and Stumler.

"Duck!" cried Grimm. "Take cover!"

They jumped into action like startled rabbits, spurred by two more bullets whistling close. The anger, the fear, the utter futility of the moment, were horrible. Stumler realized they were caught like rats in a trap, against the curve of high cliff. He jumped for one of the coral hummocks and dodged behind it, an inch ahead of a bullet.

After a moment he peered forth cautiously. Smith was paddling in to shore, Morris was standing up with rifle ready. He stepped ashore, and Smith followed, gun in hand. They stood eyeing the coral rocks, then Morris spoke.

"Come out o' that or we'll run you down and finish you!"

"Go to hell," retorted Stumler. Morris fired and the bullet chipped the coral at his ear. He dodged away and peered out anew. Grimm was lying doggo.

"Tell you what," called Morris placatingly. "Throw out that tobacco pouch you got last night, Grimm! Throw it out, and we'll go and leave you in peace."

"And our canoe?" came the voice of Grimm.

"Sure thing. All we want are the babies. Hand 'em over, and we quit."

Stumler snorted disdainfully; he knew better. But Grimm was somewhere on the other side of the place. And, after a moment, Grimm obeyed the behest, tossing the pouch out to the white sand. Instantly, Jack Smith fired.

"Got him!" he yapped jubilantly. "Now for the Yank!"

Morris scooped up the pouch and stuffed it into a pocket. That was his undoing; for in this split second, Bill Stumler went to work.

The thought of Grimm, shot down by trickery, sparked his brain. At his feet were small water-rounded fragments of coral. There was not an earthly chance, he knew; here was murder, and no mercy shown. As all this flashed through his mind, he shot erect and his arm swung.

Straight to the mark sped a coral chunk; not for nothing was Bill Stumler chief pitcher on the fleet team. Jack Smith whipped around and fired, but the chunk caught him smack in the face and tumbled him backward. Morris, stuffing the pouch in his pocket, got his hand free and jerked up his rifle. A coral chunk was coming straight for him. He dodged it, lost his footing in the loose sand, and came to one knee. By that time, Stumler had stooped and was up with three more chunks in his grip.

He let fly and missed. The rifle spanged out; he felt the bullet tear at him and whip him about. Quicker than the bolt could work, he let fly again. This time his aim was dead center—straight to the bearded face peering over the rifle-sights. Struck between the eyes, Morris dropped like a shot.

Jack Smith was coming to his feet. Stumler took a step into the open, whirled, and put one smack in the groove. It hit Smith just above the belt, and doubled him up and left him sprawled in the sand. Stumler darted out, caught up first one rifle then the other, and stumbled across the sand, frantically calling Grimm's name.

To his amazement and wild delight, Grimm arose, wiping a streak of blood from his brow.

"Are you hurt?" panted Stumler.

"I guess not—the bullet knocked off a rock splinter that laid me out. But here, here!" cried Grimm. "Your shirt's all blood—let's have a look!"

Stumler took a look himself. His first anxiety passed; that bullet had struck a rib and glanced aside, leaving nothing more than a bit of torn flesh. A laugh burst from him.

"Come on, Grimm! Get your pouch and let's go! Leave 'em here to think it over!"

Grimm hesitated, looking at the two sprawled figures, then nodded. "I guess you're right," he assented. "It's a temptation to murder—and we're not murderers."

He went to the senseless Morris, frisked him, then frisked Jack Smith and came erect. He had two pouches now. He hurried to the dugout that had brought them and shoved it out into the water; the ebb tide caught it instantly. Then he helped Stumler with their own craft, and tumbled in.

They let the paddles be. After a bit of work they got the mast stepped and the mat-sail well enough in place to catch the wind. Grimm, in the stern with a paddle, steered; the canoe, steadied by its stout outrigger, rippled through the waves of the channel like a fish.

"Hurry!" yelled Stumler joyously. "She works and we've got two rifles and—holy smoke, what's that?" he added with a gasp. "Grimm! Look!"

They stared off southward and west. A smoke was visible along the horizon, then a second smoke.

"Some of your navy craft?" asked Grimm.

"From that direction? Not a chance! There's a third smoke showing up!"

They went dancing across toward the rapidly growing masses of Vangunu, whose outer islets seemed coming to meet them. And as they went, the smokes to the west and south grew more numerous and closer. When they were a scant mile from the refuge of the reefs and islands ahead, a low shape was clearly visible.

"Destroyer," said Stumler, standing up to see the better. "And be damned—she's making for where we were! What's the name of it?"

"Viru," said Grimm. "They're all making for Viru! You know what that means."

"Sure as shooting, the Japs have come back to take possession! And we can lay up among these islands ahead, then beat it when darkness comes—say!" Stumler broke off and looked at his companion. "What about Morris and Smith? They'll be caught, by golly!"

Grimm, his eyes on the reefs ahead, glanced up at Stumler for an instant.

"Yeah?" he said. "Well, I know what I'd say about it if I was a missionary!"

"I'll bite," said Stumler. "What?"

"That God moves in a mysterious way, His wonders to perform! You get into the bow and watch for coral, and keep a damned sharp lookout!"

"Aye, aye, sir," said Bill Stumler happily.

(Editor's Note: The Japanese are by recent reports occupying both Shortland and New Georgia islands, and establishing air bases there, which our forces are bombing. No word about Morris and Jack Smith.)

III

ALL QUIET ON THE TANKER FRONT

*Who Would Have Thought International
Discussions Would Break Out Amidships?*

E IGHT BELLS and the watch was changed. Three of them were in the galley getting a spot of hot java—Reilly, the pumpman; Macleish, the chief gunner's mate; and Sasha, the docile, yellow-haired Russian deck-hand who had been put aboard at Pearl Harbor to fill the place of Jack Leary, gone with a burst appendix. Sasha knew enough English to obey orders and was a good seaman.

Reilly was in an argument with the Navy man, who had also come aboard at Pearl Harbor.

"You may be a chief gunner's mate," he sniffed, "but what you don't know about oil tankers would fill a book."

Macleish grinned, "Mister, I had three years in the Aruba run before this war. I've handled pumps aboard the finest tankers afloat, ships that'd make this little doo-dod look like a child's toy. So don't get personal."

"I'd not get personal with a Scot," re-plied Reilly bitterly, "under any circumstances, because he has too much agin' him in the first place. This here is a Diesel electric, the latest and most efficient tanker going.

"Her hydraulic handling is so far ahead of your old east coast boats as to laugh at 'em. She's not big, because she runs California high-test over to the islands to supply your gunboats and planes; without us, you'd be Jap dogmeat. That's why you and your lousy guns are aboard us—to make sure your Navy can operate."

"Well, God save me from arguing with an Irisher!" said Macleish.

"Then don't start what you can't finish," said Reilly, and rolled out of the galley, while Sasha and the steward grinned. Reilly was heavy set and rotund in build, but muscled as became a pumpman. Macleish gave the steward a dour look.

"I riled him. Why was he talking so careful?"

"That's his Old Potstill," replied the steward. "Two gulps of that bottled smoke he calls Irish Whiskey, and he talks like a preacher. Him and Mike Tobin, the second mate, keep a supply on hand. A pumpman on this run's like God—he's got a cabin to himself, and can have liquor aboard and welcome. Mart Reilly's the best pumpman in the tanker fleet. And right now, us tankers are the first line of defense for the islands."

"That's correct," said Macleish, and Sasha grinned at them knowingly. He was blue-eyed and brawny. He had turned up amid the thousands of construction men that had been rushed out to the islands, and had been shifted to this emergency job by port officials.

Now Pearl Harbor was half a day astern; Mart Reilly stood on deck, looking up at the blazing stars and waiting for Tobin to come off duty. He was assigned to the deck department, the chief mate having charge of loading and discharging cargo; but at sea his main duties consisted of keeping the pumps, valves and gear in first-class condition, and standing night watch.

The *Hawaiian Princess* was heading for California with water in her trim-tanks to balance her lessening fuel oil, and Reilly cherished his usual grouch after the frantic turn-around. All tankers are operated on a quick turnaround basis, each crew member a link in a precision team whose tanks are like clockwork; but with the islands in bitter need of aviation gas, it was even more so. This trip they had made it in twenty-two hours and not a soul had stepped ashore; even the Old Man had got his clearance brought out to him. And at the home end, it was

two months since Reilly had set foot in his California bunga-
low or glimpsed his wife.

"Be damned to such a war!" said he, looking at the phosphorescent streamers alongside. "We're in war service, they say, and
tankers is a front like a battle-line. Yah! Supposed to get a
voyage off with pay every two months—but not the pumpman.
He's too bad needed. It's poor policy, if you ask me that knows.
Poor policy!"

HE CURSED the inflated jacket that must be worn at all
times, even in sleep; he cursed the stringent blackout aboard,
and the Navy gun-crews and chief gunner's mate. Somewhat
assuaged by these vented oaths, he turned as Mike Tobin came
from the bridge ladder.

"That you, Mart?" said the second mate. "I've got some startling information."

"Where from?" growled Reilly.

"Port engineer, back at Pearl Harbor. It's the real dope."

"Come on," said Reilly, and led the way. A pumpman does not rate a cabin, but space aboard the *Princess* was going begging these days; and after all, Reilly was a personage.

In the cabin, he switched on the dim-out bulb, opened a big corrugated-paper box, and from it took a fat, ripe pineapple. He laid out two clean spoons. Lifting the tufted top from the pineapple, Reilly sniffed and beamed all over his bronzed face.

"It's ready," said he. The fruit had been neatly cored and the space filled with Irish whiskey, which had now absorbed into the yellow pulp. "Dig in, Mike; age before beauty!"

For a space there was no talk to spoil the savor of that golden fruit. Then Mr. Tobin sighed and licked his spoon and broke the silence.

"Mart, that's grand! A great invention. Well, ye know the islands are still jittery about spies and such. It's the opinion that the Nips will send out some subs to cut off the gas supply; the islands are dependent on us tankers, you know."

"That's no news, much less startling information," sniffed Reilly. Mr. Tobin laid a finger alongside his nose and winked, a habit he had picked up on the east coast.

"But wait! Word about the tanker runs has been sent out by some spy's short wave. It was intercepted and decoded; told about our course and so on. I know they informed the Old Man, for he's jumpy as a skittish colt. And we're takin' a different course eastbound. So don't be layin' any bets about not sighting a sub, like you usually do."

Reilly winced. He had already taken a couple such wagers. The engine-room crew always bet that subs would be sighted, not to win but to keep it from happening. Like insurance.

"And," went on the mate, "there's particular new orders about the blackout. Keep an eye peeled. Of course them island fellers and the Navy hands are nervous as a bunch of old women, and no blame to 'em; but they claim the Japs are starting a reg'lar campaign to sink tankers, and any light showed at night would be just too bad. S'pose a guy was planted aboard us to show a light at a certain time—huh? Sweety gravy!"

"Like this Russian we took aboard," said Reilly. "We got to look out for Russians."

"He's all right. Government brought him out to the islands; you bet they looked him up plenty! They wouldn't have put him aboard us, without he was safe."

"Government!" Reilly sniffed. "Even if them officials was efficient, which they ain't, and I was a spy, I'd set out to fool 'em proper and I'd do it. Why can't the government be run like the Navy? That's what I say."

"There's reasons," said Mr. Tobin sagely. "Anyhow, Sasha ain't no Jap. He's a durned good AB. Good as any quartermaster, too. Well, let's finish it."

THEY FINISHED it and dumped the hull over the lee rail, and Reilly turned in.

Like all pumpmen, Reilly regarded himself as the most essential man aboard, and with some justice. He was neither a deckhand nor an officer, but mingled with both alike. Morning found him in the pumphouse amidships, testing valves and putting a shine on the brightwork. The chief engineer stopped by to see about some repairs, which must be made before raising the Coast; then along came Macleish and stopped to eye the pumps knowingly.

"Neat gadgets," said he. "Fifteen hundred bar'ls per hour, eh?"

"I see you know pumps," said the chief.

"He'd ought to," put in Reilly. "By his sayso he was pumpman on Noah's Ark. Macleish, ain't you glad you ain't pumpman away down in the belly of an old-style tanker, these days?"

The chief gunner's mate nodded.

"Deck-pumps are safer, I admit," he said mildly. "But this toy ship has drawbacks. Can't carry any but light oil; needs all sorts of special tanks, must carry heavy overdraft at her berth and look at those automatic shutoff valves!"

"Well, there's no gas pockets in this ship, no slack tanks, no ullages to take," broke in Reilly.

"Nice work," said Macleish. "About right for an Irisher to handle. It takes a Scot to run the pumps on a real tanker; they need brains."

Reilly was breathing hard. "Sure," he retorted. "That's why you got in the Navy. Takes the Irish to stick to the job and risk torpedoes!"

"At wartime pay," barked Macleish, reddening. "You don't see any boghopper changing into uniform to fight for his country, when he can earn soft money on a safe run—"

That was a mistake, because Reilly smacked him slap in the eye; then they were at it hammer and tongs. The inflated jackets prevented much damage, but the chief gunner's mate had a fine shiner and Reilly a swollen jaw when the Old Man came along and stopped the show with a burst of profanity you could hear almost to Pearl Harbor. He gave them both a hot raking over and a promise of the brig unless they shook hands.

So they did it, looking into each other's eyes with looks that belied their words, and it was ended for this time. When the smoke blew away, Reilly saw nobody around except the yellow-haired Sasha. The Russian, being off duty, was rubbing up the brightwork, unbidden.

"You good faller," said he with a wide grin. "You don' like them Navy faller, eh?"

REILLY EXPRESSED himself in regard to the chief gunner's mate, and Sasha laughed.

"You're all right! Aye show you how to shine brass."

He did, too; he put a mirror gloss on everything in sight. Reilly was so grateful and pleased that he invited Sasha to his cabin, and put out a glass and a bottle of Dublin cream. Sasha poured the tumbler full to the brim and downed it at one vast gulp.

"My good lord!" said Reilly. "Have another!"

Sasha took him at his word and repeated the performance.

"That way we drink vodka," he said, beaming.

"You're a blasted Communist to treat Irish whiskey like that!" said Reilly.

"Communist? Me?" Sasha leaned forward and shook his finger in the air. "No, no! White Russian! Aye was officer in the navy of the Tsar, me! Aye come all the way across Siberia, fighting the Reds. They catch me, to try to shoot me!"

"That so?" said Reilly. He felt a bit sorry for the Russian. Not even a vodka tank could stand two such shots of potstill liquor, which has a sly way of blowing up like a grenade when the pin has been pulled. "Then how come you ain't dead now?"

"Them fallar save my life," said Sasha earnestly. "Pull me away quick, bang-bang! They give me good job in Nagasaki, plenty money, plenty girl, you bet!"

"In—where did you say?" asked Reilly, picking up his ears. But Sasha was not regarding him; a torrent of amiable Russian was pouring from his lips, and he wanted to embrace Reilly, who shoved him off.

"Aye help build a big naval base," said Sasha. "Paramushiro base, you bet! Aye don't tell Navy man that. You don't like Navy faller, you my friend. Pratty soon, quick, aye show how much aye lof you, Mister. Now aye go sleep."

He got up and departed, despite Reilly's implorations and offers of another drink. He shook his head, grinned vaguely but amiably, and went off muttering a blue streak of Russian.

"Pratty soon, quick!" said Reilly to himself, sitting over his pipe and brooding. He was still at it at eight bells, noon. A little after, Mike Tobin, released from the bridge, looked in, entered, and closed the door.

"One hell of a note!" said the second mate. "The Old Man is mad as blazes. Howcome you got to pick on the Navy?"

"Hey! Sit down and have a drink before mess," exclaimed

Reilly. "Lookit, I got some real news! This here Russian we got aboard, you know what he is?"

"Yeah. I looked up his papers; all clear. He's no communist. Been working for ten years past in Seattle and Vancouver." Mr. Tobin poured a drink and examined the bottle. "Here, who drunk all that? You?"

"No. He did, in two drinks." Reilly's brain clicked. "Mike, listen here! Vancouver, hell! You know about the Jap base at Paramushiry or some such name?"

"Happens I do," said Tobin, nodding. "It's their latest up-to-the-mark mystery base, where they can bomb Alaska from. Naval and air base, just built."

REILLY LET out a yip. "That proves it!" he exclaimed. "Listen. This here Sasha puts down a pint of Irish in two drinks, see? You know how quick it'll work.

"Well, he talks. He was a White Russian officer, naval; you know how them Japs use the White Russians, right now, against the Reds! He says the Japs saved his life in Siberia and gave him a job at Nagasaki, and he helped build the Paramushiry base. Ten years in Vancouver, my eye!"

"What you driving at?" asked Mr. Tobin, nursing his drink.

"Why, he's working for the Japs here and now! He cottoned to me because I hit Macleish and he misunderstood the matter. He thinks I'm agin' the Navy. So is he, savvy? He's a Jap spy, that's what he is! That's why he was working at Pearl Harbor!"

Mike Tobin reflected on this.

"You're excited," he said at last. "Now, look. The guy licks up a pint or so and it hits him. So what? So he opens up with a lot of his past history. Like all these Russkis, he's been used to lying all these years, putting on the dog, claiming to have been a general or an admiral or a prince. He dishes out a jumble of it; and you fall for it."

"Might be," said Reilly, dubiously. "How about working at the Paramushy base?"

"A figment of the imagination," declared Mr. Tobin. "He hasn't the brains to be a spy."

"That's what I'd like the other feller to think, if I was a spy—"

"Well, we got fresh island pig for noon mess, so come along before we miss it."

Reluctantly, Mart Reilly passed up the argument; but the more he pondered the whole matter, the more he became convinced that he was right. And he set himself, warily, to keep an eye on Sasha, whose last name was too Russian to be pronounced anyhow.

He even forbore to indulge in any small talk with the chief gunner's mate, for the moment. Macleish, whose gang was in charge of the three-incher forward and the two ack-ack guns aft, put his men through their paces that afternoon at target practice. And at mess that night, following orders received before he came aboard, he gave a little talk about the danger of subs. They were facing it now, according to the best Navy opinion, for they might expect subs to lurk halfway between the islands and the Coast; therefore it behooved all hands to obey regulations strictly and to keep an eye peeled. The peril would be greater at night than by day, said he—and just then, as though to mark his words, came the signal for boat drill.

All hands piled out into the darkness. Reilly, assigned to No. 3 boat, came upon Macleish heading for the big forward gun.

"Oh!" he said. "So you're ready to catch a boat ride instead of working your guns, huh?"

"You're a liar!" snapped the Scot in righteous anger.

"That's all right," said Reilly, sinking in his unjust barb. "Your crew can fight the gun while you stow your duffle in a boat—"

Macleish let him have it, and they were going hot and heavy when Mr. Tobin jumped in and hauled them apart.

"You fools, the Old Man will skin you alive if he gets wind o' this! Stations, and damned quick about it!"

They obeyed, and there the matter rested. But as the drill

ended, Reilly became aware of one figure lingering behind the
others, and coming to him. It was Sasha, speaking soft.

"Hey, Mister! Why you not shoot that Navy faller?"

"Oh, it's you!" said Reilly. "Well, I ain't got a gun, for one
reason."

"Aye get you one."

"The hell you will! Where'll you get one?"

Sasha merely laughed in response and, coming back into the
lighted mess-room, winked at him in good-humored understanding. Reilly was startled by those words; then reflected that
it must be the Russian's notion of a joke. It was obviously impossible for any gun to have come aboard; things were too
closely watched back at Pearl Harbor. And then he forgot the
matter, on seeing that Macleish was rapidly acquiring another
shiner.

"Got a crack in the dark, hauling the gun around," said the
chief gunner's mate to the inquiries showered upon him. But
his gaze met that of the gleeful Reilly with promise of vengeance
to come.

Recalling the episode next morning, he confided in Mike
Tobin. The second mate bided his time, slipped down into the
fore-peak, and met Reilly later with a shake of the head.

"I went through his duffle. Not a sign of a gun, Mart. You'd
better get this guy off your mind."

"Yeah, I guess he was joking," assented Reilly uneasily, and
let it go at that.

Toward noon the Old Man and Macleish came along past
the pumphouse and stopped by the rail, talking. Macleish was
again expounding the Navy theory anent the subs lurking in
these waters, not only for tankers but for westbound convoys
bound for the islands and Australia. The Old Man was plainly
jittery about it; though, with the *Princess* now full of water
instead of aviation gasoline, to sink her would be no easy task.

"Well, hope for the best. I got to shoot the sun," said the Old

Man, and departed. Macleish turned to the pumphouse and came over to Reilly. The dour Scot looked serious.

"Look," he said. "What price letting our discussion wait till we get ashore?"

"Okay," said Reilly. "But if you give me any of your lip I'll crown you, even if there's a sub alongside!"

With an effort, Macleish controlled himself.

"I'll give you something harder than lip," he retorted. "But it's a deal, Irish. You lay off and I will. Likes and dislikes aside, we got the men to think about; won't do to get 'em disorganized. This thing is too serious."

"It's a bargain," agreed Reilly. "But from what we've heard of these Jap subs, they're a messy pack of amachoors at the business."

"True enough," Macleish assented. "But a torpedo don't know it, so don't count too strong on that."

With a nod, he stalked off.

EVENING CAME on with a high, light haze that dimmed the stars and blackened the sea. Everybody was restless, uncomfortable, irritable; to be deprived of radio and news in these war-days, to have cabins and ship-bowels lit only by faint dim-out lights, to wear inflated jackets at all hours, was bad for the disposition. Even the card and crap games reacted in quarrelsome fashion. The night watches were doubled.

Early in the evening watch—two bells, to be exact—a wild yell went up for'ard, the gun-crews pattered to stations, the engines quickened, and alarm shot through every soul; but it was only a playful porpoise darting ahead of the ship and stirring the water in a luminescent streak. Sheepish laughter and jokes sounded on all sides as the tension dropped and curses consigned the sportive fish to farther depths.

Reilly, free until eight bells, was in no mood for slumber and got into a crap game in the fore-peak with some others, including the Russian. Just before four bells, Sasha drew out of the game and vanished. Reilly went to the deck for a breath of fresh air—there was no rule against smoking on the empty run, a hydraulic tanker having no lingering gas pockets—and stood leaning over the starboard rail, idly watching the dark water.

Then he saw it, and his jaw dropped in sheer disbelief. It came again and yet again. Three times in all—a strong though momentary beam of light flashing down along the side of the tanker and touching the water.

Reilly gulped incredulously, then stiffened, craning across the rail, watching for a renewal of the thing. He crouched, intent, squeezing as far outboard as he dared, looking to see whence that damning light had come; in his amazement he had neglected to spot the point.

Swift conjecture fluttered across his brain. Carelessness? Impossible; not three times, anyhow! Accident or reflection? It might be, although unlikely. And suddenly his mind leaped— the Russian! Sasha was off watch, had drawn out of the crap game and disappeared.

"Be damned to him for a spy and worse!" thought Reilly in a startled alarm. "It's all true and more! There might be a dozen subs nosing the surface within a mile of us, and we'd never know it. He flashes a light three times, and the sub knows it's a tanker. By the saints, that's it!"

He quivered as he hung there, waiting; but the light came no more, and uncertainty grew upon him. Suddenly came a step and a voice, and he jumped as a hand grabbed him.

"Hey, what you trying to do, commit suicide? Who is it—oh, it's you!" It was the chief gunner's mate who had found him. Reilly twisted about.

"Mac, did you see it?"

"See what?" growled the Scot.

"A light. It flashed three times, a steady down beam—work aft and see who's hanging about the rail! It came from some-where amidships."

Macleish departed swiftly, and presently returned.

"Not a soul in sight. Are ye sure of it?"

"No, bad luck to it!" replied Reilly slowly, and drew a deep breath. He could make no accusation without proof. "But I can swear to it just the same. Somebody showed a light, not once but three times."

"Hell! Nobody aboard would be doing that a-purpose," said Macleish. "Still, might have been a reflection from a cabin door opening—don't seem likely, with all hands knowing what it might mean."

"Wait and see if it comes again," Reilly said. "'I'll look around below."

He was struck by a sudden thought, and hastened back to the forepeak. The game was still going and Sasha was there—in fact, had the dice. Reilly nudged the man next him.

"When did the Russian come back?" he breathed.

"Why, I dunno! About four bells, I reckon. He went out and come back again."

Reilly smothered an oath at such stupidity. His suspicions were absurd; Sasha was laughing and joking in his broken English, with broad good-humor.

Still, there was the fact. And, the more he thought about it, the less Mart Reilly liked it. The *Princess* was not following her usual course back to the Coast—but the Japs might be clever enough to keep up with such changes. Any signals made at certain hours, in a certain stretch of sea, might or might not be picked up by a sub awaiting just such signals.

"It could be," Reilly told himself. "It could be—and he could be the guy! Let's see, now. S'posing I was that guy, and framing it all up beforehand, or acting on orders already framed up? I wouldn't be running much risk shipping aboard an empty home-bound tanker, for the crew would get clear if we were hit The orders would be to send the signal on certain nights, and at certain times—most likely, every hour on the hour, so far as possible. And it was around four bells when those lights showed. Hm! On that basis, the next time would be six bells, most likely on the sta'board side, same as before."

He hauled out his silver turnip; ten-thirty. Without more ado he quit the game and went on deck again. Half an hour to wait. The *Princess*, a specially built job, had no catwalk; he went up and down the passages and found no sign of Macleish, somewhat to his own relief. He was sorry now that he had taken the chief gunner's mate into his confidence, on impulse.

In fact, the whole thing looked pretty nonsensical. In this gloomy frame of mind he turned in at his own cabin and sought a drop of consolation, and brooded unhappily over it. Suddenly he leaped up. He had intended to keep an eye on the forepeak ladder to see if Sasha emerged, and it had slipped his mind.

Darting out, he made a dash for the starboard passage, emerged by the pumphouse and came to the rail, straining his eyes aft. All was black, and he relaxed, blinking down at the faint luminosity of the water alongside. Tanks had been trimmed that afternoon to balance the used-up fuel oil.

Reilly heard the three double-strokes of the ship's bell; eleven o'clock. Another hour and he would turn to for watch duty. The sensible thing would be to snatch a bit of—

He jumped as he saw it—a broad, steady beam shooting down from the rail a bit aft of amidships. It flickered out. Then it came again; but by this time Reilly was off the rail and padding aft in furious haste. He caught the voice of Macleish uplifted in an oath; next instant an electric flashlight, still burning, dropped to the deck without going out, and in the radiance two figures appeared interlocked.

A shot spanged out. One of the figures went sprawling, and by the uniform it was the chief gunner's mate. The shot was answered by a cry from the bridge—then by a wild, frantic yell from the lookouts.

"Torpedo!"

Scarcely conscious of the tumult raging from stem to stern, Reilly bore down on his man. Sasha stood in the glow of light, a pistol in his hand. He recognized Reilly and lowered the weapon and started a wide grin.

"Ye damned double-blasted spy!" yelled Reilly, and went for him.

They crashed together into the deckhouse side and the pistol went skittering along the scuppers in the ray of light.

Meantime, with feet padding the deck and voices in a roar, the *Princess* spurted as the engines quickened and the wheel was put hard over. She swung, wrenching and heaving and groaning, in a quarter-circle arc—a panic-struck blind thing desperately trying to dodge the phosphorescent streak in the water that was plunging at her. And somehow she did it; the stern watch said afterward that it slid past not a foot from her rudder.

REILLY WAS taking punishment; that Russian could hammer in slogging blows like nobody's business, and not even the inflated jacket stopped the low ones. For a moment the two men were toe to toe until Reilly, gasping under those crunching smashes, ducked and grappled. Macleish, raising himself on one elbow, was shouting, but nobody heard him in the uproar. Then Sasha and Reilly together fell over him, and with a groan he collapsed under them. The *Princess* was by this time heading for the north star; she seemed to jump with terror.

Reilly now was lashing away in a frantic ferocity that matched the Russian's fury. They went rolling under the rail, first one atop and then the other, kicking, gouging, grappling. In one turn, Reilly got home his knee under the Russian's belt and caught the gasp of agony it drew, then he howled a bitter oath as the reaching fingers clawed for his eyes and tore the skin from his cheeks instead.

What he did not see, the other did. Sasha loosed him abruptly, pitched forward, and got the pistol. He twisted around and began to fire. That maddened Reilly with fear as the bullets whined and he hurled himself bodily on Sasha and damped his teeth in the man's forearm. They fought for the gun, savagely, blind to everything around, blood on faces and fists, blood salt in their mouths. The pistol fell, clattered, and was knocked somewhere beyond the ray of light.

From the bow watch lifted one shrill and awful yell. It was echoed from the water dead ahead—echoed by more shrill voices. A gun exploded almost under the tanker's bows; it exploded again, and somewhere within her came the blasting explosion of a shell. As though frantic with the pain of it, she lifted. Her bow came up and up; underfoot was a rending, crunching crash and the sound of little shrill voices screaming—then something was crunching along her keel and gone.

Of this, Mart Reilly knew nothing; sheer mad ferocity blinded and deafened him. He went rolling under a terrific smash—then was up and caught Sasha afoot, and rocked the yellow head back and back again with gasping jabs, till he sank his hard fingers in the thick throat-muscles and hung grimly on like a terrier. Then came a blinding glare of light, as someone picked up the fallen torch and played it on the two gory shapes.

A hoarse, screaming bellow of defiant fury burst from the Russian. He kicked Reilly loose, hurled himself at the men of the gun-crew swarming around, knocked them aside like ninepins, and went swarming over the rail. Then he was gone—only Mart Reilly, gasping and drooping on one knee, and Macleish being helped to his feet and a bullet-hole clear through his body that streamed scarlet over his deflated Mae West.

Reilly came dimly to himself with someone sloshing water over him and wiping the blood from his battered face. His hands were useless swollen things, knuckles broken; his face was a purpled mass, and he was still gasping air into his spent lungs. From the babel of sounds around, one voice began to come clear—that of the Old Man.

"Hey!" piped up Reilly. "I thought we were torpedoed?"

"Missed us," said the Old Man, his arm about Reilly's shoulders. "And we plumped square into her and run her down! It was the greatest piece of bull luck ye ever saw! But," he added at Reilly's ear, "ye don't have to be telling anyone, Mart. About it being luck, I mean."

Reilly quavered out a laugh. "Aye, sir. Where's that damned Russian?"

"Jumped over and gone. Macleish told us about it—come on, if you're able. We'd better see to him. It was grand work, Mart, grand work! If it hadn't been for you, nobody would have suspected him. And the way you fought him! But come along."

Reilly staggered along to the cabins. The chief mate, who was an amateur surgeon, had Macleish in a berth and was bandaging his wound while Macleish cursed softly.

"How is he?" asked the Old Man.

"Looks like a good clean puncture, sir," said the mate with relish. "Never saw a finer one. Might be a good idea to give him a toss of grog."

"Get it out o' my cabin, sir," spoke up Reilly. "There's a bottle of ten-year-old Irish in the locker." He went to the berth and looked down at Macleish. "That is," he went on, "if your principles will permit you to drink real potstill liquor! I'll be honored."

"The honor," said Macleish, "is all mine. Gimme your hand, you durned bog-trotter! I'm proud to shake it."

"Same here, you blasted Scot," said Mr. Reilly happily, and did not even wince under the hard grip as they shook hands.

THE OLD MAN OF ICELAND

Up in the North Men Stand Guard
Against a War That Seems Far.

.

A N A R G U M E N T was going on in the battery hut, as Jon slid into warm garments for his lonely vigil on the cone of Keilir.

"Listen, the jeep speedometer says it ain't only twenty-five mile to Reykjavik!" someone declared. "I don't give a durn what you call it in kilometers; me, I go by miles. And we ain't but five mile off of the shore highway."

"You walk it, brother, and it'll be fifty," came response. "This here lava is sure hell underfoot! Them Marines and their searchlight battery up by Gerda may or may not be working. They only got about thirty minutes in the whole night to operate. They'd better call it a day."

"Along about November they'll call it a night, all day long," jeered another. "This here twenty-three-hour daylight does things to you, too. Boy, I wish a couple them Heinie bombers would come over and give us a real chance! Geese, you keep your eye peeled up on the hill!"

Jon Gissleifson nodded, grinned in his easy-humored way, and leaving the hut, started for the cook-shack to pick up a thermos of coffee.

They were into June now, and night was practically day. The sky was just a dark streak for an hour or so, until the sun bounded back above the savage black peaks to east and south, lighting up the snowy radiant crags that never melted, and rosily tingeing the eternal vapor floating and drifting above the craters of Mount Hecla.

For them, the mighty harbor of Reykjavik and the wood-and-stone buildings were gone, as the rest of the world was gone. Theirs was just an Iceland vista of hills and lava, but a mighty important vista. The hut, snugly covered with sandbags, the camouflaged ack-ack battery, and the conical hill of Keilir up above, was everything in sight; their horizon was, however, enormous.

From that lava cone one could see far north across the roads and the smokes of Hafnarfiordur; westward lay the Reikjanes, as they called the lava bad lands stretching to the sea at this southwest tip of Iceland; southward were higher peaks and the far white sea-horses of the ocean; southeast and east stretched the snow-crests and glaciers above the lake-country. And all of it wild, desolate, inhuman, with only occasional smokes to hint at man's presence on lonely farmsteads in hidden valleys.

The cook was of Danish birth and could talk with the natives. He gave Jon the thermos and package of grub, then nodded amiably at him.

"Say, Geese! There was a feller here a while back while you was asleep, asking for you. Him and me had a talk."

"Asking for me?" said Jon Gissleifson, surprise in his broad, strong features.

"Uh-huh. A farmer, by his looks; an old guy with a long beard and only one eye. He was bundled up in a blue cloak. Says he knew your folks back home, but he hadn't been out of Iceland himself. I didn't savvy him at all; if you ask me, he was plumb nuts."

"That's funny," said Gissleifson. "Maybe he was someone from Reykjavik who had heard about me and my folks. What did he want?"

The cook shrugged. "He just didn't make sense. He says you had the gift, whatever that means, and that there was blood on the Keilir, and that all the enemies did not come by way of the

sky. Just like a gabbly old preacher, he was. I guess he wanted a handout of cigarettes or grub. He says he might see you later. Look out for him, up there."

Gissleifson nodded, and went trudging away on the path that went up the bare conical hill called the Keilir. The observation post was located up there; and if it was cold now, it would be worse than cold when the snows of winter came.

"Said I had the gift, eh?" he reflected. "How did he know about that? Not that it means anything to me, but the old folks all said the same, that it ran in the family. Hm!"

Second-sight, the Scots folk would have called it—the gift of seeing things unseen. To Jon, this was all a pack of nonsense; or rather, something beyond his comprehension.

PERHAPS JON GISSLEIFSON should never have been sent to Iceland; once there, he should have been utilized to the full as interpreter. His people had emigrated from there to Wisconsin, a couple of generations back, and he knew the language perfectly well. However, he had landed as a mere cog in the army machine.

"Geese," the boys called him for short; little he cared. He

was tall, dark, raw-boned, with laughter deep in his eyes; but back of the laughter was a somber glow, a leashed fury that told of dark tragedy. He had not talked about it. Not even his buddies knew of it; but it was there, waiting, waiting hopelessly but implacably, burning like hell-fire.

As he mounted along the path, he could hear the distant crepitation of machine-gun fire from the ranges outside Reykjavik faintly shaking the cold thin air. There was no war here, but it was creeping closer. Occasionally a German bomber or two appeared, dumped its load and fled swiftly. Reconnaissance planes, high and far, sounded now and then.

The path curved. He looked northward to the distant peaks of Snaefels purpling the horizon. Out there to the north was the old land of heroic saga stories—there, and eastward. He had heard those tales as a boy, he had read them since in books; once it had been his dream to visit those lonely parts some day. Now he had another and darker dream, without a hero but stark with tragedy. If ever the occupation force moved on to Norway....

HE CAME to the hut, high up on the conical hill and elaborately camouflaged. Bennie Nolan, glad of the relief, welcomed him and replied to his first question.

"Naw. Not a thing stirring. I hear they had an alert over on the Hecla post last night; plane of some kind. Nothing developed. Well, me for grub and shuteye! Take over, soldier."

Gissleifson took over, reported in by the portable field telephone, adjusted the instruments to suit himself, swept sky and far sea and nearer landscape with the high-power binoculars, and settled down to his lonely vigil. Some day something might happen; not today, with this bright sun and sky.

He re-thumbed the letter he had received from home two days ago, and turned again to the paragraph he already knew by heart. He could not keep away from it; just as one cannot leave alone the thing that hurts worst of all. The words stabbed again at him:

"Bill Johnson has had a letter from his cousin Bergdolf who

recently escaped from Norway and is now in England. It said that B saw Mr. Helms in a concentration camp there. No news of Frieda."

He folded up the letter carefully; there was an ugly set to his mouth. The Reverend Luther Helms had left Wisconsin on a visit to relatives in Norway—and the Nazi influx had trapped him there. With him had gone his daughter Frieda, whom Jon Gissleifson had expected to marry on their return. Nothing more had been heard from them, until now.

Opening the case of his wrist-watch, Jon took out the little round snapshot, his favorite picture of the vanished Frieda, and propped it on the instrument-base, where his gaze could touch upon it from time to time. Her smiling, merry face was his constant companion up here on the lookout job. Engulfed now in the hell that Norway had become, lost in that maelstrom of conquered folk all this long while—alive or dead? He could not know. He could only hope for the best, and pray.

Gissleifson did pray; he was that sort, deep and steady-hearted. There were queer depths in him, though; throwbacks to ancient days and forgotten times—some said, to other lives. Good-humored he might be on the surface, but scratch the surface and there came a hard and astonishingly bitter stratum, especially these latter days.

The far sparkling sea, with its fast-tumbling white horses, was bare except for a few fisher-craft, easily identified. The sparkling summer sky was empty, except for a Spitfire and a racing P-38 on reconnaissance. The bleak dark crags eastward, the white streaks of waterfalls, the glittering far glaciers, showed no life; only—

He looked again, in surprise, at the moving object coming up the lava cone from the east side, where there was no path and apparently nowhere to come from. He focused the glasses on it; a man, who seemed to get over that jagged lava without difficulty. An old man walking with the aid of a stout staff. His gray beard was blowing in the wind; a faded blue cloak was wrapped around his tall, erect figure. On his head was an odd pointed cap striped with black and red; it was the characteristic headgear of men on the Faroe Islands, off eastward.

"Why the devil is he coming here?" thought Gissleifson. "No one has ever been up here, or knows about this lookout—still, I suppose all these islanders know more than they let on. Hello! This must be the same old fellow who was asking for me at the battery!"

The description answered, sure enough, for on closer approach the old man proved to have but one eye; very bright and keen it was, but in that weathered old face Jon Gissleifson was aware of shrewdness and a crafty spirit. As though he knew the spot intimately, the stranger came straight to the hidden lookout. He halted, peering in at Jon, and spoke in queerly accented words.

"*Goddag, min herre.*"

"It's a good day so far," said Jon. "Come in out of the wind and sit down." The other complied, looked around, and his eye rested for a moment on the little picture of Frieda Helms. Then it struck out at Gissleifson.

"So you are Jon Gissleifson," he said. "I heard of you in Reykjavik."

"Oh! So that's how you came to look me up at the battery, eh? And who may you be?"

"Ole, they call me," said the old man, with a slight smile. "It is a long time since Gissleif Arneson went to America. I knew him and his father Arne before him."

JON LAUGHED. "Then you're a lot older than you look, Ole! Maybe you're thinking of someone else."

Ole shook his head. "No, young man. I shall gather dust a long while yet."

"What do you mean by that?" asked Gissleifson, puzzled by the words. That piercing eye made him feel a trifle uneasy.

"Age, young man, is only the dust of the road home, which lies thickest in the day of return; for me, that day is far distant."

"Oh! You're confident enough. Did you come here looking for me?"

"*Ja.* You think of the young woman there; she is far away in Norway. She has lost the ring that you gave her."

At these words, Gissleifson was absolutely struck dumb for a moment; he could only sit there and stare at the old man in amazement.

HOW COULD this graybeard know about Frieda? Guesswork, perhaps. But how could he know about that ring? It was an old one of twisted gold that had belonged to his mother and had been made long generations ago—it had been in the family hundreds of years, by report. He had given it to Frieda, after having the worn gold reinforced, as an engagement ring.

"You seem to know a lot," he exclaimed. "Perhaps you guessed at that, too—what was the ring like?"

"It came from an old tomb here in this land, where one of your ancestors found it."

"Maybe so," Gissleifson responded. "But what was it like?"

"Like knotted ropes twisted together endlessly."

"By George! You hit it, all right!" said Gissleifson. Then common sense came to his aid, and he smiled. "Oh, I see! Maybe you did know my great-grandfather; you knew the family anyhow, and so knew about the ring, and guessed that I gave it to Frieda—eh? Ole, you're all right. Have a swig of coffee."

He opened the thermos and poured his visitor, who seemed amused by his words, a drink, and took one himself. Meantime, he did not neglect his work, but sea and sky remained empty.

"A new drink to me," said Ole, wiping his bearded lips on his cloak. "Not bad, but I prefer good honey-mead, myself. So you are a soldier. You listen here for the enemy, eh? But if he comes by night you cannot see him."

"The searchlights will."

"Maybe. They did not see the plane that came during last night's darkness."

Gissleifson frowned. What had Benny said about an alert?

"Did one come?" he demanded. The old man nodded.

"It came and went again, emptier than it came."

"What d'you mean by that?"

"It was lighter by two men when it went, than when it came."

Gissleifson stared at the speaker for a moment, slowly comprehending.

"Look here, Ole! Do you mean that it landed two men?"

"They came down from it, yes."

"The devil! Do you know what you're saying?" exclaimed Gissleifson excitedly.

"I usually do." Ole remained quite calm and unperturbed. "I was up on the Langjokull. One of them floated down and fell into the Hvitarvatn and died there in the water. The other man came down near here and is hiding."

Gissleifson stiffened. This old man up on the Long-glacier? Well, likely enough. And one paratroop man had gone into the Hvitar Lake, perishing in the icy glacial water—that sounded likely, too. But if another had landed safely—why, this was important news! With an effort, he controlled himself.

"See here, Ole. It might be that a German plane landed spies or saboteurs; if so, we must get them at once. But don't fool me. Be sure of what you're saying, man!"

Again Ole seemed amused, smiling slightly as he pawed his gray beard. One man or a hundred might have landed and taken to shelter; once down safely, a man could hide as long as he liked in this jumbled terrain of peaks and badlands and tiny hidden valleys, until ready to creep forth and go about his business, whatever that might be. The story certainly sounded plausible, though how Ole knew so much about it was a question.

"Do you know where this man is?"

"Of course. We can get there in two hours; that is why I looked you up."

"You mean you'll lead a squad of men there?"

Ole shook his head. "No. Why take many men to kill or capture one?" he replied. "It is your affair, Gissleifson; yours alone. A man of your blood, a man of the old race, should not need help when it is a question of one enemy alone."

There the old man stuck and would not be budged, bribed or argued with. Gissleifson talked in vain. For some reason Ole refused pointblank to lead any party to the spot, but was willing enough to lead him. At length he grew angry, came to his feet and picked up his staff.

"Very well; if you are a niddering, a worthless coward, let it pass," he cried in a new voice—a deep, roaring diapason quivering with contempt and fury. "I did not know I was talking with a man afraid, one who dare not face an enemy unless friends are with him! Besides, I said this is your affair, not theirs. So it is, Jon Gissleifson! I do you a great service and you are too cowardly to accept it—"

"Hold on, hold on!" cried Gissleifson, reaching for the telephone. After all, the battery commander had instructed him to pick up anything useful from the country folk that he might find. "I'm on duty here, Ole; can't leave here without orders. Wait, now!"

THE OLD MAN was sincere, he felt convinced. Further, he had a queer and unreasonable feeling that there was something cockeyed about the whole thing. He could not account for it, but it was there. This old man was obviously a simple peasant, yet had a strange and almost majestic air; he might have been a king. Many of these mountain oldsters possessed this same characteristic, as though living far and high held them above their fellows, but with Ole it was more pronounced. That flash of anger, that rolling voice, had given him a new aspect altogether.

Over the phone, Gissleifson told his story. If the thing were true, it assuredly demanded prompt investigation; since the country folk had by this time become entirely friendly to the forces of occupation, there was no fear of trickery or anything in the nature of a trap. The old man's positive refusal to lead others to the place was the only queer thing about it all.

"Very well," came the decision. "I'll relieve you at once and detail you to make the investigation. Meantime, I'll send word to headquarters to have a search made at the Hvitar Lake—that's well north of here. I needn't warn you to take no chances, and if there's anything to the story, your old peasant shall be well rewarded."

"Thank you, sir," replied Gissleifson, and hung up. He nodded to Ole. "A relief is on the way, and then I'm with you. So take it easy."

Ole granted assent.

By the time his relief came swinging along the path, Gissleifson was ready to turn over the post and go, inwardly glad of the change from the monotony of lookout.

A pistol was weapon enough; he wanted no avoidable burden, knowing only too well that the trip would take him through some pretty tough country. Whether he could keep up with this old mountaineer was his chief worry.

Art Hunter was the relief. Before he arrived, Ole strode out of the hut, saying he would wait on the lower slope. Hunter came in, with a query that showed he knew nothing of what was up.

"Hey, Geese! What kind of a rabbit's foot you wearing, huh? Can't you stick it out?"

"Special detail. You saw that old country fellow?"

"Huh? Saw nobody. Who you talking about?"

Gissleifson pointed down the slope, to where Ole stood. "Him."

"I don't see anybody," said Hunter, gaping.

"You're nuts. Or else I am," said Gissleifson. "Anyhow, I'm off. See if you can see me go."

He started after Ole, who was awaiting him. Hunter's words had angered him; perhaps Art, who was a notorious joker, was trying to put over some game, he thought, and his anger died out.

Ole led him a stiff pace over the rough lava ground, and although no path appeared, seemed to know exactly where he was going. The Heiler cone vanished; as far as Gissleifson could perceive, they struck off toward the east and north, now following stony gullies, now clambering over bleak hill flanks. Before an hour was up Gissleifson knew that he was traveling, tough as his muscles were. They rested briefly beside a leaping waterfall whose spray feathered on the air. Ole pointed to it.

"Men died here," he said, "in the old days. By this water is the place where the sons of Sigfus were killed. It was a famous fight."

"Never heard of it," said Gissleifson. "How long ago was it?"

"A thousand years and more," replied Ole. "Those men are forgotten now; but others shall soon die and be better remembered. When we find this man we seek, look out that he doesn't kill you by stealth. He will pretend to be a man named Helgi Gudmundson from Krisuvik; but he is not. When you tell him that eight days ago he was in Norway, he will be afraid."

This was singular, thought Gissleifson, a trifle suspiciously.

"I thought you said he was a German?"

"It was you said that, not I. However, he is a German, one who has been here and who knows this country well, and speaks our tongue."

"If you know so much about him, what's his real name?"

"Hans Munster. Are you ready? Soon we come to a path; *folg mig.*"

Follow me! Easy to say, hard to do. As Gissleifson clambered on in the wake of Ole, he thought uneasily of this information. How had the old fellow learned so much?

There was only one answer. Ole must have known this paratrooper from other days, and perhaps had run across him and helped him to take hiding. Then had gone to turn him in. This would explain the whole thing, and nothing else would. None the less, Gissleifson did not find it entirely plausible.

He was mystified by his graybeard, who moved across the roughest ground with the grace and ease of a goat and showed no evidence of weariness. By his own story he must have been continually on the go since last night, yet he was fresh as a daisy and his one eye was blazing with energy. These Icelanders certainly seemed to improve with age, particularly these back-country peasants. Jon recalled that his own grandfather at ninety had outchopped him in the woodlot, and was tough as iron.

HANS MUNSTER, eh? Well, the game was to capture the fellow if possible; take no chances, but bring him in alive. The task force wanted trophies and information. No doubt this Munster had been planted here to act as a spy and perhaps signal to lurking submarines off the coast. In Norway eight days ago, eh? In Norway!

"And I'd give my right hand to be there eight days from now," thought Gissleifson.

Ole turned around, the one eye burning at him, and spoke.

"Not in eight days, young man; but, perhaps, in much less than eighty; though I cannot say what you will find when you get there."

He turned and strode along. Gissleifson swallowed hard; was the old man a mind reader—or had he himself spoken those words aloud? Perhaps; he could not be sure. And yet, from this moment, he regarded Ole with a touch of fear and awe. Indeed, the old fellow seemed to take on dignity and stature the farther they went. Here in these jagged recesses of the badlands he was in his own place, supreme, master of all around—a desolate supremacy, with scarce a tree or shrub to bring a touch of green to eye.

Abruptly, in a winding gully strewn with great tumbled masses of riven rocks, Ole came to a halt, and waved his staff like a spear at the gully ahead, which was small and narrow.

"There lies your man," he said in a stately manner, like a king dismissing some subject. "I go no farther. Press on, and bring to a close the web of destiny woven by the Norns, Jon Gissleifson, for the Disir are by your side. You need no further guidance."

Dim memories of old tales flitted through Gissleifson's mind—this talk of the Norns, or fates, and the Disir, or guardian spirits, was a throwback to heathen days. The old man must have gone a bit dotty, he thought; probably much loneliness and age had unsettled his wits when in such places as this. Desolate and lonely it was, and vaguely sinister.

"But what about getting back?" he queried. Ole looked at him and laughed grimly.

"Fear not! You'll find your way; if you get lost, I'll not be far. Farewell."

So saying, he swung around and in ten seconds was lost to sight among the rocks.

Gissleifson uttered one angry grunt. Well, he was in for it; no backing out now! He loosened the pistol in its holster and headed up the little ravine. A good place for a man to hide out, certainly; there were almost no shrubs, but the strewn rocks were of all sizes and shapes.

Less than eighty days? What had made Ole say that? More guesswork, of course; with the Axis being pushed out of Africa and new fronts opening up everywhere, the task force wearing the emblem of the Arctic bear might well look forward to Norway. It was anybody's guess, in this war!

Then all thought of Ole fled away, as he heard something up ahead—the voice of a man singing softly, as one sings to himself when enveloped by loneliness. But the words were German.

He went on, alert in every nerve, threading his way among the rocks, stepping with care, straining to catch sight of what lay ahead. The singing had ceased. The wind whistled eerily along the black crags overhead. Gissleifson caught a faint whiff of tobacco smoke; then suddenly sighted his man.

A SLIM, young, bare-headed man who sat on a boulder and inhaled from a cigarette he had just lit. He had fair, thick hair and a bonily handsome face. He was roughly dressed in the crudely fitting garments of the country, and heavily booted. There was no parachute in sight, nothing at all to indicate that he was not the peasant he seemed. As a stone clicked under Gissleifson's foot, he sprang erect with startled air, then relaxed and waved a hand in smiling greeting.

"Oh! *Goddag!*" he exclaimed. "Soldiers are everywhere, eh? Or do you understand me?"

"Jag forstar," said Gissleifson, approaching warily. *"Hvad heter de?* What's your name?"

"Helgi Gudmundson from Krisuvik on the shore. So you speak our tongue! What a happy surprise! But you're an American?"

Gissleifson nodded. He lost courage; this, he thought swiftly, might be some form of joke. This fellow was certainly an Icelander by tongue and costume, and seemed unarmed. Best step warily. A pleasant, handsome, cheerful fellow, this.

"Yes. I got lost," he replied. "Can you tell me where I am?"

"A long way from the city!" rejoined the other cheerfully. "Keep bearing south and you're bound to come out at steads or shore farms. Reykjavik lies west and north."

Gissleifson sniffed the cigarette smoke. Ha! English! He had tried to smoke some of those English cigarettes when he first came here; the Limies had scads of them to swap.

"Where," he asked, getting out his own smokes, "did you get those cigarettes?"

Instantly, reassurance came to him. The other looked startled at the question, glancing at the cigarette, then at him.

"These? I traded a soldier for them. One of your soldiers."

"Not much you didn't!" said Gissleifson. "We don't like them. We don't have them. Maybe you got them in Norway when you were there eight days ago?"

Gudmundson stared at him, then broke into a laugh.

"Me? In Norway? My friend, what are you talking about? I live in Krisuvik, down on the south shore. I've never seen Norway, although," he added wistfully, "I've often thought of going there with the fishing fleet. Perhaps I shall, after the war."

NO USE; that illusion had failed of its mark. Perhaps, thought Gissleifson, he had been too quick to jump at conclusions. After all, the cigarettes might mean nothing. Again he became irresolute, uncertain.

He had lugged his canteen with him, although water was never very far in these hills. He took it off, drank, offered the other man a drink, but Gudmundson shook his head. He laid down the canteen and reached for a cigarette.

"Where," asked the other, looking at him curiously, "did you learn our tongue, the Danish tongue that our shore-folk speak? Although you do pronounce it something like a Swede. Do you know the old language that the northern folk speak?"

"No," said Gissleifson. "Dansk is good enough for me—"

He had a cigarette in his lips and was fumbling with a book of matches, when he saw it. Something hard and deadly leaped through heart and brain. His words failed; for an instant his pulse stopped. Then he gulped, and forced himself to light the match, but as he lifted it his fingers were shaking. And he could not take his eyes from the other man's hand.

"Yes? What is it?" came the laughing question.

Gissleifson dropped the match, took the cigarette from his lips, flipped it away.

"What's that ring you're wearing?" he asked, trying to keep his voice casual.

"This?" The other glanced down at his hand. "Oh, an old family ring—"

"*You're a damned liar!*" The words burst forth suddenly, with abrupt violence. In a split second, Gissleifson had his pistol out and was covering the other man. "Hold out your hand—quick! Let me see that ring!"

Gudmundson went white, then extended his hand with a laugh.

"Why, certainly! Have you lost your wits, my friend? Be careful with that gun—"

There was no mistake. There could be none. Gissleifson touched the little gold ring, made like three twisted strands of rope; he slipped it off the man's little finger and looked at it more closely. The same, the same! There was the place where the gold had been added at the worn shank. There was the place where it had been cut and joined together, to make it fit Frieda's finger.

He looked up, and his eyes were frozen, and his face was thin and hard.

"I'll give you a chance for your life, Hans Munster," he said thickly. "Tell me where you got this, where she is—speak up!"

At the sound of that name the other man stiffened in nerve and muscle. His eyes changed; they became queer and hard and inhuman—the typical Nazi eyes, as of a man who has lost his soul. The handsome features shifted into queer animal lines of ferocity.

FASTER THAN eye could follow, the Nazi moved. The edge of his palm struck the inside of Gissleifson's wrist, knocking the pistol to the stones; the other hand darted in with a crushing blow, a deadly blow to the throat, a blow to kill one instantly. The American's chin came down, taking that crack full force but saving his throat. He was dealing with a man trained in killing. But the Marines knew those tricks too.

Gissleifson staggered under the ferocity of the attack that swept into him. He had dropped the ring. But Frieda would never have given it up; it had been taken from her—and through his brain tore visions of fearful possibilities. This man knew— this man knew! And thus thinking, he woke up.

It was almost too late. Knee and fist were hammering into him, nausea was drifting upon him, his head was rocked back and the hard fist was smashing in again for his Adam's apple—he blocked it. Then he went to work on his man in grim earnest.

Not a pretty fight; a bare-handed fight for life is never pretty. Once, as they staggered back and forth, Gissleifson saw a glint on the stones, where the ring had fallen; the ring, that this man had taken from Frieda or from her body. It stripped from him the last veneer of civilized habit; if Munster had become a devil, he became ten devils in one, slugging, rending, tearing. Both men were so well trained in this deadly butchery that for a space each avoided vital damage from the other.

Then they were down, grappling and slashing, exerting every trick. Blood was running from Gissleifson's mouth and nostrils; but, more horrible to see, Munster's left eye was ripped from its socket and lay out upon his cheek. They rolled, they writhed, and Gissleifson came uppermost, jamming the Nazi's head against a rock. He checked his effort.

"Speak up!" he gasped. "Where—did you get it? Where—"

His breath came in a groan, as a savage jab in the groin went home and sent him toppling. Munster was up and at him with the boots, but he brought the Nazi down again, falling across him, twisting the foot he had caught, bringing a wild scream of agony from the red-bubbling lips. Then Munster caught up a sliver of rock and hammered him over the eyes with it, before the leg could be broken, and crawled away from him on hands and knees.

Crawled—reached out—caught up the fallen and forgotten pistol, with a gasping croak of triumph. Before he could use it, Gissleifson was upon him again, locking with him, sinking iron fingers into that iron wrist and turning the weapon aside. It exploded; powder burned, the bullet went wild. They lay almost motionless, yet with every nerve and muscle at frantic utmost, arms trembling, faces strained and bloody and terrible. The gun was twisting, twisting—Munster's head darted forward like that of a snake and his teeth sank into Gissleifson's neck muscles.

A twisting, convulsive effort shook both men; once again the pistol exploded, with more muffled report. Munster's body jerked. His teeth lost their grip and he threw back his head, gasping air into his lungs; then he went limp and inert, and lay senseless.

FOR A moment Gissleifson was helpless to move. Then, gathering energy, he wiped blood from his face and examined the other man, after knocking the pistol away. That second bullet had pierced Munster's body—a deadly wound, he thought. However, he had his orders.

He bared the wound and bandaged it, having his first-aid kit in pocket. He shoved the left eye back into its socket and bandaged that. He applied first-aid to his own hurts, as far as possible, and stumbled to his canteen. A drink, a slosh of water over his face, and he felt better instantly. Back to Munster, and he poured water over the hurt face and into the puffed lips; but the Nazi lay silent and unconscious.

Gaining strength and energy, Gissleifson searched about until he located the fallen gold ring, and slipped it into a pocket. He looked around, and painfully limped a little way up the ravine, peering here and there among the rocks, looking for such a hiding-place as he himself would have chosen.

Presently he found it. There was a pistol, a knapsack well packed with rations and flashlight and neat cylinders of explosive and fuse; and among these effects was a little book in English and German and Danish giving all sorts of information about Iceland and its people. He lugged the stuff back with him to where Munster still lay inert, and sank down to rest beside the dying Nazi. Idly, he took out the little book and turned the pages. A sentence struck up at his consciousness; he read it again, and read on.

"It is believed that the old heathen gods still linger in the recesses of the fells, and chiefly the greatest of the gods, Odin. They say he sometimes appears to men in the shape of an old man with one eye and a long gray beard, wrapped in a blue cloak, and calls himself by the name of Ole—"

Gissleifson caught his breath. Oh, it was absurd, absurd! It was all nonsense, of course.

Yet the queer things that old man had said and done lingered with him. He thought about himself, and the gift of second sight that ran in the family—

Munster groaned and moved, and Gissleifson forgot all else. He gave the dying man more water. Munster opened his good eye, looked at him, and spoke faintly.

"You win, American."

"Tell me!" breathed Gissleifson quickly. "The ring—where did you get it? Where is she? You were in Norway eight days ago; you took the ring from her—where? Where?"

A flicker of life came into the face of the dying man. A faint, terrible smile touched his swollen lips with venom.

"Yes," he said, almost inaudibly. "Yes. I was in Norway—and she—and she—"

He paused.

"Where?" urged Gissleifson. The one eye flashed up at him.

"Go—go to hell!" gasped Munster. His body wrenched, a strangled sound broke from him, and he relaxed in death.

Gissleifson stood up. Through him passed a wave of anguish, of hopeless despair; then, when his fingers touched the gold ring in his pocket, his heart firmed and his shoulders squared once more. He had learned nothing; her fate, her whereabouts, remained hidden from him. A deep breath escaped his lips.

"But he was in Norway eight days ago—at least she must be alive!" he murmured. It was queer about that old man, Ole. He recalled now that Art Hunter had not seen the old fellow at all, or had pretended not to see him.

He headed back for the Keilir cone, dragging his aching hurt body along. A later party could locate Munster and the other things here. Perhaps, en route, he would meet the old man, who had promised to guide him if he got lost.

He got back without need of guidance, and without seeing Ole again. Nor was Ole ever seen again. None of the country folk, when questioned, could tell anything about such a person, nor was he known in the whole district. Jon Gissleifson, they said, must have imagined him.

But Jon Gissleifson had the gold ring on a cord about his neck, for proof, though he told nobody about it. Perhaps in less than eighty days, Ole had said—God! If that should come true like the rest! In Norway!

V

A WOLF IN WOLF'S CLOTHING

His Past Record Was Black, True... But
After All, He Was an American.

B ENEATH THE blazing morning sun of Tunis, the Honorable David Morton flushed with annoyance as his companion began to sing softly. They had alighted from the tram at the Avenue Jules Ferry. Although he was rumpled and unshaven and dirty from three days of prison, Dick Ravenal could sing. His words, however, were impudent; he wanted to be rid of the Englishman at his side.

> "Taffy was a Welshman, Taffy was a thief,
> Taffy came to my house and stole a piece of beef!"

Morton halted. "See here, Hobbs, I've had enough of this!" he barked.

"Well, David's the same name as Taffy," said Ravenal. "You certainly came to my prison house, and you got me set at liberty, and took your piece of beef!"

"And paid for it," snapped Morton. "Have you no gratitude?"

"None. I just don't like you. Because you're in the British consular service, should I worship you? Far from it. I've informed you on troop dispositions and the exact number of planes at the Bizerte base and the air fields here outside Tunis—"

"I helped you because you're a British subject, Hobbs!" began Morton. Ravenal grinned.

"I'm no such thing. The passport I showed you isn't mine; it was stolen. As though I'd have a name like Hobbs! That's what the Arabs call bread—*hobbs!* My friend, I'm an American

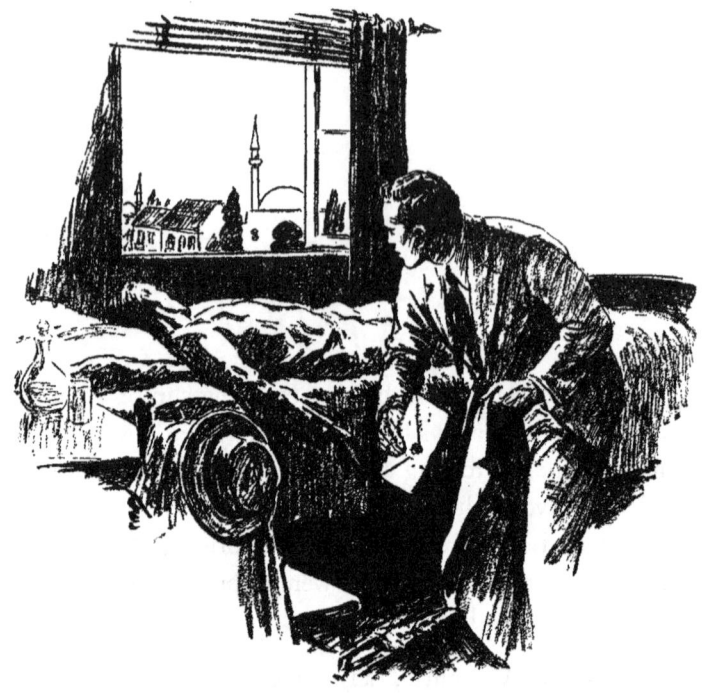

citizen. You got me free; now run along with your information. You did a good job telling the police they had made a mistake, and you're paid for it—so what? I have business ahead. Here's your pocketbook; don't be so careless with it, or some thief will grab it. I've no use for it. Good-by."

He pressed into the hand of the astounded Britisher a fat leather pocketbook, then slipped away and was gone in the passing throng, leaving Morton all astare; and this was the last he saw, or wanted to see, of the Honorable David Morton.

Doubling back the way they had come, Ravenal slipped around the corner and walked into the Transatlantique Hotel, by no means the largest or finest in Tunis. It was convenient because it stood on a corner and had two entrances. He went to the desk and demanded his key.

"M'sieu has been away?" said the clerk, handing it over.

"Yes," replied Ravenal. "For three days I have been sitting

mourning among the ruins of Carthage, my friend. No letters? Good. Send me some luncheon, and a bottle of that Monfiore Chianti."

"Ah, M'sieu! There is a trifling matter of accounts—"

"Apply this; I've had no time to get it changed." Ravenal laid down an English five-pound note, and departed to his room, anxious for a bath and a change. The Honorable David had paid in cash as well as in service for the information he got. Ravenal wondered why the devil he had been so keen to get it.

Dick Ravenal, at present soldier of fortune, was one of those not uncommon men whom most women think in need of mothering, and whom other men usually like on sight.

He was not so much a rascal as merely amoral; he had no reverence for money, his own or another's; he knew his way around in a dozen countries, and he had an air of pleasant, kindly intimacy and sympathy which was natural to him. This deceived enemies and bound friends more closely.

He was not a bird of prey; such birds prey on victims, and Ravenal had no victims. He could rook a blackguard with pleasure, he could live by his wits, he could even kill without a qualm if life were at stake; but he had a certain code which he never transgressed. For years he had been knocking about north Africa—after losing a fortune in Egypt, at cards and tables and women. He was no angel, understand; hear the worst and get it over.

THAT PLUNGE into the fleshpots of Egypt had swept away his money and his past. His young wife, back in Baltimore, divorced him, his business associates chucked him out. He could not go home, so stayed where he was, in Africa, and wandered. He slipped into easy ways of living, collecting tribute where it offered, giving generously where there was need. Because he was speaking fluent Italian with a poor devil of a runaway Italian soldier, and giving him cigarettes and money, the police here clapped him in jail as an Axis spy, until Morton convinced them he was only a mad Englishman. And in return—why the devil, he asked himself again, had the consular chap been so frantic after that information?

He reached his own corridor, started for his own room, and paused. Beside him, a room door swung open; a man appeared, clutching at the jamb, speaking to him.

"So here you are, species of canaille! I've been ringing for half an hour. Inside, inside! Abominable service in this rathole, abominable! Quick, damn you—help me!"

His first thought was that the man was drunk; then he dismissed it as the man caught his arm. Not drunk, but ill—frightfully, horribly ill, doubled up with agony. He had been mistaken for the garcon. This was not a tourist hotel with telephone luxuries; here one used the bell, French fashion, and sometimes it worked and sometimes not.

Ravenal helped the man to the bed, helped him stretch out, half-conscious. A hard, lean man, who muttered to himself in German. Ravenal pricked up his ears. A Nazi? No lack of Nazi spies hereabouts by all accounts. He looked around swiftly.

Evidently the man had arrived very recently, perhaps within the hour. A handbag was open, a grip strapped and locked, still fresh with the chalk-mark of the customs inspector. A coat and vest lying on a chair. Ravenal swooped on them, delved in the pockets, found a passport and two letters. The passport was French and told that this man was Eric Horn, a Frenchman. The letters gave it the lie. They said Eric Horn was a Nazi, outfitted in Paris with French identity; in reality, Ober-lieutenant Horn of Breslau.

Ravenal pocketed the lot. He came back to the bed. Horn's eyes wavered open in a lucid interval. Ravenal spoke to him in German.

"Shall I call a doctor? Tell me what I can do for you."

The man was clutching at his side, in a sweat of anguish, but joy darted into his face at hearing the German speech. He fell into a babble of fevered words.

"Yes, yes! The doctor, yes. But first— the summer-house in

the Belvedere—at five this afternoon! Meet Hesse there. The report on that damned American agent—important. He must be—must be removed—the Americans—fleet from England to Algiers—sh!" A groan wrenched at him and he twisted in convulsive pain. "Meet Hesse—meet Hesse—"

The man straightened out, unconscious.

Ravenal was deeply startled by those words. He swiftly examined the Nazi agent; there was no sign of injury. The truth hit him suddenly—the appendix, of course! He searched clothes and handbag again, replacing the passport on the dresser in full sight. A wallet, fat with paper money, rewarded his search. In it was a note, addressed to Eric Horn at the Transat' Hotel, written two days previously; a brief but illuminating note. It was brief and curt, but indicated that the writer did not know Herr Horn:

> Five o'clock, the Belvedere summer-house, on the 4th.
> Bring this to serve as your identification.
> Hesse.

Ravenal chuckled. Then he left the room and made his way back to the downstairs desk, and spoke to the clerk.

"There's a man in Room 39 who's very ill. He asked me to have a doctor sent. It looks like an emergency case, too."

This done, he sought his own room and lost no time in getting a bath and shave and a change of clothes. He left his door open and kept an eye on the hall. When he had dressed, he went to Horn's room and found a physician there, at work. He explained his interest and the doctor nodded.

"Good thing you called me; apparently a ruptured appendix; the fool had taken a physic. He's not recovered consciousness. I've given him a hypodermic and am rushing him to the military hospital. It's a toss-up whether he'll live."

Ravenal withdrew. In his own room, he applied himself to a hearty lunch; and then, in the expressive native phrase, sat knuckling the drum of thought. He was faced with a decision which, no matter the choice, was unpleasant.

H E   H A D   no desire to mix in the North African game of politics, which in Tunis was particularly hot and vicious. The French feared and hated the Italians in nearby Tripoli, and in Tunis itself the Italians outnumbered them. Between Nazi agents, Italians, Allied agents, Vichy agents and occasional Fighting French sympathizers, Tunisia was a hotbed of undercover action. And life was cheap here.

But two things stuck in Ravenal's craw. First, that consular chap's overweening interest in the dispositions at the airports; second, the words of Horn. "The Americans—fleet from England to Algiers—" and then about the removal of some American agent. This struck Ravenal as not only ominous, but directly keyed by destiny to pluck at his own affairs. Cards had been dealt him. If he refused to play them, he was a rat.

The choice was, in a way, a bit hard because he had a deal on with a Tunisian grain broker that would net him a cool ten thousand francs provided he put it through at once. If he did not get down the coast to Sfax this afternoon and see his man, the deal was off. If he stayed here and played the cards given him, he must chuck the other completely.

"Be damned to it!" he thought. "These Nazis are out to get some American; my job is to step in. I've been given the chance, maybe, to make up for my sorry wasted opportunities. If I refuse it, good-by to all self-respect. So I must lose a cool ten thousand francs for the sake of some chap from home I never set eyes on! Well, I'd be a hell of an American if I passed up the chance."

So he reached a decision, then found himself rewarded upon dipping into Horn's wallet. The money in it was French and Algerian, and the total was close to seven thousand francs— sweet consolation for his lost brokerage deal! This cheered him up amazingly, and clinched his decision.

There is simply no use in affirming that Dick Ravenal was a heroic figure burning to match wits with the masters of espionage; he was not. He knew too much about that grim game, and was afraid of it. He had a bad record, and from some standpoints was an arrant rogue. And yet—well, even those wretches in prison had liked him. One of them had given him a couple of racing tips, too.

With his borrowed English papers in his pocket and a few other things besides, Ravenal walked down the Avenue de Paris, bought himself a spotless sun-helmet and a swagger new white jacket of the finest material, and in its buttonhole carefully adjusted the ribbon of the Legion of Honor, which he had no earthly right to sport. He then turned in at a *boutique* half French, half Arab, and made some heavy bets on the afternoon's races at the Kassar Said hippodrome.

By this time the afternoon was wearing along, so he hopped a northbound tram, taking a ticket to the Belvedere. He got off at the entrance avenue of palms. This enormous park, with its theatre and casino, was entirely French but was always thronged with the white-robed natives, particularly as the evening prayer-hour approached, for your Arab is a sensuous soul and loves beauty. And this was the most beautiful spot in Tunis, at the day's end. Ravenal felt himself thrill to it now, as always, as he climbed.

From the open loggia of the summer-house, he stood looking across the trees and the city beyond to the Kasbah and the ragged peaks of the Bou-Cornein. The soft richness of the view, the vast expanse of white houses and roofs, spotless with distance, was enchanting. Ravenal, however, kept his eye on the figures around. He had not come here for the view. No German was in sight. A few soldiers, a number of Arabs as usual, a little group of Italians with a guide—and a woman, close by, who stood looking dreamily out across the park.

A young woman, dark, gowned in the simplest and most notable Parisian style; svelte, slim, with incisive profile and the eyes of an artist. She drew a deep breath, turned, caught Ravenal's look, and colored slightly. Then she returned his gaze.

"It is very beautiful," she said in French.

He bowed slightly, as in apology for answering. "It is called the Burnouse of the Prophet," he said. "That is the native name for the city. See, how it flows from the Kasbah, where lies the hood of the burnouse, toward the port and La Goulette! A burnouse of purest white, pricked out with the green tiles on the domes of saints' tombs and mosques; streets so narrow as to be invisible, windows all on the inside of the houses—secrecy everywhere, sanctity everywhere, a city of holiness! That is, from a distance."

As he spoke, he was wondering what such a woman was doing here, alone.

"What an odd conceit!" she exclaimed, gazing out again at the city, neither rebuking him nor showing too much interest in him. "It is more beautiful than any other city in French Africa! Why is that?"

"Beauty gravitates to beauty," said Ravenal. "These people love beautiful things, as they love perfume! The perfume bazars here are unique, you know. Have you seen them?"

She nodded. "I've been here several days. One goes first to the perfume bazars."

Her tone bespoke dismissal; she was through with him. Perhaps, he thought, she had come here to meet someone. This recalled his own errand. He bowed slightly to her and turned away. Still no one in sight who looked at all like his man; or, he reflected, the Nazi agent might even be in Arab guise.

Ah, the letter which was to serve as identification—of course! He moved closer to the square opening in the exquisitely tiled walls which gave view of the city. He took out the letter, un-folded it, held it as though perusing it, and then in leisurely fashion struck a match for his cigarette. Surely, he thought, if the man Hesse were anywhere here, he must catch sight of this significant poised figure!

Then he caught a startled breath from behind, and turned

to find the woman staring at him. She spoke softly, but in German.

"Where did you get my letter?"

"Your letter?" For an instant, Ravenal was thunderstruck, as he realized the truth. A smile came to his lips. "But it is mine, since it is addressed to me! And don't speak German here. So you are Hesse!"

"Of course," she said. "Hesse Dubois. But you—well, I would never have taken you to be Eric Horn, after what I've heard of you!"

"Neither would less friendly persons, which is my object." Ravenal forced himself to accept the situation. He concealed his astonishment and nodded at her, offering his arm. "We can't talk here. Come along. Let's take a tram and find a café and be comfortable. Did you have any trouble getting here?"

Not for nothing was Ravenal a crafty fellow. As they left the buildings and headed for the tram entrance, he got what he most needed to know; information.

"Leaving Egypt was not easy," she said. "However, I got a boat from Alexandria. And I have frightful news. The British have amassed incredible forces. American planes and tanks and men are pouring in. Already the offensive is under way and Rommel is crumbling; he cannot hope to stand up against it. What word from Paris and Algiers?"

"Nothing of moment," said Ravenal. "The most important thing at present is the matter of that American who must be removed."

"Yes, yes, that is urgent!" she replied. "I have learned everything. I got it straight from an American consular agent in Alexandria—the fool! The information must be sent on at once from here; have you any means of sending it?"

"Of course," said Ravenal calmly. She relaxed, and sighed.

"Good. Then everything's all right. Here's the tram."

They got aboard and started down the long avenue, chatting of little things. Meantime Ravenal found himself sizing her up anew. He was good at this; every rascal, like every hotel clerk, learns to do it automatically. Yet she had fooled him at first sight.

N O W H E saw her as a person not to be lightly regarded. Evidently she was a trained and supple spy, probably of French birth; her hands were slim and tapering, but they were strong, her features were vivacious and beautiful, but lacked any sympathy or compassion. She was obviously efficient, but also superficial.

At the Avenue de Londres they changed to a west-bound tram, and in time gained the crowded Place Halfaouine, with its trees and stone benches and French fountain and surrounding cafés, and the enormous Mosque Halfaouline at the far end. This was the very heart of the Medina or native city, thronged with Arabs of every hue, with grayish Berbers, with shiny black Soudanese, with magicians and story-tellers and snake-charmers, and the air a din of laughter and babbling voices.

"You speak English?" questioned Ravenal, as they settled down at a café table.

"Of course."

"Then stick to it, as the safest. Here's the soul of Tunis before your eyes," he said. "Squalor enough, but also beauty. They go in for fine clothes, these natives. Like the ancient Khmers who built the jungled ruins of Siam, they worship beauty—and the same vice. There, opium. Here, hashish. It spells decadence, effeminacy, weakness."

"How soon can you get off my information?" she demanded. She was practical, not dreaming of beauty; probably anxious and worried, thought Ravenal.

"Within half an hour. By short-wave wireless."

"Oh! And you only arrived here today?"

Ravenal waved at his hand. "Everything was long ago arranged. The superior Aryan race is most efficient. I am surprised that you did not run into any of our people."

"I did," she confessed. "But I had orders to report to you alone."

"Excellent woman!" he said, as their drinks arrived. "Now, then, let's have it."

She poured out a torrent of low, rapid speech, to which Ravenal listened without evidence of emotion. His pleasant, kindly features held their half-smile. His dark eyes narrowed a trifle; a shadowy, predatory air became visible and lent his face an incisive quality. Inwardly he fell into tumultuous and ghastly alarm.

"These special trade control officers the Americans have sent to Africa," she said, "have been here a year and a half. They are picked Intelligence men, cooperating with the Free French sympathizers. Spies, all of them—spies! Agents working against us! No one has suspected this before. They're supposed to supervise the exchange of American products and food sent to North Africa for cork and other things. Something is in the air! Berlin must be warned at once. No one knows just what it is."

She paused. Into Ravenal's brain darted the words of the sick man. "The Americans—fleet from England to Algiers!" Could such a thing be? No, no, it was fantastic!

"That is the information you must send," she went on. "This man Wright, here at Tunis, is one of those agents. He has caused us terrific injuries."

"And therefore must be removed?" said Ravenal. She nodded.

"Exactly. That is my work; it is all arranged. I met him yesterday. He's not only in contact with the military authorities here, but with the British; also with Italians in Tripoli—the swine! He has caused the loss of invaluable ships sent to supply the Afrika Korps. How far may I count upon your help."

"All the way," said Ravenal. "But the thing must be kept quiet."

"Just you and I and Kleine. He was our best man in Cairo

but it got too hot for him and he had to clear out. He'll arrive here tonight or tomorrow. You'll like him."

Ravenal doubted this, but gathered that Kleine did not know Eric Horn, which was pleasant. She went on, a vicious edge creeping into her voice.

"We'll handle this American pig tomorrow night. Wright lives at the Hotel des Anglais and does his work there. He is circumspect, but a fool. I think he must be a naval officer. He is interested in helping me, and thereby gaining some vital information."

"You're a charming woman," said Ravenal, and almost meant it. "How did you trap him?"

She smiled. "Oh, my brother is an officer in the aviation; he is very ill. He wants to give the Americans full information on the latest dispositions at the Bizerte base, also at the Aouina military aviation base here. And you are to be the brother."

She broke into a laugh and stopped there, refusing to give him any hint about her plans. Glancing at her watch, she rose. "I must leave; I have my report to finish and get in the mail. I'll telephone you tomorrow. You'll send the information at once?"

"Immediately," said Ravenal. "But if you phone me at the hotel, do not ask for Eric Horn. Ask for Mr. Ravenal. I'll tell the desk clerk it's an affair of the heart and he'll be delighted to cooperate. I find it safer not to use the name of Horn."

The sun had set. They walked back to the tram line and parted. This Hesse Dubois was beautiful, but she was a very machine of a woman and not one for philandering; nor was she more than superficially clever. Ravenal's notions of voluptuous female agents went glimmering. He began to feel the very cold, steely edge of this young woman's real personality, and it frightened him.

He returned to the Avenue de Paris, dropped in at the betting office, and to his surprised delight found several thousand francs awaiting him. That tip from the chap in prison had been accurate. Decidedly, he reflected, he was finding virtue well rewarded! So, being the man he was, he sent half his winnings by a sure hand to the poor devil in prison, and sought the Brasserie Tantonville where he dined like a lord.

But, at the back of his brain, things were jangling. An American agent and a British agent both risking much to get accurate information on the local aerodromes—Americans, a fleet from London to Algiers—hell's bells! Could his wild fantastic thought actually be true? Were his own people going to move in on North Africa?

He went to a dance after dinner, not to watch the dancers but to watch the crowd, as he loved to do. Arab women were not allowed to dance in Tunis; the performers were women from the Jewish suburban community of Ariane, but the dances were purely Bedouin. Only a native-trained eye could appreciate them, since they were neither naughty nor graceful from other viewpoints. The crowd, mostly native, would sit entranced for hours, sniffing flowers and munching burnt almonds. Ravenal munched and sniffed also, and watched the people around. He finally headed for home, determining to call on Wright in the morning.

Upon reaching the hotel, he inquired after the sick man. The desk clerk shook his head; M. Horn might or might not survive the operation. One could not say. Only Allah could foretell the event!

Dick Ravenal slept soundly.

AT NINE next morning he was walking briskly down the Rue de Portugal. Just outside a gate of the Medina, the old native city, was his destination; an obscure French hotel of small size. Ravenal asked at the office for M. Wright. The clerk looked dubious; M. Wright was usually busy. One must be announced. So Ravenal gave his name and settled down to wait.

Presently came a query; his business with M. Wright? Somewhat nettled, Ravenal made answer that it was personal, concerning the Aouina airport. He waited again. At ten o'clock a cheerful garcon appeared and led him upstairs and down a corridor to a room door, and in. There, sitting behind a desk in a room that was obviously part of a suite, a room businesslike and bare, was a man with bleak eyes and stony features. A man of thirty, who nodded at him and bade him be seated.

"You have business with me, Mr. Ravenal?" came the brisk American words.

"Yes, of a rather personal nature," replied Ravenal. "In fact, I think that I can interest you in—"

"Pardon me," broke in Wright, who was fingering a dossier that lay before him. "You can interest me in nothing, Mr. Ravenal. Let me refresh your memory. You have been knocking around the Near East for some time in a disreputable manner. Your passport was long ago cancelled. In Egypt, you were implicated in the El Arish scandal; you had a share in the Myers cotton swindle; after a most unsavory series of episodes, you were expelled from the country because of your participation in the affair of Nabhas Pasha."

Ravenal writhed inwardly; pallor stole into his cheeks as he listened to the chill, unemotional words. Wright continued with pitiless voice.

"In Algeria, you had a bad record; twice arrested, each time released with charges unproven. At Constantine you had a finger nipped in the swindle of a French promoter; you came to Tunisia and have been mixed in the same sort of slippery business. Very recently you tasted prison life, being mistaken for an Italian spy. You are a second-rate con man. The world may be your oyster, Mr. Ravenal, but I am not. Is that sufficient?"

The cold eyes bored into Ravenal. He met them squarely.

"No," he said quietly. "If I were the type of man you think me, I'd be blatting about how hard the world has used me, about everyone being down on me, and so forth. Well, I'm not. I admit frankly that I've been pretty much of a rascal. Maybe you remember a Jew named Saul?"

"Offhand, I do not," said Wright.

"You should. He made the same admission, and changed his name to Paul, and became quite a guy. I'm here because I can be of use in a big way, to you personally and to our own country. A man on the edge of the underworld often has abilities and knowledge which make him of great value—"

"I don't think we care to deal with underworld characters," broke in Wright.

"Very well." Ravenal gathered himself to rise. "I see that she was right about the Annapolis ring; navy man, eh? And her report on your work and that of other trade control agents in North Africa, including your connections in Egypt and Tripoli, was probably correct. But the matter of a fleet from London to Algiers, and the American forces concerned, probably is of no interest to you, so I'll say good morning. Pleased to have met you."

He nodded amiably, rose, and started for the door. As his hand touched the knob, a word stopped him—a hoarse, strangled word.

"Wait!"

HE TURNED. Wright sat as though shocked into a paralysis. Twice he opened his lips, twice closed them. He gestured to the chair and found words.

"Come back. Sit down."

Ravenal complied. He sat and looked at Wright, whose stony features were becoming human under the stress of inward emotion. He said nothing. He perceived instantly that his words had struck to a vital spot. Not only was Wright frightfully startled, but his cold hauteur had smashed like an eggshell.

"What is it you're after?" Wright asked, with difficulty. "You want money, eh?"

"No," said Ravenal pleasantly. "Oh, no! I'd like to be given an emergency passport and get in good standing again with the lodge, so to speak, and to be given a job without pay. I'm not selling information, if that's what you mean. I could be useful.

I have friends among the natives, you know, all through these parts. I even speak their language at times."

"Wait," said Wright, who seemed to be in panic mentally. "You said—you mentioned a woman—that she took me for a navy man—"

RAVENAL NODDED cheerfully. "Yes; you should not wear an Annapolis ring on this sort of job, Mr. Wright. A full report on you and other members of the trade control, and their real activities here, was turned in last night for transmission to Paris and Berlin; I killed it. I could tell you a lot of things, but I've no interest in telling you how wise I am. That's water over the dam."

"You seem," said Wright, choosing his words carefully, "to have picked up a lot of amazing and probably erroneous information, Mr. Ravenal."

"That's the wrong attitude," Ravenal replied, with kindly concern. "Really, it is. You're in a good deal of personal danger; that's why I came to you. It seems that you've done some very fine work, and the Nazis don't like it by half. With your Egyptian connections, you must have heard of a certain Nazi agent in Cairo named Kleine?"

Wright's eyes flickered slightly. Ravenal smiled.

"I see you have. I'll probably be chatting with him today. If there's anything you'd like to have conveyed to these Nazis, I'll be glad to—"

"See here!" Wright almost exploded. "Come across and tell me everything you know and where you got it. I'll make a deal with you. This—damn it, this is uncanny!"

Ravenal relaxed, laughed, and produced the Royal Khedivial cigarettes he was now enjoying. He lit one, unhurried. This was a hard man to deal with, but his play was won.

"No. I don't intend to empty my bag and then be kicked out. Luck has put me into a position where I may regain all that I've lost, including my self-respect, and I mean to do it. Let me give you an example. I can write letters to a few natives I know;

and in three days can have the most detailed and exact information on every aviation field between here and Constantine. Simply because I know a native or two who have connections."

"We don't need that information," murmured Wright, who was staring at him.

"Perhaps not. I might warn you about certain things; I shan't do it. You're one of those men who must be allowed to make mistakes—"

"Confound you!" said Wright. "Who's this woman you're talking about?"

Ravenal smiled, regretfully.

"You see? You've formed a certain notion of me; therefore you must browbeat and make demands. Too bad. A Nazi agent came to town the other day, via Algeria. He must have contacted some of your men there; at all events, he was bubbling over with information and surmises about American activity in North Africa. Well, he has stopped bubbling; in fact, he may be dead by now. That reminds me, I must inquire at the hospital."

Wright, by this time, had steadied and was under full control.

"Ravenal, you ask what I can't do offhand," he said frankly. "I must get instructions. That will take time."

"As a navy man," said Ravenal, "you ought to know the value of individual action and responsibility."

"True." Wright bit his lips. "Still, I must have a bit of time on this thing."

"As you like. You say you don't need information on the aviation bases here; yet in reality, you and the British both need it badly. You can't make up your mind about me, so you refuse to trust me. That's natural; I don't blame you a particle. But just stick away in your mind what I said about Saul of Tarsus—he was a pretty bad egg, you know." Ravenal rose, smiling. "I'm at the Transat, as you probably know, so you can always reach me. But, if I were you," he added gently, "I'd not waste very much time. Good-by."

This time he walked out unhindered.

"Left him flat as a pancake," he reflected. "So, by heaven, it's true about our boys moving into French Africa—ships, planes and tanks! Probably the British, too. Well, maybe I should have warned Wright about the fair Dubois and what's on the carpet; still, I gave him plenty of hints. He's a stubborn ass! The only way I can convince him is by making deeds talk louder than words. But I've sure left him flattened out, poor devil!"

Ravenal was no hero and had no ambitions in that line. How long he could keep up the role of Eric Horn was an unpleasant conjecture; particularly as this fellow Kleine was sure to be far more clever and shrewd than the pretty Hesse Dubois. He must keep it up for this evening, anyway. Perhaps Wright would have brains enough to accept the warnings given, but he thought not. That man lacked the supple mentality needed in the sort of game that was afoot.

SO, REGRETFULLY, Dick Ravenal made up his mind to the worst, and prepared for it in his characteristic fashion. Life had taught him the folly of dramatics, and the practical value of success without trumpets, and he knew that Nazi agents were brutally direct in their methods. So he made no attempt to get hold of a pistol or other weapon, although some very curious things of that character were to be had in the Medina. Instead, he looked up a grain broker whom he knew in the Suk of the grain merchants, and talked with him for a long while.

"It can be arranged," said the Arab, pocketing a thousand-franc note. "Allah is great; blessed is Allah! It will be delivered before the sunset prayer. Loaded and ready."

Ravenal went to his hotel, since he was expecting word from Hesse Dubois at any moment. He inquired at the desk regarding Eric Horn; the man had died an hour previously, without regaining consciousness. The police were now taking away his effects.

In his own room, Ravenal pondered this turn. For the moment, all was well. But the police would wire Paris; by the morrow Berlin, and later all other Nazi agents, would know that Eric Horn was dead. So it would be just as well not to overplay his role—yes, just as well to end it this same evening!

"But," he vowed, "never again—never! No more of this damned secret service. Let Wright give me a job of some sort, no matter what, but count me out as a political agent. There are better things in life so far as Dick Ravenal is concerned."

A wise decision. He had scarcely made it when he was summoned to the office telephone to answer a call. He was greeted by the voice of Hesse Dubois.

"Our friend has arrived," she said, after satisfying herself of his identity. "Can you meet us about six at the Chianti Restaurant in the Avenue de France?"

"With pleasure," began Ravenal. She rang off before he could get in another word.

Ravenal was thirty-four, at the axis of life. If he was wise in chicanery, he was all the more apt at recognizing and borrowing the wisdom of others. Now he took a leaf from the Arab book and made his way to the Grand Mosque under the hill of the Kasbah, About the Tunisian mosques were grouped cafés, often by nationalities. He seated himself in the café of the Moroccans, bought flowers from one of the countless flower-sellers, ordered mint tea and sat there for the next three hours. He sniffed perfume, sipped tea, and meditated in relaxation and repose of mind, like the burnoused men around him.

When he came back to the hotel, he was renewed and invigorated. He found two telephone calls, and laughed; they were from Wright. He ignored them, went to his room, and changed clothes. While he was at it, a package arrived; the promised package.

He opened it and disclosed a malacca stick in two pieces. He screwed them together and had a light, rather thick, quite handsome walking stick, with a carved handle in place of the usual crook. The handle was of wood, carved into the shape of a goat's head with ruby eyes. He touched the horns with his thumb and they moved slightly.

He put his fingernail under one of the ruby eyes, and it came loose—a bit of glass on the end of a pin. He examined the tiny aperture and saw a drop of moisture; he quickly replaced the pin and eye, and nodded with satisfaction.

At five-fifty he left the hotel and walked briskly down the Avenue de France toward the Italian quarter. The Chianti was a notable dining place, not far from the Place de Rome. As he drew near, Ravenal saw Hesse sitting at one of the café tables, a man beside her. He went to them, bowed over her hand, and shook hands with Kleine at her introduction.

"I shall leave you gentlemen at once," she said, "having an engagement. There is no time to lose, M. Horn. You and Kleine will await us; I'll bring my friend to you. Kleine knows where. An apéritif, and then to work."

The drink was ordered. Ravenal found Kleine devouring him with curiously intent gaze. This Cairo agent looked anything but a Nazi; Ravenal could have sworn, by looks and gestures that he was a Greek, and said so.

"You compliment me," said Kleine, with a flash of white teeth. "It is a matter of careful attention to detail, of course, from haircut to fingernails; I had the proper build to start with, luckily. But you, Monsieur—you astonish me! You do not answer to anything I have heard of the famous Eric Horn; it is marvelous!"

"Thank you," said Ravenal modestly. "What news have you?"

"All bad," returned Kleine. "Rommel is breaking. These damned English and Americans have assembled incredible strength! And that American army in England is about to strike, probably at Norway. I think we had better get our organization here together, eh?"

"We shall do so this evening, when our present task is done," said Ravenal. "I had a long talk today with your friend Wright,

Mademoiselle. He is no fool. Do you think he'll risk his neck like a lovesick boy?"

HESSE GAVE him one flashing look. "Not at all. Evidently you misconstrue my ability. Do your part as well as I do mine, and all goes excellently. Now I must be off. Au revoir!"

She rose. The two men bowed her away, and then resumed their seats.

"That woman," observed the dark, swarthy Kleine, pulling at his long mustache, "has her limitations; but within them she has the devil's own brain!"

"Apparently so. She's not too obvious," assented Ravenal. "What's our program?"

"Simple, bold, efficient. She and I have taken rooms in the St. Georges Hotel in the Rue Hoche—a huge tourist place, eminently reputable and distinguished. You and I go there now and wait. She brings him to visit her very ill brother. It is all open and aboveboard, nothing secret, you understand. He comes. We kill him; we depart."

"Hm! Bold enough, certainly, and a trifle risky," said Ravenal. "How kill him?"

"Knives. They're ready and waiting. And she has a pistol, if needed. It won't be."

They paid for the drinks, departed, and caught a tram for the Rue Hoche in the upper French city.

Ravenal was not happy about this murder-trap, but nerved himself for the worst. Wright would be unsuspicious, of course; a big hotel, an atmosphere of absolute security, a plausible story. Well, it was going to be a nasty business at best; he clutched his walking-stick lovingly. No more of this damned secret service! If he got out of here alive, somebody else could take over the job; Eric Horn was dead, and would stay dead.

THEY SWUNG into the hotel, empty now of tourists but crammed with officers and their families, with consular service people and visitors and, above all, refugees who had money to spend. It was a gay and cosmopolitan crowd.

Kleine got his key at the desk, explained that his sister and a dinner guest would arrive at any moment, and led Ravenal away. From the ornate and somewhat overstuffed lobby they passed through corridors and more corridors, until Kleine paused at a door and opened it, to show a very handsome two-room suite. Unopened luggage stood about.

"Bluff," said Kleine, kicking a suitcase. It was obviously new. "This is at the end of the building, excellent for our purpose; we can leave by the courtyard entrance. Not much time; here, into the bedroom. Throw some things about—"

He tumbled pillows and bedding and switched off the lights, leaving only a bed-lamp burning in this farther room. From under his coat he drew a weapon, passing it to Ravenal; an Italian stiletto, razor-edged, long and thin and deadly.

Ravenal dropped into a chair that stood at one side of the entrance. He put his walking-stick between his knees. The feel of that knife made him a bit sickish; he had seen Arabs at knife-work and it revolted him. If he needed anything to steel him to his own job, this was it. Kleine thumbed a similar stiletto with satisfaction, his swarthy features and glittering eyes touched with diabolic glee. The two of them were at either side of the doorway.

"As you're no doubt aware," Kleine said, "the important thing is to do it swiftly and shut his mouth. Not that noise would matter here; the court's on one side, the gardens on the other. An admirable location...."

Ravenal shivered and the words ceased to register. Assassination, foul murder—should he take care of this Nazi fiend here and now? No, wait; he wanted above all else to convince that stubborn man Wright. It could be done deftly, with luck, when Wright appeared. The trap must be sprung, must be evident, if Wright was to believe—

"Arrived!"

WITH THE word, Kleine crouched against the wall, opposite, stiletto ready. From the outer room came the slam of a door, the fresh, eager voice of Hesse in French.

"He is in the next room, Monsieur. Proceed, I beg you. Gilbert! Here is the visitor I promised! Is your light on?"

Wright came into the doorway between the rooms. Unexpectedly, he paused and turned.

"But, Mademoiselle——"

Just there, she struck him; what with, Ravenal could not see. Wright came staggering into the bedroom and groaned, and collapsed. Kleine leaped on him, knife ready—

Ravenal's thumb pressed on the horns of the carven goat, desperately. He had dropped the knife. A finger-nail had plucked out the two red eyes as he sat; he held the stick with steady aim. There was a slight hiss. Two invisible jets of liquid shot forth, straight into the face of the Nazi.

A howl of agony burst from Kleine. He hurled the stiletto to the floor and clawed at his eyes. Into the doorway came the woman Hesse, just as Ravenal rose to his feet. He swung the stick, pressed again—a fractional second too late. She was already swinging up a small pistol, her features convulsed with surprise and fury and comprehension. It exploded; then the ammoniated fluid jetted into her face and eyes. A stifled scream escaped her.

Ravenal felt that one bullet leave a sear across his cheek. He was already in motion, springing at the woman, wrenching the pistol from her and with one hearty shove sending her reeling and staggering away into the other room.

He whirled around. Kleine was spluttering oaths and grasping at the air. Ravenal aimed and fired; the bullet struck the Nazi just above the knee. Kleine howled anew, collapsed and sat clutching at his leg while his blinded eyes poured forth tears.

Ravenal swooped on Wright, who was feebly trying to rise. He helped Wright up, wrenched him about, and urged the dazed, bewildered man through into the other room, past Hesse who was gripping at a chair for support, and to the door. An instant later they were out in the corridor. Wright put a hand to the back of his head.

"Lord!" he groaned. "What is it? Who are you? See here—"

"Check it. I'm Dick Ravenal. Come along and get out of here, you blithering idiot!" He urged Wright along. What was it Kleine had said—out through the courtyard? Here were the stairs—good! He swung Wright at them. "This way! I had to shoot Kleine to make sure of him—only in the leg, though. You walked into a perfect murder-trap, and now you're walking out of it. Pull yourself together and we'll make the street from here."

They came into the cool, starry courtyard and caught a breath of perfume from the orange and lime trees. Wright clung for a moment to a carven pillar; his shoulders squared, he had himself in hand now.

"So that was it," he said. "Ravenal, I owe you apologies—more than apologies, by heaven! Will you shake hands?"

"I guess we can afford the time," said Ravenal, chuckling. "Do I get that bit of work?"

"You get any damned thing it's in my power to get for you," said Wright fervently. "And since you know so much about it, I don't mind telling you that this is the big night, over in Algeria and Morocco—the zero hour comes at dawn. American armies are landing to occupy the whole country, and British as well. It's the biggest thing that ever happened! You bet you'll get that bit of work—for your country!"

Ravenal pressed his hand. "Thanks. Thanks! Just one thing— no more of this blasted secret service stuff in mine. Anything but that; anything!"

"Okay," said Wright. "Let's go find a drink and talk it over."

VI

BRAZIL IS IN THE WAR, TOO

*A Very Hush-hush Job for Army
Intelligence, with Vital Bases at Stake.*

EXCEPT THAT it was an Army Intelligence job, Tom Herron had not the faintest notion of his present business. He did not even have an inkling whither he was bound, until he went aboard a Ferry Command bomber at Miami and was sent into the navigator's cabin. There he found his chief, General Blaney Smith, awaiting him.

"I'm en route to Africa, you're bound for Brazil, Captain Herron," said the general. "So make yourself comfortable, and if you get airsick, God help you, for I can't!"

The general was a hard-bitten old lad who ran G-2 efficiently. Herron had been a natural for the Intelligence. Before the war he had traveled extensively in South America for a big machinery outfit; he spoke Spanish and Portuguese fluently, and had come close to marrying more than one dark-eyed senorita. He was still free, however; and not even the war had taken the roguish, cheery twinkle from his darkly aquiline features.

Once in the air, the two men settled down side by side.

"This is a very hush-hush job," observed the general. "You're chosen because you know Brazil like a book, among other reasons. You're going to Sao Minaes, on the tip of the east coast budge, where we hop off for Dakar and Africa."

"My old stamping grounds, eh?" said Herron. "Where the big air bases are."

"Yes; both our own and Brazilian. As you know, those bases

are important as hell, both for the Army and Ferrying commands, and for the Freight Transport people. Brazil is with us in the war, but just the same there's a tremendous Nazi sentiment, and the country is riddled with Nazi agents."

He went on to enlarge on this unpleasant fact. One General Pereira, tops among Brazilian engineers, was Herron's present objective; the American was to pose in his old role of machinery salesman for postwar deliveries.

"This Sao Minaes situation is a headache, Herron. This Pereira is an old-school martinet, trained in Prussia in the old days. He may be pro-Nazi; he may not. No one can find out just how he stands. He has no more human sympathy than a stone, apparently, and is a devil for duty and honor and so forth."

"Never heard of him. Why is he important?"

"Because he's installing a big system of coast and ack-ack defense outside the airdromes and city. We've been given supposedly full information by the Brazilian government; but there are rumors of secret installations we don't know about. You can see what it would mean if some Nazi coup were suddenly pulled there by Fifth Columnists—if those airfields so vital to us were suddenly sabotaged or destroyed. Nothing is impossible in this man's war."

"And Pereira is a suspect?"

"No and yes. We must learn whether or not he's with us. He's an enigma. A man of forty-odd, he recently married a very attractive woman there. We've heard rumors about her, too. On the face of things, Pereira is suspect; we must know definitely. Any mistake would have most appalling results. Your job is to get under his skin and learn what's what. Those who know him say he's absolutely reliable. Your report must be as definite as possible on this conflicting case. Dispel the mystery and report to Washington."

"Okay," said Tom Herron, and this was all the information he could get on the matter.

It was an early morning when the bomber swam down the sky and landed at the Sao Minaes Ferry Command field. To Herron, the changes here were a revelation.

The city had swollen to twice its size, pushing back the coffee and tobacco plantations; the little port had developed into a tremendous dock area; above all, the airfields and hangars and sheds made up an amazing view from the air. He began to understand the worry about Pereira. Planes were everywhere, in air or on the ground. A most vital base indeed, to the whole war activity.

A handshake with the general, and he was off, putting his kit-bag into an ancient taxi and heading into the old city, once so small, now so huge. He alighted at the small but excellent Hotel de Paris, a French establishment. The desk-clerk greeted him with a cry of joy.

"Ah! Senhor Herron! What a happy surprise! You did not wire for a room?"

"No, and I suppose you're full up?"

"By a lucky chance, Senhor, we can give you your old court-yard room, gladly! Shall you be with us long?"

"Only heaven knows," said Herron laughing. "I hope so, anyhow."

A bath, a shave, a change, and he sallied forth to get an outfit of whites and have a look at the town. The old sleepiness was gone. Brisk Brazilian air cadets were everywhere, and soldiers; the dark-brown of the American Air Force was on every hand. Herron rejoiced that he was not in uniform, for salutes were legion—elaborate figure fours, regular arm-breakers, so many were the higher officers in sight.

FOR THE rest of the day he loafed about town, got established at his old club, met a few former friends, and spread the word that he was once more in the machinery business. It took a bit of time for one to get into the proper Sao Minaes frame of mind. Yet all the while, had he but known it, destiny was waiting close at hand.

The hotel had a magnificent *patio,* sweet with orange trees, heavy with great banana leaves, cool with fountains; also a courtyard used by vehicles. Next morning, after breakfast, Herron was at the desk arranging for laundry, when one of the sleek bell boys approached him with a discreet murmur.

"Senhor, a lady in the *patio* desires to speak with you."

Surprised, Herron stepped into the flowering *patio.* He saw no one, until he neared the fountain. She was sitting there on the cushioned tiled bench, and rose, her hands extended, a smile upon her lips.

"I saw you, Tomas, and had to speak with you," she said quietly.

He bowed over her hand, met her eyes, and read the kindness in them.

"What luck!" he exclaimed, smiling. "I only arrived yesterday—and today I find you! Two years since we parted, Sonia. Then you were the most beautiful woman in Brazil; and now your beauty has come to new perfection!"

This was a lie. Tom Herron always voiced what a woman would most love to hear. There was no woman in the world he wanted less to meet, just now, than Sonia Leontoff. Not because of their old love affair, which had been a joyous interlude, but because of what she was and had been. She was no company for a G-2 agent.

One of the many refugees from Baltic lands who had flooded into South America, Sonia had quite frankly been, in those first days, a German agent. She was slender, pale, perfectly poised; not in the least beautiful, but charmingly exquisite in every detail. As he dropped on the bench beside her, Herron was throbbingly alive to danger; he felt it envelop him like a misty cloak.

"Time has been good to you," she said. "The same springing life in your eyes, Tomas, and only a touch of gray at the temples! It becomes you."

"And you seem both younger and happier," he replied. She showed a golden circlet on her finger, smiling slightly as she met his eyes.

"You see? I have found my place. No longer Sonia Leontoff, but now Senhora Pereira. My husband is a general. I should like you to meet him, Tomas."

The devil! Herron swallowed hard, but gave no sign of his startled alarm. Pereira!

"Did you marry for love—-or duty?" he asked. At the significant words, a flicker came and went in her eyes; fright, he could have sworn.

"All that is long ago ended, since before the war," she said earnestly. "I've had no connection with them these two years and more. Andres is a good man, a splendid man! But tell me what you're doing here?"

"You take the words from my very lips!" Herron laughed lightly. "Just now I'm selling the same old machinery. I've a big shipment on the way, by good luck. And you, at this hotel?"

"Our apartment is being done over, so we're living here for the week. This place has a good wine-cellar, you know; you used to like it for that reason." Her gaze touched upon him gently, lingeringly, but she shook her head when he suggested luncheon. "No, it would not do. Andres is lunching with two influential men of the coffee cartel; it would not be proper for me to appear. Why not come to our suite this evening?"

"With the greatest pleasure," Herron responded.

She departed, slim and poised and exquisite. Herron sank back on the bench. He blinked at the flowers, at the delicate green of the banana trees, at the splashing fountain. Married to a general, a man of importance—and no longer a Nazi agent? Not likely. And she was afraid. Of what or whom? She was not the sort of woman to know fear.

"Be damned if she hasn't a soft spot in her heart for me still! Charming woman; I was lucky to escape her," he reflected. "Once a Nazi agent, always one. Well, now we can savvy why Pereira leans toward the Nazis. I think I'll lunch right here, too."

So he did, and watched with interest when the party of three men arrived. Pereira was a stiff little man with a stiff mustache, graying hair *en brosse*, and a hard eye in a red face. With him, two men in mufti who did not gesticulate or look like Brazilian coffee planters. At the moment, Herron scarcely noticed them; he was trying to appraise Pereira, and found it a bit difficult.

The man talked little, was unemotional, curt, decisive. Not once did he smile. How had such a man won the radiant Sonia? When Herron left the dining-room, Pereira was speaking, and a scrap of his words reached the American clearly.

"In war there is only yes or no," he was saying crisply. "There is no perhaps. There are no sympathies, no allowances or excuses. It is simple; orders are orders."

There was the man, a man of hard rock, unbending as flint. Herron lounged about the hotel entrance until the three came out. He was rewarded by a glimpse of Pereira's face emerging from cool shadow into hot sunlight. The face startled him as it changed and hardened to meet the world's eye. For, in the shade, something appeared that was gone an instant later; ere this,

Herron had seen the brand of hell in a man's face, when no one was watching.

He almost forgot this, he almost forgot the two Germanic coffee planters, when he saw the driver of Pereira's car standing at attention. A trim Brazilian sergeant—but sight of him gave Herron a violent shock and sent him hastily back into the hotel.

"The devil! The devil!" he murmured in dismay and alarm. "I know that man! Altman, by the gods; Dirck Altman! With his mustache gone. He was Nazi attaché first at Rio, then at Caracas; many's the time we've played bridge together. And now a Brazilian soldier, a sergeant, detailed to drive Pereira. And Pereira's wife a Nazi agent. Boy, would I burn my fingers if I tried any monkey-work with our general of engineers!"

He was profoundly disturbed; Pereira must be wholly pro-German. And yet—and yet—that glimpse of the man's face emerging from shadow into sunlight lingered with him, like a half-sensed clue that somehow eluded his grasp.

TAKING HAT and stick, he struck out for a walk to clear his desperately fogged head. There were plenty of old friends he knew and should look up; he wanted none of them now. He left the downtown district and headed for the old and now poor district near the river, where the early Portuguese had builded. He came at last to the strange, lonely old church fronting the river, its yellow stone carvings half effaced by time and ruin.

Here by the cracked and desolate majesty of past days, he paced along and tried to reach some coherence of thought. Altman! He had vivid memories of the fellow; a sardonic, handsome devil among devils, famed even before the war for his cruel blood-lust. Where did he come into this picture? Brazil was at war with Germany; therefore Altman was an out and out spy.

The soft old yellow masonry of four hundred years towered silent from amid its crumbled arches and eroded carvings. Now, as always, Herron gained a certain peace of mind from this vision of ancient beauty. It soothed him, left him alert of brain, keen of eye and thought; when he turned back into the city, he was relaxed and rested. And a good thing he was.

THE AFTERNOON was wearing away when he reached the hotel. He approached the desk to get his room key. With it, the clerk handed him the card of one Senhor Paolo Mendez, bearing the miniature emblems of several Brazilian decorations.

"Senhor Mendez asked for you half an hour ago," said the clerk. "Ah! Here he comes now, by the greatest marvel! On the stairs."

Mendez was, indeed, coming down the stairs that went to the upper floor of the hotel; a deft, polite man in his forties. Herron recognized him instantly as one of the two men who had lunched with General Pereira. He introduced himself and shook hands. Senhor Mendez would like a few words in private? But certainly; the *patio*, perhaps.

They stepped into the *patio*, found it empty, and Mendez came straight to business. He understood that Herron was interested in machinery and had a large shipment en route here, released by United States authorities. He talked rapidly and convincingly. He was willing to pay well. The machinery was vitally needed here.

Herron listened, probed shrewdly, and ticketed his man. Of German origin or descent, most certainly; a Nazi sympathizer, perhaps a Nazi agent. Who had told him about this mythical machinery? Sonia, of course. And where the deuce had Mendez just been for the past half-hour? Upstairs. With Sonia. Therefore she must have phoned him—

Aloud, the American was more than willing to deal with Senhor Mendez. Not at the present moment; he was awaiting the invoice of the shipment. Perhaps tomorrow at five? Very good. Senhor Mendez shook hands and took his guttural leave, highly gratified. Herron turned to the desk.

"General Pereira has rooms here, I think?"

"Suite B, Senhor."

Herron nodded and went upstairs; there was no elevator. So

the general's luncheon pals had been Nazi agents—poor Pereira! They had him under their thumbs all right. Why had Sonia told them about that machinery shipment? Diplomacy be damned! Tom Herron was angry, and he impulsively swung away from the direction of his own room, passed down another corridor, and came to the door of Suite B. He knocked, and after a moment knocked again, imperatively.

The door was opened by Sonia.

She stared at him blankly, wide-eyed; her pale face bore the traces of tears. Recognition brought color into those pallid cheeks. Then she caught her breath.

"What do you want? You know you should not come here now—"

"What about Mendez?" asked Herron. The name was like a blow; she quivered under it. "I'd like a few words with you," he went on, more gently. "Come downstairs if you prefer. I suppose it's unconventional for you to receive a visitor when your husband's not here."

She opened the door wider. "No; come in. The worst has happened. What does anything matter now?" she said drearily. "Come in."

Herron stepped into the sitting room of a suite, and she closed the door.

"What do you mean by the worst?" he demanded sharply. For a long moment she gazed at him, emotions bursting in her face, then shook her head.

"No; it was not you who did it. Never would you do so despicable a thing!" she began. With an effort, she got herself under control. "You mentioned Mendez. Why?"

"I've had a talk with him. He broached the matter of that machinery shipment; I had told no one but you. Therefore he learned it from you. He was here."

"Yes, he was here," she said quietly, steadily. The color had seeped out of her face anew; she was stricken, helpless, desperate. Again Herron saw fright in her eyes. "Yes, I phoned him about it. He's not a bad sort. It was to help you I did it, Tomas, for he has much money to spend. Then he came here and told me—he told me—"

Her words died; her very breath of life seemed to die. For an instant Herron thought she would collapse.

"For a Nazi, he seemed rather decent," he said. "Come, Sonia! I understand—"

"You understand nothing!" she broke in, her voice dead and dreadful. "It is Andres, my husband. Mendez came to warn me. Someone has told Andres that I—about the past—how I did work for the Germans—and has convinced him. You do not know what that means, but I know—"

Again she quivered, caught her breath, then suddenly broke down. Shaking with sobs, she dropped into a chair and put her face in her hands. Herron stood looking down at her. She was not acting; this was real. And dimly, he did begin to understand her emotion.

"Tell me, my dear," he said gently. "Let me be a friend; there is always some way out."

"Not for me." Her words were muffled, then choked by sobs. Emotion mastered her. Herron pulled up a chair, seated himself, waited. Presently she looked up at him, tears streaking the admirable makeup on her face.

"For nearly a year—I have been in hell," she said brokenly. "He—Andres—never dreamed that—that I had worked for them. I never dared to tell him. He hates them virulently."

"Hates the Nazis? Your husband does?" Herron echoed incredulously.

"Yes. His son was at school in Germany when war was declared. He was thrown into a concentration camp. He hates them virulently, with his whole soul! But for the boy's sake he must pretend; he has been trying to get his son released. He hates everything German. And he loved me, Tomas, he loved me; and I came to love him. That is the truth. And he never knew how I had been one of their agents, in the past; I never dared confess it to him."

"Naturally not, I suppose," said Herron. "And now—someone has told him?"

"Worse!" She was pouring out everything. "Last year two of them came to me, threatening to tell him about it unless I did as they wanted. Well, I did so, in little things, tricked them, played them along. They were mad wolves; not like this Mendez, who is a—decent sort. It occurred to me that I could get the son of Andres set free. They promised it if I would help, and I did. They had lied. He was not set free."

She paused, then went on. "Then came the question of the new defenses here that Andres is installing. They wanted the plans. I never even knew about them—never! But somehow they got the plans, found I had been tricking them, and in revenge went to Andres. It was this very afternoon. Mendez told me. He says they showed Andres old letters from me— everything! Even Mendez was outraged. He says it was need- less. He does not know who did it—"

"Perhaps I can help," offered Herron. "If I have a word with your husband, eh?"

"No! For God's sake, no!" She half started from her chair. "You do not know him. He has been in torment, also; about his son, and other things. The Nazi influence here has been hard on him. He has seen Brazil betrayed by these people; he even had to take their orders, until war was declared. He is a man of the highest honor! He was forced to do things that seared his very soul! I was his one confidante, his one friend—and now he finds me a traitress, as he thinks! It means the end of every- thing between us. Nothing can help me now. To him, honor is so much, so dear—"

SHE BROKE off, staring at empty air. By this time Herron understood; that glimpse of Pereira's face coming from shadow into sunlight—yes, he had the clue.

"If only I had been able to get his son set free!" she went on.

"That would have meant everything to Andres. It would have excused everything. It would have meant all the world! He lived for that son of his—"

Herron had no time, no chance to speak or think. With a sound like a moan, she shot to her feet and froze there, listening. Then she flung herself upon him, dragged him from his chair and propelled him violently to the doorway that opened into the next room.

"It is he—his step!" she panted. "Quickly—leave by the other door—for the love of God, quickly, quickly!"

So he was shoved into the bedroom adjoining. She slammed the door so hard that it banged open again an inch or so.

He had caught up his hat and stick, luckily. Dismay crowded him—worse to be caught here in the bedroom, than there! Run? Be damned to it! He heard a key grate in the entrance door, and the door open.

Then came the voice of Pereira; and so startling was the dreadful note in that harsh voice that Herron stood transfixed, listening.

"Ah, Sonia! I must speak with you," it said. "Yes, now—at once. And you may well be afraid of me, my dear. You have every reason. Apparently you know what I am about to say, but your tears will have no effect, for I have been given full evidence."

"Yes, I know what they have told you." Sonia sounded collected now, desperately poised. "And you would believe them, without giving me one word?"

"What, my dear? Is it not true, what they told me?"

"Yes; but—"

"Precisely. You admit it." The laugh that came from the man was even more dreadful than his heart-wrung voice. He went on, with growing anger.

"You cannot deny the evidence written by yourself. It spoke for you, my dear. And the crowning infamy of all—not content with spying upon me, with outraging my honor as a man and a soldier, you betray my country itself! They know all about the work I have been doing. They have the defense plans, they know everything."

An instant of silence. Evidently she was too proud to counter with the least denial, or too afraid. Then her voice came, very calmly.

"Very well. And thus jumping at conclusions, what do you intend to do?"

"What I should do," came the response, "if instead of my wife, it were my dearest friend or my own son who had thus betrayed the honor of a soldier and his country—"

Tom Herron gathered his wits swiftly. He knew these Latins; his knowledge of their psychology, his ready sympathy and invention had made him tops as a salesman. Now, upon sudden impulse, he shoved open the door; and barely in time. General Pereira stood there with a pistol in his hand. At sight of Herron his words failed; he was paralyzed by the intrusion.

Before he could speak, Herron seized the chance, stepped into the room, and bowed.

"Ha! Do you know, General, that I made the same mistake myself? Yes, upon my word!" he said, lightly, easily, confidentially, as though to an old friend. "This woman, I understood, is a Nazi agent. I have seen the proofs of it. So I shall denounce her to her husband, General Pereira himself! And then what? Why, in the very act of coming here—I learned the truth about it!"

Audacity—always audacity! It was the one slim chance. Pereira stood as though thunderstruck, his eyes widening on the American, who laughed softly and extended his leather-framed Intelligence card. Now or never was the time to nail his man!

"Permit me; my name is Herron, captain in the Intelligence of the United States Army. An American of the north, who dared to enter your rooms like a thief—because I have some vital information, news of the greatest importance, about several things. About your son in Germany, for one thing. About Madame, here—"

H E   B O W E D to Sonia, who was absolutely frozen by his sudden appearance and also by his words. Before she could find voice, he hurried on to get his most important point over.

"And lastly!" he exclaimed, with a burst of vehemence for more effect, "about the person who is the actual traitor—this damned Nazi spy whom you have trusted implicitly, and who has sought vengeance on your wife because she would not join in his treachery!"

Pereira, who had listened in cold hauteur, unbent at these words.

"Senhor! You—you are aware of what you say?"

"Oh, yes. The imperative thing is to undo these mistakes and catch the rascal who is responsible, and who stole the plans of your defense system." Herron was working on the man now as upon a pliant instrument. "Yes," he continued musingly, "it is quite true that in past years one Sonia Leontoff did indeed act as a very minor German agent here in Brazil. It was of no consequence; one of those things we do, and regret, and cease doing—as she ceased long before she became Senhora Pereira."

"Senhor, you appear to know a good deal of my private affairs!" said the general, stiffly.

"That is my business," Herron replied, smiling. "You see, after her marriage these blackguards tried to force her into resuming the work. She refused. Later, in the hope of getting your son released from Germany, she pretended compliance. They discovered that she was tricking them. They denounced her to you—however, the chief thing now is to get hold of this Nazi spy who wears the uniform of Brazil."

These brisk words stung Pereira, jerked at him, brought him to life.

"That is true, true!" he exclaimed. "Who is this man you accuse?"

"The sergeant who drives your car."

"What!" Incredulity widened the flinty gaze of the general. "Impossible! Joao Morales is a faithful soldier, well known, decorated—"

"Sure; the Nazis aren't fools. They don't wear spy badges," said Herron. "Get him here, if you like, and we'll prove the charge in short order."

"If this is American bluff, Senhor, you'll regret it!" Pereira took refuge from his amazed chagrin in anger. "Your impudent effrontery shall be put to the proof. Sergeant Morales is now waiting in the courtyard with my car."

HE STEPPED to the telephone and ordered that Sergeant Morales be sent up. His service pistol vanished. He swung around and eyed Herron in critical appraisement.

"This intrusion, Senhor, the strange story you tell—"

"Will carry its own proof, General." Herron took a chair by the door, settled himself comfortably, and produced a cigarette. "I don't wish your faithful sergeant to get a look at me before he's well inside the room. And if I were you," he added, "I'd keep that gun handy. Sorry I haven't one myself. And send the senhora into another room. Don't think for one minute this spy will bow politely and hold out his wrists for the handcuffs!"

"I stay here," spoke up Sonia. She was staring at Herron in genuine amazement. "Senhor, is it true that you serve the North American Intelligence?"

"Quite, Senhora," replied Herron. He knew that Pereira was hanging on every word. "If you doubt it, my dear general, permit me to say that you lunched today with two Nazi agents."

Pereira flushed. "Those gentlemen are public officials," he said stiffly.

"But also Nazi agents. And you knew it. I don't accuse you, mind!" Herron went on. "I have no doubt of your integrity. Possibly those two men could help in procuring the release of your son from Germany. But you perceive, my dear general, how deceitful appearances may be. You might be accused of dealing with the Nazis—just as your wife was accused."

PEREIRA'S MUSTACHE moved as his lips compressed, but he made no reply. This shot had finished him. He was still wearing his army kepi; now he removed it, and with his handkerchief mopped sweat from his forehead.

He had changed. No longer was he the sternly dramatic Spartan nerved to kill the thing he loved. Something had broken in him. He shot queer probing glances, now at Herron, now at Sonia, across the room. A knock sounded at the door.

"Enter!" he rapped out.

Into the room came Sergeant Morales, and stood at attention.

"Close the door and come here," said Pereira. The sergeant obeyed, paying no attention to Herron. He stood before the general, his back to the American. And now Herron spoke, calmly and quietly.

"Good afternoon, Dirck—or should I say Herr Altman?"

The sergeant did not move a muscle. For a moment the room seemed engulfed in a monstrous swollen silence. Herron's chair creaked as he rose, leaning on his stick. He stepped forward and swung around to face Morales.

The brown, hard features of the sergeant quivered slightly in recognition, then became stolid and composed again. Herron nodded amiably to him.

"So you remember me. Well, the game's up. Mendez and the others were arrested a little while ago; they split on you to save their own necks. You're out of luck, Altman."

Morales remained absolutely impassive; he was yielding to no such bluff. But now Sonia took an unexpected hand. Her laugh rang upon the room—a laugh soft and deadly.

"I can also identify this honest fellow," she spoke up. "Altman, you call him? But I knew him as Z-3S, operating direct from Berlin, and—"

At this, Altman abruptly cracked—so swiftly that even the alert Herron had not the slightest warning. Perhaps he feared lest Sonia clinch his fate as a spy; perhaps she might indeed have done so. At all events, Herron's prediction was only too well verified.

Altman took one slithering step backward. An imprecation broke from him; a small pistol seemed to leap into his hand. He fired, and General Pereira pitched over sideways. He fired again—just as Herron's stick swept up and struck the inside of his wrist, unflexing his finger-grip. The bullet went wild, the pistol dropped to the floor. The stick went to the floor with it, as Herron leaped in on his man. He met a savage blow that rocked his head back and staggered him, and Altman darted to the door—

TOO LATE! Herron caught him just as it opened, knocked him off his feet and dropped to pin him down. As easily pin down the whirlwind! Tom Herron got a bad surprise there. Hard and fast as he might be, the Nazi was harder and faster, a thing of coiled steel fighting for very life. Herron got him by the throat, then felt his hold broken, as a whirl of agony swept over him.

Altman was giving him the works, and he could not save himself. He fought desperately, lashing in cruel blows, but another knee-punch stretched him out and Altman was on top of him with fingers gouging. Herron barely did save his eyes—and there, not two feet away, lay the fallen pistol! Altman reached out for it.

A yell of pain burst from him. Sonia's heel came down squarely on his outstretched hand, grinding it against the polished hardwood. The pistol went skittering away. Altman leaped upright as though on springs. He struck the woman heavily across the face, knocking her sideways—then he was off—out of the room and gone. Sonia recovered, scooped up the pistol, but the door slammed before she could use it.

Herron, sick and dizzy and faint, came to one elbow. Pereira was clutching at a chair, his right leg dragging. Herron came swaying to his feet, half fell against the wall, then summoned his last energy and stumbled across the room.

Sonia had just unclasped the French windows that opened on a small iron balcony above the courtyard. As Herron came to her side she stepped out and went to the balcony rail. The general's car stood almost directly underneath. Altman appeared from the hotel entrance, hurrying to the car. Sonia called at him and he turned, pausing, looking up.

The pistol in her hand jumped, then jumped a second time. Herron remembered, later, that he did not hear the explosions at all; nothing registered except that little kick of the flame-spurting pistol.

Altman's hand fell from the car door. He spun around, sank down, and lay in the white sunlight with a dark splotch growing on his tunic.

For Tom Herron, the next events were dully fogged. He was sick and hurt and his brain was paralyzed; one bad crack across the nape of the neck had almost finished him. People were rushing about, and the air was filled with excited Brazilian voices that showered Portuguese in steady volleys.

Presently the room quieted. Herron found himself comfortable in a chair, with Sonia pressing a cool drink upon him. General Pereira lay upon a sofa; a surgeon was just turning away from him with laughing reassurance.

"You'll be all right in a day or two; a mere leg puncture—"

Drilled in the leg, eh? And the general had never used his ready pistol at all! Herron gulped his drink gratefully, and his brain cleared, Pereira was talking at him, but he missed the words; something about Altman, and keeping the thing quiet. The fellow had gone out of his head and tried to kill his general, and Sonia had finished him. It would never do to tell spy stories.

Herron finished his drink. He looked at Sonia, who sat holding her husband's hand. Rather, Pereira was holding hers, and bringing it to his lips. Her pale face was happy, her eyes were warm and richly eloquent of many things.

"Senhor," said Pereira, "I owe you a great deal. Permit me to

offer heartfelt thanks and my sentiments the most distinguished!"

"Thanks," said Herron. "I presume that you'll now make
complete changes in your system of defenses about the city and
airfields, since the Nazis seem to have copped your plans?"

"That will, obviously, be necessary."

"Then may I suggest that you make the changes with the
greatest secrecy, and meanwhile offer Mendez or some similar
Naziphile all details of the present system—in exchange for
the release of your son from Germany?" Herron chuckled as he
spoke. "It will do no harm, and I shall be happy to lend any
assistance that may be required."

Pereira surveyed him for a long moment. The hard eyes
chilled and glittered, the stiff features firmed, and the ghostly
suspicion of a smile touched those uncompromising features.
Then the general extended his hand.

"My friend, they have excellent champagne in this hotel," he
said solemnly. "As you say in America of the North—shake!"

VII

A TOAST IN WATER

*Neutral, Yes.... But Death Walks
the Streets of Dublin.*

D ARROW WAS on the public phone in the lobby of the Shelbourne, Dublin's famous old hotel of spacious comfort and leisurely ways. He got Morley, at the United States Consulate, without trouble, and gave his name.

"Oh, hello!" said Morley. "Had no idea you were over here. How are things back in Cleveland?"

"Pretty tough," said Darrow, "what with rationing and so forth. Look, Morley. I'm buying some woolen goods and need advice. Take time off and run around to that Cottage Industries place in Dawson Street. Say, an hour from now."

"Woolen goods!" repeated Morley in a shocked voice. "Oh, very well. In an hour. Okay."

Satisfied, Darrow hung up and went into the dining-room. He had arrived only an hour previously, and was hungry. The head waiter took him to one of the tables by the front windows, where he could look across at the lush spring beauty of St. Stephen's Green, and one of the wise old waiters came hovering for his order, and smiled like a friend.

"Oh, sir, I took you for an American!"

"So I am," said Darrow, surprised.

"And with that tongue on you? One can't shed the old-country tongue, sir."

Darrow chuckled. "True enough. I went from Galway to America when I was fifteen; but that was many a long year ago—after the last war, it was."

The waiter departed. Darrow settled back in his chair, looking out across the sidewalk and the street at the park.

It did not seem true. This could not possibly be the late spring of 1943; why, there was no war here at all, no sign of war, scarcely! It was incredible. Fresh from Ulster, where American jeeps jumped the hedges and the American base camps stretched over the countryside, fresh from his own uniform and reports and mountains of red tape and papers, Darrow found this like another world.

Here all was peaceful, brisk but unhurried. True, Dublin feared nothing, for the Irish Free State was neutral; but Darrow had forgotten what a peaceful world looked like. As a boy, he had gone with his family to America. He was an American now and proud to serve his adopted country, proud of the double silver bars he had worn until his recent change into civvies. Still, he had not forgotten the things of Ireland. And the Gaelic, too; he could speak the old tongue adopted by the Free State and rescued from oblivion. It was coming back to him with the very air of Ireland.

He hoped nobody would suspect it. Dublin was neutral, but under the calm surface was a boiling current.

Darrow looked much younger than his thirty years. Laughter glinted in his eyes; he had an air of irresponsible gayety and his smile held an undeniable charm that lent him youth. It was a constant irritation to his superiors, who wondered how this cheerful young sprig had attained captain's bars in what was a very hard service. Whoever picked him for this Dublin errand, however, knew what he was doing.

HIS MEAL over, he lit a cigar, left the graceful old portals of the hotel, and sauntered along to Dawson Street. He passed the Mansion House with curious glances and went on to the office and shop of the Cottage Industries, where goods of all descriptions made by the country folk were offered for sale. He was just buying a woolen necktie when Morley came in—a trim, brisk, stick-swinging man, quite the career diplomat.

"Hello!" said Darrow. Morley nodded as though they had just parted that morning, instead of a year and more ago in Cleveland. Darrow got his change and they left the shop together. Darrow handed over his purchase.

"Have yourself a cravat, Bill. I can't use it. And suppose we don't walk, but stop here on the curb. Apparently you smelled a mouse from my message."

"A rat," said Morley. "I heard last year that you were in the Intelligence."

"And I don't want to be seen with you, any longer than must be."

"Right. Dublin's lousy with all sorts of agents. What's the game?"

"Know a chap here named Lafarge? In the ministry, with some innocuous title; actually an aviation shark, an expert who did some flying in Spain and so forth."

"Sure," replied Morley. "What about him?"

"Give me the lowdown on him. There's a rumor out that he's built up the supposedly non-existent Irish Air Force into quite a thing. I've got to meet him and so forth."

Morley grunted and looked thoughtful. "I understand he's got about four hundred first-class planes cached away, and is getting more."

"And if this Free State of yours ever let loose with anything it's got on Ulster, you can see what'd happen to our forces up there," said Darrow. "Go on."

"Lafarge is around thirty-five," Morley said. "He's straight as a string, I believe. A fine chap, but he's had domestic troubles, which wrecked him for a while. Now he's free. He's Irish-American, like yourself. You Army chaps had better be jittery, too. Lafarge is hand in glove with Colonel Luhring, the German attaché here."

"Go on," said Darrow grimly. "Luhring's a gay blade by all reports."

"He's gay, all right, and he's clever, and he's got us worried," said Morley. "Well, Lafarge does quite a bit of gambling, and more drinking; also, he's in love."

"I don't know any gambling went on here."

Morley winked. "*Sub rosa*, strictly. There's a private house at Lucan, in the far suburbs, seven miles out on the Liffey, where the diplomatic crowd and others gather of an evening. It's the Boyle house. I'll have someone not in the consulate phone Boyle and a card of admittance will be sent to the hotel. When d'you want it?"

"Today. This is a rush job."

"Can do," said Morley, nodding. "Boyle will see that you meet Lafarge. What else?"

"He's in love, you said?"

"Yes. She is Foraine, the artist; Mirabelle Foraine. She etches. She has a beautiful old house in Mountjoy Square. Has her press there and a little shop or picture gallery, open any time.

She's a bit Bohemian, and may possibly be a Nazi agent. She runs with the sporty crowd and is a friend of Luhring."

"A Nazi agent wouldn't be a friend of Luhring," said Darrow reflectively.

"Well, that's all I know. Anything else?"

"Yes. The most important thing of all. Does this gal love Lafarge?"

Morley met his eyes for an instant, and smiled.

"God only knows! Plenty of others would like to know. I don't."

"Thanks, old man. I think I'm all set. And I'll want that card, remember."

"Right. Glad I'm not playing your game! There's too damned much secret service in Dublin already. Well, give me a ring any time."

Morley walked off as though their meeting had been a casual affair, and Darrow headed back for the hotel.

A BRAVE and noble city was Dublin, dingy like all ancient cities, but nervous in these uncertain days. Four hundred planes or more—whew! If the Free State made a sudden jump to grab the four northern counties and throw the English out of Ulster, it would be just too bad. The American forces based there would catch it coming and going, and might have to get into the row. Nobody wanted this. But nobody knew what the Free State might do overnight. Especially with Nazi prodding.

Nobody, that is, except Lafarge, a member of the government and a potent force to reckon with. And Darrow's job was not only to acquire information, but more particularly to make sure where Lafarge stood. If he were merely a pawn in Nazi hands, the situation was sheer dynamite. For, with the Nazi strength crumbling and wasting in Russia, and the Nazi army in Tunisia being blasted aside to make way for a sweep into Germany—the desperate gangsters of Europe might well try to create a bloody diversion here in Ireland, where their agents and diplomats and private citizens lived an untrammeled life.

At the hotel, Darrow got directions, then walked over past the Bank and Trinity College gates to the O'Connell Bridge. A tram took him the length of O'Connell Street and out Summer Hill, and he made the rest of the way afoot to Mountjoy Square. Once the center of fashion and great homes, this park was now surrounded by decay; he had not far to seek his destination.

This was a charming little Georgian house, with an addition which was evidently the picture shop. It had a separate entrance, and a sign on the door stated that the hours were three to five. Darrow rang, and the door was opened by a slatternly maid.

"Is Miss Foraine in?" asked Darrow. He was told to enter, and the maid vanished.

He found himself in unexpected luxury. Paintings and etchings, yes; but the place was like a room in a private house—as indeed it was. Rich rugs on the floor, fine old furniture around, glimpses of other rooms adjoining.

Then he caught a voice speaking Irish, a voice soft and intimate, an excellent thing in women. Darrow liked her at once because of the voice. She was at a telephone, as her words indicated. She switched from Irish to English and back again, but Darrow followed her speech without trouble, as he could follow that of the people in the street.

"But you must, you must, you must!" she exclaimed urgently. "I cannot bear it, Leo! You simply must stop this incessant drinking. It's absurd to say that life lies behind you. Am I nothing? Is the future worth nothing? It's all the fault of that scoundrel Luhring—oh, I could curse that man!"

A door slammed shut; the voice was cut off. Tom Darrow, standing in front of a magnificent proof etching of the Four Courts, stared at it unseeing. Leo—Leo Lafarge, of course. So he was drinking hard, and life lay behind him—poor devil! And this woman who loved him was a Nazi agent—or was she? No, by heavens! Not with a voice like that!

She was in the room before Darrow realized it, standing

looking at him. She wore a stained smock, her bronze hair was in disorder; she was a slim woman of perhaps thirty, with large gray eyes. She was not beautiful. She seemed colorless, almost lifeless.

"Well, sir?" she asked. Yes, it was the same voice. But her face was a mask.

Darrow had his own ways of working. He could act on sheer impulse, and now he did, flinging all reason to the four winds. After all, the Irish blood can get away with anything.

"You are right, Miss Foraine, you are right!" he exclaimed, as though resuming an interrupted discussion. The ghost of his gay smile warmed his eyes. They might have been old friends by his air.

"I overheard you. Absurd—indeed it is absurd to say that life lies behind him, especially at this moment! You know the old saying that no gate closes but another opens? It is true. We must make him see this, see the new road opening before him! You can do this. I can help: That is why I have come to you. Those Germans would destroy him merely to serve their own ends. We must prevent this."

It was, certainly, an astonishing speech from a perfect stranger. Her eyes widened upon him. She balanced between startled amazement and quick anger.

"Are you an insane man, or a drunken poet?"

Darrow laughed in hearty, unassumed laughter. "Neither one. I heard your voice, and I trust it. I trust you. Leo Lafarge must be ready to act when the gate swings open, the gate of destiny! Not as Luhring would have him act, in mad desperation; no. Instead, he must realize that ahead of him is opening a new future, that the past is closed and gone!"

HE PICKED his words to run with her thoughts, and they caught at her. Her eyes weighed him as he spoke, appraised his incisive features, his whimsical air, the keen friendliness of his smile. Color stole up her pale cheeks. His fantasy touched the artist in her and she became a different person. Sinking upon an overstuffed leather cushion, she motioned to a chair.

"My unknown friend, you interest me. I am curious. Sit down, I beg of you."

With a lightning change of tactic, Barrow bowed to her; it was his best bow.

"My name is Tom Darrow; I am an American. I'm here on a certain errand to Lafarge. I've been told you're a Nazi agent; I don't believe it. I've come to you, because the most important thing just now is Lafarge—important to me and to you, I think."

She studied him. "I am not a Nazi agent," she said quietly, "though I studied art in Germany and still have a few German friends. Yes. To me, as to you, the most important thing is Leo Lafarge. What a shrewd, wise man you are to try that opening gambit!"

No resentment, no idle talk about his prying into personal affairs. She was suddenly all vibrant energy. The mask had vanished. Her features were now alive and radiant. She was a woman whose mental powers were exceptional, and whose personality, once released, was almost hypnotic in its charm. A great soul, here. Darrow bowed again.

"I do not propose to play chess with you, madame. My errand is urgent; a matter of days, of hours, almost of minutes! Where stands Lafarge?"

She caught her breath; then the glint died from her eyes.

"Ask him, American. Once I knew, now it is different. He has been drinking like mad. It is that devil Luhring's doing— oh, I'm a fool to say such things to a stranger! Yet one trusts you instinctively. An American here in Dublin, knowing so much! Then you are an agent, a secret agent; of the Intelligence, is that it?"

"Perhaps." Darrow saw that she had fallen again in to uncertainty. "I must see this Lafarge and talk with him. How can I help him to reassert himself? What's Luhring's game?"

This steadied her. "They tempt him in a dozen ways—money,

power, promises. To do what? Move suddenly, even without authority; throw his entire air force upon Ulster. De Valera would never countenance it. They are trying to break Leo down with drink, with gambling debts, with talk of his blasted future. He was all but wrecked, you know, by domestic troubles. It is a pity; he is so fine a man—"

Her words trailed off; tears were in her throat. All this seemed rather fantastic and unreal, but Darrow perceived how terribly real it was. With a dipsomaniac, a man whose nerves were so drenched with alcohol that he might go off the deep end any time, nothing was impossible. He reached out, took her hand and patted it gently.

"You took the wrong course with such a man," he said. "Don't say to him: You must! Instead, show him what might be. Show him the new road opening for him."

"You mean, you have something to offer him?"

"Self-respect, perhaps." Darrow rose. "I'll be at Boyle's house tonight. Shall you be there?"

"Yes. About nine-thirty." She accepted his knowledge of the place without comment. "But there's so much you don't know! This Luhring is a devil of cleverness. He has Leo under his thumb, lies to him, stops at nothing. And Death walks the streets of Dublin these days. Oh, be careful!"

"Thank you. Until tonight, then."

He walked out of the place without looking back. He had accomplished a miracle in thus breaking down her reserve and making her talk freely; but what had it got him? He now knew definitely that some Nazi stroke was being planned; but what could he do? He had no idea. At least, however, she was a friend.

He had already gained one very distinct impression—that in Dublin was a hatred for England and everything English which amounted to an obsession. A slow-burning, ancient hatred. In the secret ranks of the Irish Republican Army, who hated everything around them, it was a wild and senseless hatred. But in hearts generally it was a deep emotion.

It was four in the afternoon when he reached the hotel. He left a call for seven o'clock and went to bed. Like all good gamblers, he knew the value of sleep and its proper place in the scheme of things.

When he was wakened, he dressed and went down to dinner. The card of admittance had arrived from Boyle; Morley had done his part. Darrow liked this stately dining-room and took his time over dinner. The hotel had been rebuilt in recent years, yet retained its air of quiet dignity, as though fully aware that it was one of Dublin's historic items.

Darrow learned that he could reach Lucan by tramway from the O'Connell Bridge, or by bus from Aston's Quay. Instead, he chose to hire a car. The best he could get was a charcoal-burning taxi, but he engaged it, and was presently on his way along the north bank quays.

The driver was a cheerful, garrulous old fellow who bemoaned the darkness that kept the points of interest hidden, and lamented the good old lost days.

"Ireland's a different place now, and be damned to it," said he. "And first thing we know, we'll be getting Ulster back again, and be damned to that too!"

"It can't be done," said Darrow, laughing.

"A felly hears talk," said the driver darkly. "The English, bad luck to 'em, are too busy to hold out. A fine bold stroke might make it in jig time—then we'd have war again, and be damned to that too."

It might be done, thought Darrow. With four hundred planes or more, it might be done. And how these people did hate England! Well, that was their business. He was an American now, and racial hatreds had died in him. He admired the English.

They reached the old watering-place of Lucan at last and the driver let him out at Boyle's. It was a most ordinary house. The door was opened by a maid who looked blank until Darrow displayed his card, then smiled and admitted him. He was passed upstairs, and in a reception parlor was greeted by Mr. Boyle, a hearty, cheery fellow, who asked if he cared to meet anyone. Darrow shook his head.

"Thanks, I'd just like to look about. I'm waiting until Miss Foraine comes."

"The place is yours," said Boyle, and showed him into a series of back parlors, the gaming rooms. Except for the roulette table and croupiers, he might have fancied himself at a party in some private home, by the furniture and pictures and rugs. Which, in fact, was what it was.

He had come a bit early, on purpose, but a goodish throng was already on hand. A few uniforms were visible, more evening clothes, and there appeared to be more than a few city folk of the fast set, a mixture of Irish and foreign in all. Women both old and young were sprinkled through the crowd.

Darrow loafed and watched and listened. He edged into these who lined the roulette table and began to make small wagers. At one side were two dark-faced young fellows who had obviously been drinking, and who spoke between themselves in Gaelic, little dreaming that anyone around could know the tongue. They were intent upon a man who sat playing at the far end. They cursed him savagely in low tones. Their words leaped with bitter passion, even with hatred.

Suddenly aware that he had stumbled upon drama, Darrow listened, amused. It was a question of a woman, he gathered. The other man had got some girl into trouble and thus earned the venom of these two, for venom it was.

Darrow looked at the man, who was the center of a group exchanging pleasantries with him as the croupiers droned out their sing-song phrases and shuffled money with nimble rakes. A man in evening clothes. A handsome man, bronzed and alert and vigorous, with a small brown mole over one eye that lent his features an oddly unbalanced air. A man of striking personality and of such magnetism, such evident charm that Darrow's interest was roused.

He moved about, trying to learn who the man was, without success. The two young bloods, who were obviously of a lower class than most of the clientele, being little better than toughs, grew more objectionable. The handsome Lothario ignored them; but presently Boyle came up to them, spoke in a low voice, and they departed—quite evidently breathing fire and fury. The place slipped into gaiety and peace again.

Darrow's curiosity was answered in an unexpected manner. The man with the mole drew in his money and chips, rose from his seat, and went to greet a couple who had just come in. Darrow, glancing after him, found himself looking at Mirabelle Foraine. He started, scarcely knowing her again. Then the man with her was Lafarge—and this Lothario with the mole must be no other than Luhring!

FORAINE INDEED, and what a change! Her make-up was subtle and triumphant, her gown was of plain silver lamé, with a girdle and necklace of handsome gold and coral. She was radiant. Again Darrow got the vivid impression of exceptional mental qualities. She was not voluptuous in any sense; her power came from within, and it was brilliant. Almost reluctantly, Darrow took his gaze from her to glance at Lafarge, already the center of an eager group of men.

An odd fellow, this Lafarge. A strong face, marked by a scar on the cheek; flushed with drinking. He was not handsome, but vitally strong and impressive. What struck Darrow was the haunted look in his eyes. The man Luhring hooked arms with him and drew him a little apart. Darrow advanced and caught the eye of Miss Foraine.

"Ah, Mr. Darrow, what a surprise!" Laughing, she extended both hands to him. "We have not met since London, two years ago! Leo—Colonel Luhring! Come and meet an old friend of mine, one who proves that an artist can be respectable!"

They all shook hands. When Tom Darrow exerted himself to please, as he now did, he definitely succeeded. An American? Oh, yes; but one of those Americans not particularly concerned with the War. A few deft hints conveyed the impression that he was a peace-loving artist, a bit of a radical who lived long abroad, and for whom it was just now healthier to stay away from the States.

Lafarge showed reserve, but Luhring proved extremely agreeable. This man, who seemed anything but the typical Nazi, was quickly aware of Darrow as a possible friend and ally, but not as a foe.

"You must come along to the studio with us, Mr. Darrow!" cried Mirabelle, a twinkle in her gray eyes. "We only stopped in here for a moment, to pick up Colonel Luhring and give me a tiny fling at the tables." Her face did not change, but her eyes did, as she added a low word under her breath. "I have lost. That devil has won. Tonight is the end of everything for us—everything!"

Darrow could guess at the truth. The Nazi agent had completed his conquest, Lafarge had gone over to him; Mirabelle must have had a terrific scene with Lafarge, probably had provoked him into a violent quarrel. For her, indeed, everything must seem at an end. And here might be the cue he himself so desperately needed in handling Lafarge—

"It will give me great pleasure to accompany you," he said. She broke into a gay little laugh.

"And tell me—what number shall I play? Give me luck! I have only one pound ten to lose, so give me a lucky number!"

"Nothing easier!" replied Darrow cheerfully. So it was now or never—then devil take caution! "What's the date—the ninth, I think. A lucky day for Ireland! Great things impending, great decisions made in the ministry, they say; a plot discovered, an intrigue unearthed—yes, play the nine, by all means play the nine, for it must win!"

His words carried, as he intended. Startled astonishment and sudden silence fell on those around. The very air of Dublin was electrically charged, fed by rumors of the wildest; eyes probed at Darrow from all sides, as Mirabelle promptly turned and went to the roulette table. Luhring came to the American, his gaze sharp.

"Those words might have meant anything or nothing, Mr. Darrow," he said almost with challenge. "Has something happened? Have you some news that hasn't been given out?"

Darrow smiled. "Perhaps, perhaps, my dear Colonel!" he said lightly. "Perhaps we shall have a welcome end to tension, an end to wine and flowers and love and lack of hope; tomorrow's a new day!" Then he added a rapid, apparently careless phrase in Irish, which Luhring would assuredly not understand, but Lafarge would. "*Na caithtear thusa in's na nealtaibh*—don't let yourself be thrown under the clouds of sorrow, for I bring you hope!"

His air was whimsical, gaily irresponsible, but men scented peril in his words and exchanged glances and drew away. Lafarge was undeniably startled by those last words, but Luhring nodded.

"Decidedly, we must have a chat at the studio," he said softly, "and—hello! What's up?"

An explosion of voices was coming from the roulette table, in high excitement.

"The nine! The nine wins—it has won twice. On the nine—quick, get this on the nine!" And then the impassive French phrase of the croupier: "*Rien ne va plus, messieurs et 'dames!*"

The ivory ball was whirling and clicking and settling down. It plugged once again into the nine.

Amid tremendous excitement, Mirabelle gathered up her winnings. Luhring went to her assistance. But Lafarge, coming to Darrow's side, spoke under his breath.

"What the devil is your game? Who are you?"

For one flashing instant, Darrow lost his gay air and looked soberly into the man's haunted eyes.

"Destiny," he replied. "Destiny, come to tell you that it's never too late—even now. Especially now! Don't let yourself be grounded, Lafarge, just before your ship takes the air!"

DARROW'S PREDICTION about the nine was being passed around. There were murmurs of talk regarding him. Conscious of the stir he had made, he chuckled to himself as he accompanied the other three to the doors. What a devilish stroke of luck it had been! He himself stood dumfounded at it.

Lafarge had a car near the entrance. Mirabelle Foraine was in open delight over her winnings, which were considerable.

"Champagne instead of coffee when we get home! Darrow, do you always bring your friends such luck?"

"Always," replied Darrow, holding open the car door. "That is, if they take my advice as you did."

"And what good luck have you in store for me?" demanded Colonel Luhring as he crowded into the little car.

"Oh, the very best, my dear fellow!" exclaimed Darrow blithely. "But not in a tiny English car like this—oh, the devil! Your pardon. The breath is squeezed out of me!"

There was laughter and readjustment, but Darrow had discovered what he most wanted to know, in the hard, hard lump under Luhring's arm. Lafarge, at the wheel, kept silent.

They made the return trip to the city by the Clondalkin and Drimnagh Castle road, and Mirabelle kept up a rapid fire of conversation with Luhring. When they reached Mountjoy Square, Lafarge left the car in the street. The house was set well back, and Darrow accompanied Mirabelle, while Luhring waited behind, coming more slowly with Lafarge. His voice reached them in a scattered phrase or two:

"—received imperative word today. At once, at once, do you understand?"

Mirabelle, despite her gay air, was a prey to convulsive emotion. She pressed Darrow's arm, pressed it against herself in an almost spasmodic gesture. Under her thin wrap the back of his hand was against her breast. She was unaware of it. She had no thought for herself; she, too, had caught those words. She was tense and strained, as she halted before the studio door and fumbled for a key.

"Courage!" Darrow murmured at her ear. "We've not lost; don't give him up. Our friend carries a pistol. That means he's afraid. Courage!"

She laughed in response; a hopeless laugh that had a sob at its heart. Then the door was opened. Her key was needless. The slatternly maid admitted them.

"Champagne, as you promised!" cried Lafarge. "Champagne laced with brandy, Mirabelle; a real celebration!"

"And water," said Darrow cheerfully. "Water first, Miss Foraine, to humor me."

Luhring laughed. "You're an odd chap, to offer toasts in water!"

"Ah, but it's a queer toast I'll offer," said Darrow.

The studio broke into light. Mirabelle spoke to the maid, told her she might now depart for the night, and vanished in search of the champagne and glasses. The three men lit cigarettes, and Luhring turned to Darrow, smiling but intent.

"Well? What's the good luck that you promised me?"

"The best in the world, the best luck you could possibly have! But here's our hostess—"

Mirabelle returned, bringing a tray and glasses, and departed again for the liquor. A coal fire was burning in the grate, for looks more than for warmth. With the rugs strewn about the polished floor, the pictures on the walls, the touches of feminine grace, the place was heart-warming.

"What's all this about water?" growled Lafarge. "Tonight we should celebrate with the very best!"

"And I claim the first toast," said Luhring.

"Not so; the honor is mine!" Darrow exclaimed blithely, as Mirabelle returned with bottles. Lafarge struck in with gloomy haste.

"No, no! I tell you, I'll give the toast, in champagne and cognac! A toast to great expectations, to startling events about to happen—"

Mirabelle looked from one to another, lips parted, with bated breath and eyes large. Then she broke into a quick laugh.

"Quarreling over a toast! Well, I'm the one to say who shall give the first toast, my friends! The decision is mine. Colonel Luhring, what's the subject of yours?"

Luhring bowed to her. "Fame, most gracious lady! Fame, opportunity to be grasped by a hero!"

"And yours, Leo?" Mirabelle turned to Lafarge, then gestured. "Oh! But you just now announced it. And yours, Mr. Darrow?"

"A toast in water," said Darrow. "We're not drinking to the great expectations of Mr. Lafarge, because they're visionary. We're not drinking to Colonel Luhring's toast of fame, because fame and treachery don't mingle. But we are, my dear Luhring, going to drink to your great good luck."

"Very well!" Mirabelle extended a glass of water to him, smiling archly. "You shall propose the toast."

Luhring, however, had flushed at Darrow's words. Now he turned, intent and angered.

"I'd like an explanation of your statement, sir," he barked. "Do you apply the word treachery to me?"

"No, no—merely to your fame. And be careful, or you may spoil your luck!"

Luhring was suspicious now. "What are you aiming at, Darrow? What luck?"

"Why, you have the chance at the greatest luck in the world— that of leaving Dublin alive and on your two feet!" said Darrow. "That's my advice to you; and, if I may add, do it fast! So I say that we drink this toast in water. Especially Lafarge. It's no time for a famous war bird to be drowned in debts or liquor or lost hopes, when he has great things to accomplish in the world!"

"You must be insane!" spluttered Colonel Luhring, standing stiffly.

Almost time; he had nearly brought the Nazi to the point, thought Darrow. His intent was simple. Provoke a quarrel, hammer the Nazi, waken Lafarge out of his liquor-fuddled dream into sharp realities, call for a complete showdown—and after kicking Luhring out, go at Lafarge with cold facts. He had an argument now to use with Lafarge, and a good one, thanks to Mirabelle.

But he had bargained without his Teuton. Either Colonel Luhring was warned by some sixth sense, or he was just plain clever.

"So, Mr. Darrow, you are not the careless artist you pretend!" he said. "In fact, you are not careless at all, but very adroit. An American secret agent, come to spy out the land in smart American fashion!"

"And to prevent you making a fantastic hero out of Leo Lafarge," said Darrow quite pleasantly. "A foolish, murderous hero befuddled with your lies and liquor. The time is close, with your armies in Russia lost, with your Nazi empire crumbling!"

As he spoke, he was gathering his muscles. Almost time, indeed! A silence fell upon the room, an instant of stupefied silence at these words.

Then Luhring acted first. With no warning whatever, he took a backward step and his hand slid the pistol out from under his arm. A flame was in his eyes. His words crackled out upon the room like electric sparks.

"So it is a trap! A trap set by you, Mirabelle—by you and this simpleton from America! I know you hated me, young woman, but I did not give you such credit."

Darrow had lost his chance. He had been too sure of himself. He had told too much. In that wild, handsome face, in those flaming eyes, he read murder.

He leaned forward calmly as Luhring spoke, quietly touching his shoelace—then suddenly caught hold of the rug and jerked. Luhring stood on the other end of that rug. It slid on the polished oak floor.

Luhring lost balance, and Darrow was springing at him. But the pistol exploded with a roar like thunder in this confined space. It exploded again. Darrow's feet went out from under him; he pitched down in a limp heap and lay motionless. Luhring staggered back, put his hand against the wall, and recovered.

"Ach! Fools, all of you?" he cried out, and darted from the room.

So rapidly had all this transpired, that Lafarge stood stupefied, all astare; but the crisis was driving the liquor-fumes from his brain. Mirabelle Foraine looked at the prostrate figure with horror in her eyes.

"Dead! Leo, he is dead—Luhring killed him—"

"Devil a bit," said Darrow. Grunting with pain, he tried to rise. Lafarge stirred, darted to him, helped him erect. Darrow grimaced. "Slipped on the floor—got a nasty crack on the head from that chair-leg. Well, I fumbled it. He's gone. What a prize chump I am!"

He slumped into a chair; it was unpleasant to see himself as a bungler. That moment of hesitation had been costly. But he might still retrieve the loss. He straightened up and looked at Lafarge.

"I suppose you know I have the details of the whole plot?"

"The plot?" Lafarge stared blankly. "What plot?"

"You and your big secret cache of battle planes by the hundred—a grab at Ulster in defiance of your own government—you and the cursed crazy Irish Republicans who'd like to see the Free State destroyed!"

Lafarge made a helpless, futile gesture. "Yes, that was it," he said.

A little cry came from Mirabelle. "Oh, Leo—how could you? You, of all men—honored, trusted, a hero of the air! How could you let them turn you into a drunken fool?"

Lafarge jumped as though stung, and wild anger leaped into his face.

"They? But it was your doing!" he cried out in sudden passionate agony. "You pretending that you loved me, promising anything—oh, I know the whole truth! That you're really a

London agent, an English spy! Luhring told me all about it, showed me the proof. That's why life meant nothing to me, why the future meant nothing. To think you lied to me, to think you were joking about it behind my back, joking even to him about my devotion to you!"

So thereupon the room stirred tragedy and pathos, the woman breaking into horrified protests, Lafarge raging wildly, both of them talking at once. Darrow listened while the man poured forth his broken heart, and the truth came to him.

"Wait a minute!" His voice struck in upon them commandingly. He went to the tray, dashed seltzer from the siphon into a glass, and thrust it at Lafarge. "Drink this—then listen."

Lafarge obeyed, his hand trembling as he drank.

"So you hate the English—like everybody else in this city," went on Darrow. "Well, that's your affair. Now look at this. It'll show you who I am, that I'm not English, at least." He took out his pocket-book and displayed his Army card of identity. "Satisfied? Well, so am I. First, that Mirabelle is about the finest woman in Dublin, and the truest. Wake up! Can't you see they lied to you? Can't you see they forged proofs and showed them to you, trying to break up everything between her and you? They turned you into a liquor-sodden fool, made a tool out of you—get it through your head!"

Lafarge stared at Darrow with those haunted eyes of his—stared, and began to see the light. He closed his eyes; a low groan escaped him. Mirabelle Foraine, a shining glory in her face, was watching Darrow—then she started, turning her head.

Upon them all broke a realization of noise and tumult in the night outside. A cry broke from Mirabelle.

"Something has happened—oh, what is it? Who's there?"

"It's me, miss."

The slatternly maid came into the room, panting and terrified, her face white.

"It's him, miss!" she gasped out. "It's him—Colonel Luhring!

He was killed out yonder in the street—two lads from the city shot him—it's about a girl, they say—"

Darrow stirred and came to his feet. He remembered those two young fellows at Boyle's house. Everything was clear.

"Too late now to make Luhring confess," he said. "Well, Lafarge? How about it?"

Lafarge went to the tray. He poured brandy into a glass, held it up, looked at it a moment—then hurled it with a crash into the fireplace and turned to Mirabelle.

"I've been a complete idiot," he said chokingly. "Can you— can you ever forgive me? Can you ever trust me again?"

She stumbled to him, hands outstretched.

"All my life, my dear," she whispered, and caught hold of him, and his arms went about her.

Darrow cleared his throat. "No gate closes but another opens," he said. "And a true saying it is. Looks like my errand's done. Lafarge, a drop of champagne will clear your head. How about a spot all around—just to celebrate a toast to the future?"

They turned to him, and tears were mingled with smiles. There would never be any raid on Ulster.

VIII

NAGASAKI SCOTCH

*No... the Sharks Aren't All in the Sea, and
the Pirates Ain't All Dead, Neither.*

S COWLING, CAP'N WINGO tamped his pipe
and refilled his glass.

"If you ask me," he observed darkly, "the sharks ain't all in
the sea, and the pirates ain't all dead, neither. If I was your age
I'd do something about it. Not to mention this piffle about men
too old to serve. Too old! Me! It's a lie and a calumny!"

Cap'n Eben Wingo was a wispy little man, bent and shrunk-
en. With his white gallagers fluttering, he looked as though a
stout breeze would blow him away, till you saw his alert, bright
blue eyes. He was caretaker aboard the palatial yacht *Whatcheer,*
now laid up for the duration unless the Navy took her over.

His guest, Cap'n "Red" Ketch, had rowed down for the
evening from his own floating home, the *Arethusa,* bringing a
bottle of Scotch along. He was a picture of youth and robust
energy, comparatively speaking, if one did not count his wooden
leg. His grizzled red thatch framed gnarled, salt-weathered
features, but he was far too easy-going to suit Cap'n Wingo.

"You should worry," he said, glancing around the cabin.
"You're setting pretty."

Cap'n Wingo snorted. "Dang it. I should be in service! Coastguard turned me down again today, durn 'em! Blasted age limits.
Why, I'm a better man than half these goldbraid snippets in
uniform! What's more, the fighting ain't all in foreign parts.
Right here on the home front we're liable to have shooting any

day, yes, sir! All them Japs want is to get next to some o' these shipyards. I can see it coming right here on the West Coast."

He brooded for a moment, then added, "What's more, I don't get took in like you, neither, which goes to prove my words."

"Meaning what?" demanded Cap'n Ketch. "You ain't lost your berth. I hear the Navy won't take over this craft, and her owner ain't getting his gold braid. So what's worrying you?"

"Your doings."

Holding his visitor in suspense by this accusation, Cap'n Wingo held a match above his pipe, with due regard for his chin-fringe of white whiskers. A drift of music came in from the yacht club. All yachts, even this elegant craft with her twin Diesels, were laid up for the duration in San Ysidro channel, but the club still functioned.

The two old cronies sat at the festive board which not so long ago had been graced by millionaire sportsmen. Few millionaires, these days, could afford the upkeep of a yacht like the *Whatcheer*. Cap'n Wingo, thanks to his master's ticket and his unblemished reputation, got a hundred and fifty a month for caretaking her.

"Bilge, that's what it is!" He pointed the dead match to the bottle on the table before them. "Bilge!"

Cap'n Ketch reddened at this insult to his liquor.

"There's a proverb about gift horses," he said acidly. "And I give Tony Sung two seventy-five for it as prime Scotch. And he's an honest Chink."

"Huh! Don't call him no Chink!" sniffed Cap'n Wingo. "He's a Korean and one of our allies, and his wife's a China woman; they got papers to prove it. And he's allowed to go to sea with his stinking old fish tub, while you'n me got to stay in harbor. A spy, that's what he is, a Jap spy!"

"Don't try to change the subject," broke in Cap'n Ketch. "What's wrong with my Scotch, anyhow?"

"Look at the bottom of the bottle."

Cap'n corked the bottle, turned it upside down, and looked at his host.

"I don't see anything. What about it?"

Cap'n Eben Wingo pointed to a tiny protuberance.

"See that pimple? If you was an old China hand like me, instead of being a lumber-barge skipper from Seattle, you'd know by that pimple and by the taste. The Japs cat a pin-head hole in the bottom of a bottle, steal out the whiskey till air-lock occurs, fill it up with rotgut, and seal the hole with hot glass. There's the living proof that Tony Sung's a Jap spy. And something had ought to be done about it, is my idear, before he blows up the shipyards!"

Cap'n Ketch, disconcerted by the undeniable evidence, tried to shift the topic.

"Yeah, you Boston guys always say idear for idea—"

"South Boston!" snapped Cap'n Wingo.

"It's all the same out here on the West Coast. Now, I'd like to get the rights of your brush with the Navy yesterday. I hear all sorts of rumors about it."

"Rumors be danged!" said Cap'n Wingo. "I give them fellers

a piece of my mind, that's what. Too old to serve, they says to my face. Too old—me!"

"I don't mean that," said Cap'n Ketch. "I mean about this here craft and its trial run. I hear your owner had a run-in with the Navy examiners, and somebody had sabotaged your Diesels and they blew up. And in consequence the Navy won't take over your floating palace."

Cap'n Wingo let out a blast of Cape Horn profanity that curled his white whiskers. He was furious at the Navy anyway, because he was sitting in a retired berth instead of employing his talents at sea.

"It ain't so!" he stormed. "I told him not to push her! I warned him and the engineer warned him. Like most owners, he knew it all; he was anxious to show off her speed to them Navy examiners. He kep' calling for more revs until one engine was burned out, the stubborn fool! However, the Navy wants her just the same; they'll take her over and make the repairs."

"Wish 'em joy of her." Cap'n Ketch ran his eye over the red teak paneling and brasswork. "Varnish palace full of chromium and lady gadgets. A reg'lar workhouse to keep in shape, what with scraping and varnishing and spit polishing, and one of them damned patent electric air suction sweepers on carpets—"

"Where," broke in Cap'n Wingo firmly, "did Tony Sung get this here Nagasaki Scotch?"

"How do I know?"

"How you ever got a master's license, I don't see; must ha' bribed the examiners. Well, there's no such stuff in this country. Therefore, it come from a Jap submarine. And Tony Sung made the contact with the sub. And that proves everything."

"Says you. Naturally, you know more'n Navy Intelligence and all the authorities who have given Tony the okay. He's got papers to prove what he is, too."

"Every danged spy has got papers to prove what he ain't. That reminds me. Your old tub, the *Arethusa,* can run out to sea any time; your owner, Dibble, has got permission."

"How you know?" demanded Cap'n Ketch suspiciously.

"I was talkin' to Dibble today, uptown, and a couple Navy men. They may take her over to use for a tender and give Dibble a commission."

"So you talked to 'em! I've been afraid of that." Cap'n Ketch regarded Cap'n Wingo gloomily, and sipped his drink.

"Trouble with you is you want to hang on to your caretaker's job," said Cap'n Wingo. "You got no patriotism. You know good'n well what would happen to the shipyards if a Jap sub ever got into this here channel and opened up with her deck gun."

"Might's well talk about a sub warping up alongside the moon," Cap'n Ketch said sourly.

"Sure. Thoughtless people like you would soon ruin this country. Just because Tony Sung claims to be a Korean and has papers to prove it, you take for granted he's okay."

"Well, you claim to be a master in steam," Cap'n Ketch said softly, "and you got a ticket to prove it, too."

Cap'n Wingo looked hard at him. "So what?"

"So everybody takes it for granted you're okay, in consequence."

Cap'n Wingo pondered this for a moment, but let it pass.

"Well, he looks Jap and he talks Jap and he acts Jap. Now he sells you this here whiskey, which could only have come off a Jap boat. Ain't that enough?"

"Not on your sayso. Even s'posing he is a Nip, which he ain't, how can he do any hurt?"

Cap'n Wingo sucked noisily at his pipe, made a wry face, caught up his glass and drained it, then attacked his pipe stem with a cleaner, savagely.

"When your owner, Dibble, bought the *Arethusa* last year, I taught him navigation. He's got sense, even if you haven't. Anyhow, if the Navy gives you a trial run, sniff around the Todos Santos islands, and see what can you see."

"The islands?" Cap'n Ketch stared at him. "The coast is pa-
troled, ain't it? Ever since you seen that cockeyed reporter's
dream in the newspaper, about how a sub could shell the living
blazes out of the shipyards if she ever got into the channel, you
been nuts on the subject. You and your Jap subs and your Nagasaki Scotch! I'm going home."

He did. He had to row home, as the *Arethusa* lay at moorings
down the channel. The two men parted grumpily, and Cap'n
Ketch took his bottle with him.

THE *WHATCHEER* lay at her slip, not at moorings.
Cap'n Wingo could get away whenever he liked, by making
sure the dock watchman kept an eye on things. So, next morning,
he was sitting in the rather dingy office of a young man who
wore the stripes of a lieutenant-commander, and who was very
much in charge of San Ysidro harbor. After a good deal of time
and talk, the young man stopped being polite and took a firm
grip on the situation.

"Cap'n Wingo, it's all nonsense to resent the fact that none
of the services can use you. When a man is seventy-three, he's
off the active list—definitely."

"I've got more sea sense than all you younger whipper-
snappers put together," said Cap'n Wingo in a positive way.
"I'm hale and hearty. I ain't afraid to take action, neither, like
you brass-stripes who are scared to get a mark on your records!"

"No doubt, no doubt," agreed the young man. "But you lack
sufficient sea-sense to know that at seventy-three a man can't
stand up to the demands of an active job."

"It ain't so," barked Cap'n Wingo. "I can take a ship around
the Horn this minute!"

"If there's one to take around the Horn, I'll see that you get
it," the young man said with crushing finality. "Now, as to your
spy scare, you're barking up the wrong tree. Tony Sung has been
thoroughly investigated. He's been here for years, and is the
only Oriental remaining around here. He came to this country
long before Japan seized Korea; his people there were killed by

the Nips. You haven't one particle of evidence for any accusation and I strongly advise you to button your lip. Your whiskey bottle story means nothing; others than Japs can needle a bottle."

Cap'n Wingo rose, bitterness personified.

"You know best, of course. Only, if I was a Jap and fixing for a spy or sabotage job, you bet I'd be able to stand all sorts of investigation by young gentlemen of the Navy! If anything at all was to give me away, it'd be some little thing—like, maybe, Scotch whiskey from Nagasaki. It's got a flavor an old China hand can't mistake."

The young man laughed. "So has Tony Sung, Cap'n—a regular aura of fish!"

Cap'n Wingo stamped out stiffly, pausing at the door for a final Parthian shaft.

"Every morning afore dawn, he takes out his fishboat. Time after time, like I say, I've watched him. And he's always loaded up with gasoline tins that don't come back, too-—"

"Nothing to it, Skipper," said the young man hastily. "Forget it, forget it!"

Muttering in his white whiskers, Cap'n Wingo walked over to Sixth Street and had noon dinner with his grand-daughter, Minnie Leary, whose husband was an inspector in the shipyard. He had lived with the Learys until the war sent him spurting back into harness as caretaker.

"Why didn't you fetch Cap'n Ketch for dinner, like I told you?" demanded Minnie.

"Too far for him to walk with that wooden peg." Cap'n Wingo champed his hash vigorously. "Sides, he's feeling brash and uppity. Not that he ain't a good man in his way—"

"So you've had another row, eh? That reminds me. Here's a call for you."

CAP'N WINGO glanced at the telephone number. "That's Dibble's law office. He owns the *Arethusa*, y'know."

"Is he the one you taught to navigate, last year?"

"Yep. Lemme at that phone, now."

He hunched over the phone and soon had Dibble on the wire.

"Oh, hello, Skipper! Remember what we were talking about yesterday—the Navy taking over the *Arethusa?* Well, they're going to try her out sometime next week: since your hooker burned up her Diesels they'll give me a chance. But I want to take the boat out for a couple days. I have a crack engineer who thinks he can get her a few extra knots by tinkering with the engines under sea conditions. Cap'n Ketch doesn't get around very spry, you know, and I wondered if you could come along too."

"Sure," said Cap'n Wingo promptly. "Don't blame you for wanting one real sailor aboard. When you going?"

"Monday's a legal holiday. How about leaving Sunday morning and coming back Monday?"

"Okay. Might run over to the islands and outside, if you can get Navy permission. It's a half-day trip each way and you might want to shoot some goats. Does Cap'n Ketch know about it?"

"Haven't seen him yet. "

"Good." Cap'n Wingo's eyes glittered. "I'll break the news to him."

LATE THAT afternoon when Cap'n Ketch went uptown for his mail, Cap'n Wingo hailed him and he came aboard the crippled *Whatcheer* with an eye cocked for weather. To his surprise, Cap'n Wingo set out a bottle of rum and was exceedingly cordial; and presently was going on his favorite topic of Tony Sung once more.

"Y'know, he heads due south every morning he goes out; where does that take him? Smack into Point Reyes, if he holds it long enough. It's a blind; twice I've thought I seen his light shift west'ard. If he shifts to a course sou' by west, where'd he get to? The middle of Todos Santos islands and reefs!" he concluded triumphantly. "And outside the kelp beds. And all them

Japs know the kelp beds like they know the palms of their hands."

"So what?" asked Ketch.

"So come Monday morning, you and your mate, which is me, will be out where them reefs give cover from the currents and prevailing winds, a hell of a ways off the coast. Yes, sir, we're going to sea on Sunday, with me along to keep an eye on your seamanship."

So he spilled his exultant news and savored it exceedingly, and waxed the more affable in view of Cap'n Ketch's chagrin. Another drink and he was in high good-humor. Then along came Tony Sung's bluff-bowed boat heading for the fish-wharf, with dish-faced Tony at the wheel and his son, an equally dish-faced boy of sixteen, ready with the lines. Tony waved at them in passing.

"Man and boy working that boat!" snorted Cap'n Wingo. "Should have a crew o' three."

"Help's hard to get," said Cap'n Ketch. "He brings in quite a bit o' fish, too. With things quiet, they let him and them sardine boats down to Pedro keep working."

Things were certainly quiet; the scare about Jap subs off the coast had long ago died away. San Ysidro, being distant from the canneries, had never attracted fisher-craft. Even before the war, a bare half-dozen had been located here; now all were gone except Tony Sung.

Cap'n Wingo had watched that dish-faced man during weeks and months; he knew that the Korean came in with his catch on Saturdays, spent the night in town, and took his wife and dish-faced son to church on Sunday, being a convert of no little renown. But on Monday, well before dawn, as on every other day, Tony Sung's fishboat chugged out of the channel and never varied her course. Having nothing else to do but scour brasswork, Cap'n Wingo had plenty of time for his fixed idear.

On Saturday night his shoulder hurt him, and still hurt on Sunday morning. That shoulder had been broken long years ago; ever since, it had been an infallible weather prophet. Off this coast a blow could come up very suddenly. So, although the glass showed no appreciable drop and the morning was fine, Cap'n Wingo knew what was what, and prepared accordingly.

His relief watchman came on Sunday morning. Dibble and the engineer showed up, and laughed to see Cap'n Wingo loaded down with oilskins and sou'-wester this grand sunny day.

"Afraid of spray, Cap'n?" the lawyer asked jovially. He was a well set-up man of forty, out of the war with heart murmurs but now hoping for a Navy place. "Coastguard tells me there's no sign of any weather making."

"Well, I got m' reasons," Cap'n Wingo said dourly. "Let's go."

The *Arethusa* was a forty-footer, of no particular luxury but built for comfort. Cap'n Ketch ventured no comment on the oilskins. Dibble, very much the owner-yachtsman, took the wheel and they went gaily down the channel. The course and objective was left entirely to Cap'n Wingo, who, as a matter of professional courtesy, deferred to Cap'n Ketch as skipper. Both owner and engineer had fish at the back of their minds, and the idea of lying up among the islands was quite satisfactory.

Outside the lee door of the wheel-house, Cap'n Ketch gave Cap'n Wingo a nudge.

"I ran into a missionary uptown yesterday," he said softly. "He had been in Korea, too. Asked him about your private nightmare. He says sure, Tony is well-known as a Korean convert. He's the only one in these parts and they handle him mighty proud and precious. The sky-pilot says there's no more chance of Tony being a Jap than of him running a honkytonk."

"I never said he run a honkytonk."

"I'm talking about the preacher."

Cap'n Wingo's chin-whiskers jutted forward as he set his teeth on his pipestem.

"Well, you ain't got around that Nagasaki Scotch! And you'd

better keep an eye on your owner-master and sheer off from them kelp-beds ahead."

The day passed in lonely futility; they saw no gulls, hence no fish. The engineer laid them up an hour at a time, readjusting engine gadgets. The seas were empty; even the kelpboats that had once worked so steadily along the coast were no more, since only the Japs knew what depth of kelp held the magic agar, and they had kept their knowledge secret. No more slim yachts and spidery fishing-craft and squat fishboats; all gone. Made you think twice, said Dibble rather vaguely.

The Todos Santos were a group of reefs and islets, barren, raising nothing except a few occasional goats. They were thoroughly charted, with every depth and shoal known. Cap'n Wingo had no use for his oilskins; with them he had deposited below a long package wrapped in newspaper. By sunset, Dibble said they might as well lie up for the night, because the engineer wanted to get in an hour's work before darkness and supper.

SO CAP'N KETCH headed for San Tomas, one of the larger islets. A haze had lifted to the southward and the glass had fallen a trifle; not much, however. Under the north shore of San Tomas, in fair shelter, they dropped anchor in eight fathoms on account of currents, and Dibble went to work with the engineer at what they hoped were the final adjustments.

Cap'n Wingo broke out a bottle below. Cap'n Ketch stumped down and joined him.

"I figure," said Cap'n Wingo, "that if Tony Sung's making for these rocks, he'd ought to reach 'em at six forty-five tomorrow morning. I'd like to take the boat and look around on shore. It's a fine lonely spot, fitted to land saboteurs and dynamite or leave messages."

"If it'll put your mania to sleep, let's do it," volunteered Cap'n Ketch. "I notice we're anchored off the one place a body could land on San Tomas. You prob'ly had in mind to make a landing."

"Yep," said Cap'n Wingo.

So they rowed ashore. It was ebb tide. Cap'n Wingo landed on the barren, slimy rocks and clambered around and peered and searched, finally coming back to the boat with nothing to report.

"No buried treasure?" asked Cap'n Ketch. "No dynamite, no gun emplacements, no airplane field, no Japs?"

"No," Cap'n Wingo replied unpleasantly.

"Haze is thickening to the south'ard." Cap'n Ketch nodded at the next islet, a craggy rock fifty feet above the sea and half a mile long. "We might look at High Rock, yonder. The only landing's on the west side—ain't in sight from here, but it ain't far. I hear tell there's a wide ledge by the landing, ten foot depth, where abalones are thick, and it's steep-to. A Jap sub could lay along that ledge and haul in abalone steaks—"

"Go to hell," said Cap'n Wingo. They returned to the *Arethusa*. The haze was thickening with night, and the glass was down a point, but they were well moored in the lee of San Tomas.

That evening Cap'n Wingo, whose shoulder was really hurting, retired early from the seven-up game. The sea was kicking up a bit, and nobody said anything about an early start next morning; he had a distinct notion that Cap'n Ketch resented his presence aboard, and he was more than cool toward Cap'n Ketch, and the engineer, by all the signs, was going to be seasick before the night was over. The *Arethusa* was kicking a bit at her moorings.

So, when Cap'n Wingo turned out on deck at two bells, or five o'clock, he had the whole wide world to himself and plenty of it. He got into oilskins with supreme satisfaction; a drizzle was blowing up out of the southeast, and dirty lay the sky in that quarter.

Night and subconscious cogitation had come to Cap'n Wingo's aid. As he got himself a quick bite and a mug of java, he reviewed the situation very happily. He had been a fool to waste time landing on San Tomas. Thanks to the rain and scud, the *Arethusa* would be invisible to anyone coming from San Ysidro; the islands covered her, too. And anyone coming would probably land on High Rock's western shore, protected from this southeast wind.

"Yep, I'd better take Red Ketch's tip and land there," he soliloquized. "From seaward, too, it has a good approach with plenty of depth; anybody could steam up slap alongside, where it's steep-to by the chart!"

So he tumbled into the boat and made for High Rock, after first getting his long package wrapped in newspaper. Getting there in the dinghy was a job, but the lee of San Tomas helped, and the current favored. As he toiled in to the landing, he was rejoiced to see that the end of the island quite hid the *Arethusa* from sight.

There was no surf here, but ill-luck assailed him. Newspaper parcel in hand, he stepped ashore, to slip suddenly on the wet rocks. He lost balance; his parcel shot forward to the dry beach, but he toppled and went down on hands and knees. To an old man, the shock was excessive. He struggled upright, and then saw that the kickback of his fall had sent the dingy out from shore. The current had already seized it.

"Condemn it!" said Cap'n Wingo in acute dismay. To swim out, overtake the boat and row it back was for him impossible; a tide-rip swept about these rocks. The dingy went on out and whirled around and started for the North Pole.

Bruised, miserable, marooned, Cap'n Wingo picked up his long package and sought shelter among the jutting rocks from the bursts of rain and chill wind that swept up from southward. Sea and sky were gray, the air was filled with flying spume and rain, and Cap'n Wingo had no recourse or solace save his pipe. Yet he was here, where he had designed to be, and consulted his watch methodically.

He was in no danger; by noon, at latest, those aboard the *Arethusa* would be searching for him. He had an unhappy vision of a white-bearded figure capering on the rocks at the south end of the island and waving a sou'wester to attract their attention. The thought of Tony Sung's fishboat, by this time close aboard the islands, cheered him. Six-thirty; yes, not long to wait now!

HE EXAMINED the landing. This was a long strip of shingle which ran back from the water for a few yards and ended in upheaved masses of ancient rock; not much of a landing, but it might prove wide as a church door—

A gasp escaped him. He took the pipe from his mouth; his jaw fell, for he saw the impossible. From seaward—from seaward, mind you!—a small boat was coming in to make the landing. From the open Pacific, not from any kind of craft, it came, four men lugging at the oars, men hidden by oilskins and sou'westers! It was within biscuit-toss of the beach before he realized its presence, so thick was the air. Cap'n Wingo sat stupefied, incredulous.

The small boat drove in at the shingle. The four plopped out and drew it up; they took out burdens and lifted them up toward the rocks, then sought shelter among those rocks. Cap'n Wingo got only glimpses of them. He looked at their boat. It was a peculiar sort of craft, unlike anything known to him; it looked like an inflatable boat, in fact. The thought steadied him and chilled his excitement.

A rubber boat—Japs, by Jupiter! Japs, set ashore from a sub!

The thrill was still coursing through his veins when off to the northward, rounding the far end of the island, he sighted a speck, distanced by the scud and rain. He dropped his pipe and chirruped to himself in delicious exultation. He forgot the *Arethusa*, which must have missed him by this time; he forgot everything else—Tony Sung's boat coming to the rendezvous! With shaking hands he fumbled at that newspaper-wrapped package. He tore off the wrappings as he crouched among the rocks, and brought to light an ancient double-barreled shotgun, already loaded.

He waited, tensed, squinting across the rain-squalls.

The fishboat came chugging down the island shore, and slowed. She came close, and sighted the collapsible boat on the shingle. Her siren tooted loudly; Tony Sung was at the wheel, pulling the cord. The four men came suddenly from shelter and stood clumped, waving. Tony Sung waved back. His dish-faced son appeared briefly, then returned to the engines.

She came in close, so close as almost to touch the shingle. Tony Sung came out into the bow and tossed a coiled line ashore; one of the four men caught it and ran back to a boulder and made fast. Tony Sung dropped from the bow and waded ashore. The boat backed out the length of the line; an occasional turn of the screw held her.

Tony Sung and the four men in oilskins exchanged warm greetings, it appeared; hard to see what went on for the sou'westers that hid faces and heads. But, after a moment or two, attention shifted. The dishfaced boy leaped to the gunnel of the fishboat, yeiling, waving his arms, pointing down the shore.

Cap'n Wingo knew instantly what he was pointing at; the *Arethusa* was coming. And with that, Cap'n Wingo shot to his feet and sent his old quarter-deck voice roaring downwind.

"Hands up! You, there—hands up!"

The men did not obey; instead Tony Sung hauled out a pistol. Seeing this, Cap'n Wingo let go with both barrels, quite unintentionally; he had never before fired this borrowed weapon. But he let go straight, which was the main thing.

There was a scattering of oilskins, men and sou'westers; screams and shouts and oaths poured up from the grotesque, hopping, shot-stung figures. Cap'n Wingo roared another order, and it was obeyed; Tony Sung dropped his gun and put up his arms with the others. And then a ghastly dismay swamped Cap'n Wingo, as he saw the faces of the four men who had landed.

They were not Japs at all. They were white men.

"Oh, my gosh!" he said. "Now I've done it—"

He stood motionless, threatening, shotgun covering the group; in reality, he was as empty as the gun itself. An overwhelming horror of his mistake gripped him at sight of those peppered and bleeding figures—white men! He was incapable of any motion. The dish-faced boy appeared briefly, cast off, and the fishboat went careening wildly away downwind, but he cared not. A deep groan escaped him. Everything was in a whirl before his senses—a whirl of blood and white men's faces. White men! Not Japs at all.

One of the four slumped down to the shingle. Tony Sung and another stooped to aid him; blood was flowing fast. The other two kept their arms up, bleating frantically. Cap'n Wingo was deaf and blind. Even when the gray shape of the *Arethusa* came looming in, he remained gripped by that frightful paralysis.

WHEN HE was dimly aware that Dibble was ashore, shouting at him to keep them covered. Cap'n Ketch came scrambling ashore too, waving a gun. Cap'n Wingo paid no heed; he was immobile, breathing hard, wide-eyed with awful realization of the mistake he had made. He stayed where he was. When, later, Cap'n Ketch came stumping up to his perch amid the rocks, he shrank and awaited the scathing torrent of words. Instead Cap'n Ketch nodded at him.

"Two o' them fellers are right bad hurt, seems like."

Cap'n Wingo suppressed another groan. "Condemn it! I didn't go for to kill 'em!"

"No harm if you had, Eben. Durn'd if I ain't proud of you!" exclaimed Captain Ketch heartily. "Yes, sir; my hat's off to you. I'll eat every last word I said!"

Suspecting sarcasm, Cap'n Wingo held his breath.

"They ain't Japs at all," he said gloomily.

"No. A durned sight more dangerous, Dibble says. Germans, savvy? Heinies in Jap service; they got a lot of 'em in Tokio. Same as them aviators who machine-gunned Honolulu streets during the blitz, mind it? If they once got safe into the country—"

It was perhaps two minutes, a long two minutes, before Cap'n Wingo comprehended those words. Then the color came back into his frozen cheeks. He drew a long breath. His shoulders squared. The revulsion of feeling almost swept him off his feet with wild joy, and he fastened Cap'n Ketch with his old jaunty eye.

"Ha! So you admit Tony Sung ain't no Korean after all, huh?"

"If he is, he's a good Jap all right!"

"I knew it," boomed Cap'n Wingo. "That was my idear all the time. Oh, boy! Oh, *boy!* Nagasaki Scotch, huh? That's what comes of knowing your liquor. Well, come on! What you standing around waiting for? Let's go! Too old for any use, am I? If I know anything, them smart-alec Navy officers at San Ysidro are going to eat crow, and plenty of it!"

It is on record that they did, too. Very gladly.

IX

SECOND GENERATION

*Pete Dominick's Father Had Come from
the Smuggler's Island of Sicily—and
Now His Son Was Creeping Back.*

S O T H I S was Malta! Malta the defiant, bombed with diabolic fury as no other place on earth had been, and still defiant! Pete Dominick, crowded against the ship's rail, stared as the slow convoy moved into the harbor. His own ship was one of several with the Stars and Stripes overhead and gobs manning the guns, but the majority were British.

No bombs here today; a patrol of buzzing Spitfires ceaselessly quartered the sunny blue sky. Pete Dominick, assistant steward, leaned on the rail, his left hand flung across it. The hand was gloved. He held a cigarette between its fingers. Ships' stewards do not wear gloves; stranger still when they wear a glove on one hand, none on the other, as he did.

He looked at the roaring harbor and island, for roaring it was. Everything ashore was a mass of rubble and ruin. The yellowish fortress walls were shapeless wreckage.

The houses and shops of the city, on its steep streets, were gigantic piles of broken stone and debris. Nothing had escaped. And yet, crowded upon these great heaps of wreckage, were thousands of people, cheering like mad, waving flags and handkerchiefs as the convoy came in under its guard of British warships, while military bands blared away triumphantly.

Pete Dominick was a smallish man, emphatically Italian by his olivine skin and black hair and mustache. But when he moved, there was a briskness, a poised and wary alertness, in his manner; a flash in his eye, a firm cut to lips and chin. And now, as he saw the sleek gray British destroyer nosing in along-side, his face lighted up suddenly, fiercely.

The destroyer took a line. Pete Dominick saw the mate coming, nodding to him.

"All set, Pete? Good luck."

He shook hands with Dominick and moved with him to the waist. A noosed line was ready. Dominick caught hold and set his foot in the bight. Men hauled away, grinning at him, not knowing the reason of all this, nor caring. He was hoisted up and over the rail, and lowered to the deck of the destroyer beneath, where other men caught him. He stepped free of the rope, and the destroyer sheered off. Two officers came up to him, one a Britisher, the other a United States lieutenant-commander.

"Come along," said the latter curtly.

Dominick followed them, amid curious glances from the British tars, and all three sought the stuffy little mess-cabin of the destroyer. With the doors closed, they sat at the table. The Britisher, eyeing Dominick with lazy appraisal, set out ciga-rettes. The American spoke briskly.

"Let's see your papers."

Dominick produced a small wallet. His papers were un-folded and scrutinized, and the American nodded as he replaced them.

"Right. All in order. Now, Dominick, a lot of work and preparation has gone into this thing. Our part is done. I'm turning you over to Lieutenant Watson, R.N., here, who handles the rest of the job. As I understand it, your father in New York was to supply you with full data covering the landing; data which no other man knows."

"He did," said Dominick. Not a Navy man, he omitted the usual "sir."

"Did he know the purpose?"

"I expect he could guess it." Dominick grinned faintly. "He asked no questions. You needn't worry about him. The old man

was the smartest smuggler in Sicily in his day. Mafia, too. He knew all the angles, and I've got 'em in my head."

"Don't be too cocky. You know what any slip will mean to you."

Dominick held out his gloved left hand and flexed the fingers.

"I know damned well what a Nazi torpedo done to me on my old ship."

The two officers exchanged a glance and a slight nod. The American rose and put out his hand, a sudden smile in his eyes.

"I'm off. Good luck, Dominick—and I'm proud of you, win or lose! But you'll win."

"Thanks. I'll do my best."

The American departed. Lieutenant Watson, R.N., indicated a bundle that lay on the table, and spoke in fluent Italian.

"Everything's there. You'd better change into it now and stay under cover. Sicily is almost within sight, but we can't leave harbor until after dark."

"Gosh!" said Dominick, with a smile. "You're pretty good yourself!"

Watson shook his head. "Sicilian dialect—well, a man must be born to it, really. Now, you know the risks, I take it. We'll do our best, but we can't guarantee where you'll find Nazis, ashore there, or what you'll run into."

"I'll chance that."

"I'll give you full instructions once we are at sea. In the packet on that chair are detailed maps and charts of the coast ahead. You'll have a couple of hours to study them; you'll find them marked."

He, too, departed. Pete Dominick seized upon the bundle.

Presently he had disappeared entirely. In his place sat Pietro Domenigo, clad in a frayed, worn, dirty gray-green uniform with the insignia of the 115th Calabrian on the tabs. From worn and bulging boots to almost shapeless cap, he was complete. A steward knocked and entered, eyed him with furtive British astonishment, and set a small bottle of wine on the table, and cigarettes, then withdrew.

Domenigo opened the maps, and sat poring over them, smoking and drinking his wine with appreciation. The sunlight faded, the daylight died; he switched on the lights and went back to his maps. They showed the coast of southern Sicily west of Girgenti—the sulphur shipping country; the marked place, evidently meant for him, was just off the little town of Siculiana, which lay a few miles inland. He nodded, well pleased. Here was the very district his father had known so well, back in Mafia days.

Lieutenant Watson came in.

"We'll have to douse lights and be off, and eat as we may. Ha! You look a bit of all right! Here's Nazi money for you— Fascisti money, rather. And a batch of old letters. This one in the center, in purple ink; that's the important one. Now pay attention."

WATSON'S VOICE lowered.

"Siculiana is the town to reach. So far as we know there's not a Nazi within fifty miles of it; may be blackshirts, though. At the tavern in that town, a scraggly little country place, is a man known as Paolo Fuga. That letter in purple ink must reach him. He's our link in Sicily and on through Italy, understand? There'll be landings there one of these days. If for any reason it's impossible, the ink will disappear if wet with water."

"Or," said Domenigo with a faint grin, "if I fall overboard."

"Right you are. If you reach him, he'll give you notes or verbal reports for us. Each night we'll stand in close to shore at the same spot where we land you. I'll give you a supply of wax vestas."

"Matches?"

"Correct. From two to four o'clock, strike one on the hour precisely and let it burn out. No other light is necessary. After four o'clock—"Watson gave the hour in military or Continental time—"it'll be too light for us to stand in, so don't try it. Understood?"

"Okay," said Pietro Domenigo, pocketing the paper money and several tiny boxes of Italian wax vestas. "I've got a handmade map of that particular strip of coast that my old man made. I saved it so I could study up on the trails at the right place where we land. Can I have some time to get this spot in my head?"

"Not here. Come below and you can have a berth with a light. Better get a bit of sleep if you can, too. We'll grab a bite to eat as we go."

The lights were doused. Already the destroyer was feeling the sea-roll, as she headed out of the harbor. They were on their way.

Two hours before dawn, a small boat approached this bit of Sicilian coast, shoaled by earthquakes and treacherous with rocks. A dreary coastline, this, westward of Porto Empedocle; here was neither the beautiful coastal plain, nor the fertile uplands and high beach cliffs that lay elsewhere. Here were neither fishing villages nor river-mouths to make harbors for them; emptiness and old desolation guarded the inhospitable shores.

The boat crept under dipping oars in the starlight. A coral fisher from Tunis, who knew every foot of the coast, acted as pilot. At length he found the spot he sought, a tiny indentation so rock-studded and wave-washed that only a small boat would dare enter.

All this while Pietro Domenigo had been impressing his present name and character upon himself. It was hard, for Pete Dominick was an American by birth and training and nature, and proud of it. Had he not lost his hand a year previously in the torpedoing of a ship on which he served, he would have been in the Army now; this was barred to him. Yet, when they wanted a man exactly suited to this particular errand, they had found him, as by a miracle—a miracle of knowledge and shrewdness. They could find anything, these Service men!

His past was washed up—public school, jobs in New York, steward's position aboard ships. No more savings and Victory Bonds and family spaghetti parties, no more girls over in the Italian quarter, no more anything he had known. A new future beckoned. If he got out of this job alive, there would be others of the same kind ahead; the Army wanted men who knew the Sicilian dialects, though not for fighting. So he was Pietro Domenigo now, soldier of Musso Fatguts as they called him. His father's name, too. The "old man" had been a tough citizen before skipping out for America, by all accounts. Domenigo wondered if he would light on anyone who had known the old man back in those ancient days. Probably not.

The shore rocks loomed. He had a pistol—Italian issue—and all else he might need. The oars ceased; boathooks held the rocks. A handshake with Lieutenant Watson, and off he went. It was a scramble sure enough amid jagged, slimy rocks. Bruised, wet to the waist, thankful for the starlight, he crawled ashore. The oars dipped, the boat disappeared on the starlit water.

He waited where he was, for the dawn. He had plenty of

cigarettes, Italian cigarettes, and cursed the vile imitation tobacco as he puffed in a niche among the rocks.

The day dawned slowly. With the first gray light, he was off, in a hurry to get away from the shore and reach the highway. His story was all clear. He had left the railroad at Girgenti and now was walking up to his home country beyond Montallegro. He had his discharge, an excellent forgery, and his soldier's book. All shipshape, if questioned. No one would bother to do that except the damned blackshirts. To the Germans, a man without a hand was nothing to think twice about.

Airplanes thrummed high overhead. Seaward, the destroyer had vanished. Around, the rocky country was empty of menace. Pietro breathed more freely. Hard to believe that he was actually in enemy country! If he could do it so easily, why couldn't a couple of divisions do it? Bat he remembered the secrecy which had surrounded him, the secrecy and haste, from the time they came to him in New York, until he boarded the destroyer at Malta.

He came to the dusty road, which wound through a green valley. He got his landmarks fixed in mind. He could—indeed, he must—find that spot on the shore again in the dark. He had much of his grizzled father's topographical sense, which had made the old man a chief among bandits and smugglers and Mafia artists, a generation ago. His father had left relatives somewhere in the hills around here, too—probably up near Montallegro, a town built of alabaster, and by all accounts a loathsome malarial place, now abandoned.

However, Siculiana was his goal, and only four miles up the valley. A mere hamlet of a couple of dozen huts clustered about a tumbledown tavern and a barbershop. Every Italian village had a barbershop and it was the club of the town, like a pool-room back home.

H E H A D forgotten something. Almost in a shiver, he sat down on a boulder, stripped off his coat, and carefully removed his mechanical hand—a beautifully made contrivance of aluminum. His few belongings were in a ragged bundle, and he added it to them with a sigh of regret. He should have left it aboard the destroyer or down at the shore; but he would take no chance of losing it now, risky as the thing might be. Maimed Italians did not have such things. He went on again, holding the bundle in the crook of his handless arm.

Now came an unpleasant surprise. A spurt of dust ahead grew into the shape of an open military car roaring at him, as though vomited upon him by the mountains that edged the sky. He plodded on. The car drew closer. It was filled with uniforms—no helmets, but peaked caps. Germans. Air Corps officers. The car bore down on him and halted and the officers called questions at him. He grinned and displayed his maimed arm. They spoke good Italian but he answered in Sicilian. They laughed and went on.

This meeting frightened him. What were Air Corps officers doing here?

He trudged on. Olive groves and the village came into sight ahead, poor straggling houses, with olive and lemon trees barely surviving. On beyond was stony desert.

There were more goats than people hereabouts. As he came into town, he saw a few old men, a few pinched and slatternly women and children. Several carts were toiling up the road toward Montallegro and the inland heights. Everywhere was the most appalling poverty and destitution; the place looked abandoned.

He made for the inn, a relic of the old posting days. It was a relic and no more, the courtyard overgrown with weeds, the ramshackle buildings ready to tumble down. Pietro walked in, and found a sharp-eyed woman at the bar and two bleary gray-beards playing checkers. A half-grown boy followed him in, begging for coppers. All eyed him with obvious suspicion until he began to speak; then they relaxed.

"Something to drink, madonna, and a bit of cheese, if the damned Germans have left you anything!" he exclaimed cheerfully. "I'm half dead and must rest before getting on toward home. That is, if any Domenigos are left, up in the hills."

"They wouldn't be anywhere else," said the woman, drawing him some weak wine. "Sit and I'll find you something to eat, poor fellow! Domenigo, you say?"

"Aye, Pietro Domenigo." He gave cigarettes to the old men and the boy, and they thanked him gratefully. "Well, I'm through with the army, thank the saints!" He showed his stump and made himself comfortable. "In the hills, you say?"

"Everybody who can get there," the woman said. "Between the accursed blackshirts and the thrice-accursed Germans, we're stripped bare and starving."

Pietro sipped the vile wine. "Some Germans in a car passed me on the road."

"They've built an airfield somewhere above, near the railroad." The woman jerked with her chin. "A war secret, they say; as though such a thing could be secret! Everybody who can work is up there earning bread. They'll grab you for it, too, one hand or not. Where did you come from?"

"Libya. I've seen fighting there, plenty of it; and the Germans running like hares, too!" Pietro grinned. "Came by railroad to Girgenti and got an early start toward home. I met a man in Porto Empedocle who gave me a message for someone he said was stopping here at this tavern. Let's see, what was the name? Fuga, Paolo Fuga. Is any such person here?"

He was aware of instant tension. The old men exchanged a glance; the boy scowled at him. The woman's eyes glittered.

"Do you think we're back in the days when tourists came to Sicily?" she snapped. "Those Germans you met were on the same errand, looking for him. I never heard of such a person. Fuga! What a name!"

A thin, quavering cry came from the street outside. The boy turned and fled. The two old men rose and hastily stamped out. The woman looked startled. Pietro gave her a grin.

"You needn't be afraid of a Domenigo, madonna. What's up?"

She made no answer. The sound of a car engine came from outside and stopped. Pietro did not move; he gave no sign of his inward anxiety. The Germans looking for Fuga? Then the game must be up.

Into the place stamped two lordly blackshirts, complete with all the dramatic paraphernalia from badges to dangling dagger. One went direct to the woman and began questioning her about Fuga. The other came to Domenigo and curtly demanded his papers.

He produced them amiably, submitted to questions, showed his maimed arm and was dismissed. He listened in astonishment to what the woman was saying.

"Yes, signori," she said humbly. "There was such a man as you describe. He came here yesterday. He was a party member, he said, a good Fascist, a friend of Il Duce. He was buying oil but we had none to sell, and he went on to the Marvuglia farm, where they have been pressing oil—"

"Where is the farm?" snapped one of the two party members excitedly.

She pointed. "Oh, yonder—up toward Montallegro, but to the left, by the mule-track that leaves the highway just past the Platani bridge. He hired our mule to ride."

"Can we get there with a small car?" asked one of the two.

"It is possible," she replied. "One of the children can guide you."

"I wouldn't trust any of you accursed Sicilians, children or women either!" snapped one of the two. "We'll find the way ourselves. Just past the bridge, you say?"

"Si, signori. By the big oak, you will see where the track turns out."

They stamped out brusquely, their trappings a-jingle. Pietro looked at the woman; she was flushed, bright-eyed, breathing hard. Outside, the car engine roared and lessened.

"That was a fine thing to do," said Pietro. "You betrayed him, you damned evil-hearted brute! You betrayed him!"

A laugh broke from her, a hard, excited laugh.

"Oh, *povero!* Poor wounded fellow!" she said. "Wait and see. Only two of those blackshirts—and taking that road! It's a joke to make the saints laugh. Hurry and finish your cheese, good Signor Domenigo, because the boy is getting mules and will guide you. And maybe you'll take back your harsh words about me when you see what has happened to those two princes of Italy who just left! The Marvuglia farm, indeed! It's Satan's farm that they'll find! Get on out, get on with you—no, I don't want money from one of us. Get on!"

Pietro was speechless. He obeyed her words and gesture in dumb amazement, gulped down his wine, picked up his bundle and walked out. Down the street, an old man was tending a bonfire of dried grass that sent up quite a smoke, and here came the boy riding a mule and leading another one, saddled. He waved a hand.

Memory of stories told by his father flashed into Domenigo's mind, and a sudden laugh came to his lips as the pattern came clear. The smoky fire—a signal, of course! And those two blackshirts, lords of creation, would head straight into ambushed rifles. And he, Pietro Domenigo, would follow them and find the man he sought. He was still laughing as the boy came up and halted the mules. He clambered into the vacant saddle.

"Ride hard and no talk!" cried the boy, smiting his mule lustily. "I want to get there and see! Ride hard!"

They did so. Pietro was delighted; he was accepted, then, he was one of them! The name of Paolo Fuga was simply a password—and the enemy seemed to have discovered it.

The mules scampered. Now and then planes whirred far overhead; once a tremendous thrumming came down the sky from invisible dots, and Pietro thrilled to the thought of Fortresses on a raid over Palermo, perhaps.

Sure enough, they came to a bridge and a big oak beyond it,

and a trail that branched out of the road. They swung the mules into it. All this while they had been gradually climbing, but this rocky little road seemed more directly headed for the hills.

An excited yelp broke from the boy when a motionless car came into sight ahead. The long slopes were craggy and rock-studded; it was all stony country up here, as though the hills had been tipped over and sent sliding seawards—as perhaps they had in some old convulsion of nature. The morning was getting well on, by this time.

The boy, in the lead, halted his mule beside the car and stared. Pietro stared, too. Here were the two lordly blackshirts sitting in the car, the same two; but now they were dead, drilled by a dozen bullets. The boy dismounted, crossed himself, and leaped at the car.

"Now I'll get a watch! Now I'll get a watch!" he cried, and reached out toward the nearer Fascist. Something hummed overhead, and a rifle-crack sounded.

"Away, you imp of the devil!" called a voice. "Away, and home with you!"

The boy darted back to his mule, then paused to lift a shrill cry.

"Here is Pietro Domenigo! He came to find Paolo Fuga! I brought him!"

He scrambled into the saddle, turned his mule about, waved his hand to Pietro, and hammered the beast into speed. Pietro lit a cigarette and waited.

A man appeared among the rocks and cactus; everywhere along these barren slopes was cactus, just as it had been in the day of the Greek poets who sang of it. Apparently unarmed, the man came into the trail and approached Pietro. He wore a cappo or hooded cape—an old costume that still lingered in these parts. He was trim, moved like an athlete, but on close view proved to have a closeclipped white beard, black eyes, and powerful features.

He came close and halted, looking hard at Pietro.

"I am Paolo Fuga," he said. "What do you want?"

"Proof," said Pietro, smiling. "I have a letter for you, but how do I know you?"

NOW THEY exchanged question and reply. Two other men, then a third, stole out from among the rocks and listened; wild men, leaning on rifles, bearded, intent men. It was like the old days when this was bandit country. Pietro had been well coached by his father in New York; more than one of the former Mafia passwords were exchanged. At length Fuga nodded and relaxed his hard stare.

"Okay," he said in English. "Your letter should be in purple ink."

"Right," said Pietro. "What about a reply?"

"Not here. Come along with us." Fuga took the letter that Pietro sorted from the mass in his pocket, and glanced at his three companions. "Marco! Keep guard over this car until dark, then drive it around near the new German airfield and leave it. Let the damned Nazis get the blame. Come along, Domenigo. Turn the mule loose to wander home."

For half an hour Pietro accompanied the others by rough hill trails that would have dismayed a healthy goat. He gathered that these guerrillas belongs to a scattered organization who hated both Nazis and Fascists. He told Fuga about the visits to Siculiana in search of him, and the old man merely nodded scornfully; about himself he said nothing.

Their road ended at a lonely hilltop farm where several other men showed up, together with two old women and a neatly attractive lass of twenty, whose flashing smile caught Pietro's eye. Fuga led him into a room of the tiny house, closed the door, and waved him to a seat on a pallet.

"Your departure is arranged?" he asked.

"Yes; but I'll have to be guided back as far as Siculiana at least."

"Later, then. Now to work; I must be far away from here by sunset." Fuga opened up the purple-inked letter and read it attentively. "Diavolo! Here's a pencil; write. I have some notes ready for you, but they want more. I'll give you everything; memorize it and destroy it. First, for my notes; hide them somewhere about you."

Pietro took two sheets of thin paper, covered with microscopic writing, folded them small, and tucked them inside his artificial hand. Then he proceeded to write as Fuga dictated—the position of airfields, of coast defense batteries, of army camps, and the numbers of troop concentrations, covering most of the northern coast of the island between Palermo and Messina. Pietro congratulated himself that his errand was being so quickly done; he could get away this same night. When he said as much, old Fuga nodded.

"Yes; 'Tonio Zucca will guide you. Before leaving, be sure you've memorized those data. You can't leave here until six o'clock. Come along, now, and eat with us. It'll be your only chance, for food is scarce in Sicily."

Outside, under the sprawling gray limbs of a giant fig-tree, they sat down with the other men, and the women brought food—adulterated pasta and wine and cheese. Eyes were curious upon the newcomer, but no questions were asked. Zucca was a man of forty-odd, seamed and wrinkled by long exposure to wind and sun; this was his house, it seemed. He had a hard, glittering eye and a steel-trap mouth. Fuga beckoned him to come close.

"Guide my friend Pietro down to Siculiana and around it, this evening. Don't leave before six; we don't want him picked up. You'll be responsible for his safety."

"On my head," said Zucca. "And you?"

"The rest of us leave now, immediately." Fuga extended a hand to Pietro, who took it. "Good luck! God attend you, and bring our liberators soon! You're a fine fellow; you look like my grandson. The damned blackshirts shot him in Palermo."

He rose, signaled the other men. Rifles were caught up, bundles lifted, and they went filing off among the rocks, followed by cries of farewell from the two old women. The young one, whose name was Nella, gave Pietro a sidelong glance or two, but disappeared when Zucca came puffing at a clay pipe and sat down beside the American.

"Your daughter?" Pietro asked, indicating the young woman.

"No; my niece. I had a brother Andrea; he was her father. He was killed by the Germans in the old war. I had another brother, Angelo Zucca, an older one; did you ever hear of him?"

"Unfortunately not," said Pietro politely.

Then he got a surprise. "So you are Pietro Domenigo, eh? The son of that Pietro who went to America." Zucca puffed at the pipe and gave him a queer, piercing look. "I was a boy then. Ha! So I am to guide you tonight. What if the Germans catch you?"

"Hard to say."

"Where did you lose that hand? In the war?"

No use keeping things secret now, so Pietro told of how his hand had been lost. Then Zucca rose and nodded.

"Amuse yourself, but don't wander about in sight. Sleep if you like. We leave at six."

There was, thought Pietro, something damned queer in the man's air; it made him vaguely uneasy. However, he had to memorize that list of data, so he stretched out on a bench under the fig-tree and fell to work at it. After an hour the girl Nella appeared with a sewing-basket. He made room for her on the bench, and they talked, mostly about America, an unending topic of wonder with these people.

Was she married? No; he touched on tragedy there. She had been affianced to a young man of the village, but he was dead in Libya. Then her uncle called her harshly, and she went away. Pietro got a couple of hours sleep; wakening, he tried his memory on the army data, found it perfect, and held a match to the paper.

It happened, by sheer chance, that he had said nothing to anyone, except Fuga, about the artificial hand lying in his shabby bundle. He did not want to abandon his role of maimed soldier until the destroyer was in front of him again, and escape assured. When he wakened, his first thought was of the weather. Relief seized him; the sunset was calm and peaceful, the sky clear. All promised well.

And here was Zucca. Two other men were with him, staring at Pietro; Zucca introduced them as cousins. They were tough hombres, thought the American. He noticed that the women regarded them with a trace of fear. The three men bunched together, talking low-voiced, while he conned his memory and burned the paper. The sun slid under the western peaks. A squadron of planes thrummed across the sky, high glittering dots in the sunlight that had disappeared from the earth.

The girl Nella brought a jug and poured wine for the three, then crossed to Pietro and poured a cup for him. She was white and terror lay in her eyes. She breathed soft words as she poured; he had to strain to catch the meaning.

"Careful—oh, careful! The oak tree by the bridge—look for me. They'll kill you."

Startled, he nodded and remained impassive. Who would kill him? Not the three men? He sipped the wine and lit a cigarette. Zucca came over to him, grinned, and sat beside him, begging a match for his pipe. Pietro supplied a vesta.

"Pietro Domenigo," said Zucca, as though amused by the name. "The son of Pietro, he who fled to America after killing my brother, eh? One does not forget, in Sicily. A blood-feud remains."

"Never heard about it," said Pietro. "When do we get away?"

"Now. When your wine is gone."

Pietro stood up and gulped what remained of the wine. "All ready."

He joined the three and they started out by a path running among the stones. Looking back, he had a glimpse of the white face of Nella staring after them; he waved jauntily. A fine girl,

Nella! She was worth all the rest put together. The oak tree, eh? Well, that was quite a way off.

The three men were, outwardly, unarmed; Zucca carried a gnarled staff. Pietro felt the reassuring weight of the pistol in his pocket. His nerves were jangled; he tried hard to control them. A blood-feud, eh? His old man had been a killer, all right. So Zucca and his two cousins meant to pay that old debt—regardless. It was more to them than anything else, more than the cause for which they fought, more than hatred of Nazis and blackshirts. Too bad Fuga was not here now! He would have stopped such nonsense in short order.

Alarm stirred Pietro as he thought ahead. Even if he escaped the three, he must face darkness in strange country; and escaping these rascals would not be easy. The trail led among rocks and cactus, and it was hard just to keep up with the three. The air was slowly darkening, the afterglow was dying into night, when a sharply wailing cry sounded from ahead. Zucca answered it and they halted. Into sight came the half-grown boy from the Siculiana inn.

"Germans and blackshirts in the village," he cried. "Two cars of them. They are watching the road each way from town, to catch any who come or go. I was sent to warn you."

"That's what comes of shooting blackshirts," growled one of the three. The boy was sent off in another direction, to warn some other party, and Zucca turned to Pietro.

"Come along, Domenigo. We shall have to circle around the village when we get there."

They went on. The stars were out, but their light was deceptive. Presently they came into a better track, that leading to the oak and the bridge. The car and the two dead Fascists were gone. One of the three men went ahead like a shadow and disappeared. The other two closed in on Pietro, who kept hand on pistol as he strode along with them.

The big oak-tree bulked against the stars. A whistle sounded and the third man came into sight.

"All clear here," said he. The others halted. Pietro knew the moment had come; he pulled the pistol from his pocket.

"A bad place to do any shooting," he said. "The blackshirts would hear the shots, my friends."

It took them unawares. "What do you mean?" snapped Zucca.

"That's for you to say. Too much talk about blood-feuds. Let's clear it up."

He had thought himself in full command of the situation; but pistols meant little to men who lived by knives. There was a swift stir of movement. Before he knew what was happening, Zucca's staff leaped like a snake and struck his arm. The pistol was knocked from his hand then they were on him, steel flashing under the stars.

Not for nothing was he Pietro Domenigo's son. He tripped one, smashed Zucca in the face and sent him sprawling, got the third man with a deadly kick. Curses ripped the night. Zucca was back, the staff whirling; it slammed Pietro over the head and staggered him. The first man was in at him and the knife slashed and bit. Pietro got that man with his knee under the chin and knocked him senseless.

A shrill whistle sounded at the bridge. "Tedeschi!" lifted a voice. "Germans!"

Zucca and his cousin took to instant flight; they melted into the darkness and were gone. The unconscious man moved not.

Pietro recovered his pistol, cursing his own bungling, and picked up his bundle. A figure came from the shadow of the big oak.

"Pietro!"

"Oh, it's you!" Vast relief broke within him. "Are there Germans coming—"

"No, no!" replied Nella. "I said that to frighten them. Come!"

He hurried to her. They came to the empty bridge and he halted.

"Look here, madonna; I got a knife in the ribs, and—"

"Quick! Off with your coat and shirt!" She was all briskness. "I can bandage it—oh, the evil scoundrels! When you are helping us all—what would Signor Fuga say to it? They think of nothing but old blood-feuds—"

His ribs were slashed; had it been a stab, it would have done for him. She talked excitedly as she worked. She had barely reached here ahead of them. They had meant to leave him stabbed to death on the bridge for the Nazis to find.

"But there are Nazis in Siculiana, and blackshirts, too," he said. "Can you guide me around the town? I'll have to reach the shore. There'll be a boat, later."

"Yes, I can take you. There's a road, if they're not watching it."

"Who are they watching for?"

"You," she said calmly. "Someone betrayed you this morning, I think; someone else who hated Pietro Domenigo. But my uncle 'Tonio wanted to kill you himself."

Pietro laughed. "My old man certainly left some friends here!"

"Not everyone is like that! We are not all bad!" she exclaimed passionately. "Plenty work for freedom, men like Fuga and others; there are always some bad men."

"And sometimes an angel, eh? Thanks, Nella. That feels pretty good."

He opened his bundle, took out the artificial hand, and fastened it in place. Matches, cigarettes—he had what he needed, and pushed the bundle off the bridge-rail. His head still rang from that crack over the skull, but the army cap had saved him from damage.

"A mile this side of the village we can turn out," she said. "It is only a track the goats use to get down to the stream, but it will serve us."

"See here, Nella, will you get into trouble with your uncle over this?"

"Of course; he will know," she said. "What do I care if he beats me?"

Pietro swore fervently in English, and she laughed at the sound of it. They were stepping briskly along; it could not be a great way to the side path, he reflected. Lights showed below them, ahead, where Siculiana lay—

Suddenly she caught convulsively at his arm; a white light hit them and lit the road as a car swung around a bend. There was no chance to evade. Voices barked at them to halt, the car stopped, men jumped into the road.

"How the devil do I know his name?" said a voice. "Can't mistake our man, with the left hand gone—here, you! Who are you? Speak up?"

Pietro slipped his arm about Nella, kissed her cheek, and laughed.

"Soldier on furlough, signori! Domenigo, of the 15th Calabria—my papers are all in order—"

A searchlight from the car spluttered blindingly at them. Pietro produced cigarettes and fumbled one out, holding it between the fingers of his artificial hand. He asked for a light, and someone scratched a flint lighter. The men around were blackshirts.

A laugh broke from one, coarse jokes resounded from the others, and they piled back into the car.

"Never mind your papers," sang out one of them. "Keep your arm around the girl!"

The car roared away.

"A miracle!" breathed Nella. "A miracle! What did it mean?"

"They're looking for a man with one hand; I have two. One here, and one here—"

"But you had only one at the house!" she exclaimed, too astonished to protest against his arm remaining where it was. He explained, laughing; she freed herself quietly and took his arm.

"That's better, Signor Domenigo. Remember, your family has a bad reputation! But if any others find us, you have my permission—"

"Not until then?" he demanded in mock dismay. She laughed. The war, the dangers of the night, were all swept away for the moment. They were close in spirit and in body.

THEY CAME to the path and she steered him into it. From the village came a chorus of voices in maudlin song; Germans or blackshirts, they were making merry. Pietro felt Nella shrink against him, then she hurried on. They were silent and watchful now.

But, as the moments passed, his heart soared. The village was behind them, and they headed for the road once more. The danger was lifting, at least for him; but what about this girl beside him? The life to which she must return would be hell— even were she not handed over to the blackshirts by Zucca. That old devil was capable of anything.

The starry canopy drew down. They came into the road again; Pietro could smell the salt tideless sea beyond the trees. Sea and sky together welcomed them, pressed close, and the stars were friends. He was telling Nella that some day he would be back to look her up, and he meant the words. Then it came, with a shock.

They almost walked on the two men before seeing them. Two helmeted men with rifles. Germans; a hard voice barked at them, a flashlight leaped and lit them with its beam. One of the Germans spoke fluent Italian.

"Halt! Account for yourselves—oh, a soldier with a girl, eh?"

Desperately, Pietro tried the same trick that had worked before, got out cigarettes, asked for a light. No go this time.

"Your papers, you Italian swine! None of your fine words; I saw enough of you in Africa. Hand them over! Get away from that girl. Hold her, Otto; We'll talk to her ourselves. A wallet, eh? Into the light with it."

The speaker pawed over the papers. The other man caught hold of Nella, laughing; she stood motionless. The first man thrust the wallet back at Pietro.

"Quick, now! Down the road with you, at the double—march!"

"Go on, Pietro, go on!" came the girl's voice, desolate but brave. "Go, go!"

Pietro thrust the wallet into his pocket—the sagging right-hand pocket.

"Yes, go!" barked the German. His companion laughed. "She stays here—march, you rascal! March, or I'll break your head in!"

The rifle swung up. They represented power and armed might, those two; they bulked against the darkness, owning the world and all that was in it. The flashlight was switched off. The rifle drove at Pietro, to smash him with the butt. He leaped nimbly aside. Fire spurted from his hand; the man before him doubled up with a clatter.

From the other broke a wild oath. He leaped forward. Pietro fired again and the man fell.

"Nella! Here—to the shore! Out of the road!"

He had her by the hand. They ran side by side, breaking through the trees to the rocky land at the roadside. From somewhere ahead burst a shout, then another; it was echoed from behind. Pietro cursed softly. To be cut off so close to safety—

Figures broke the starlight, two or three of them, boots pounding the rocks, voices hammering. Be damned to them! Pietro fired, fired again, blasted them with bullets, cleared the way in a white-hot fury.

Then, with the girl panting at his side, off among the rocks and away.

They ran desperately, frantically. With a stifled sob of relief, Pietro recognized his landmarks in the starlight, the rocks, the trees, the spur of granite ahead. A car came roaring along the road behind, and halted. Shouts dinned up, and lessened. They had got clear, they were almost at the shore.

"This way! Here!" he gasped, and drew her with him, clambering over the rocks.

Nothing escaped him; his own mental notes, the tracks on that map the old man had made. The soughing surges of waves among the rocks beckoned them. He found the almost invisible trail he sought and led her on. They were at the shore itself, and there below them was the dark little niche where, in time, would come the boat.

Down among those dark rocks they scrambled, and into the niche. He drew her down beside him; behind and above towered the jutting blackness that hid the stars. They waited there, trembling with effort, lungs quieting by degrees, neither of them daring to speak.

She began to sob—dry, heaving sobs of hysteria. They passed into tears. Clumsily, he tried to comfort her, to reassure her. Coldness and damp crept upon them. She fell quiet, quick enough, when feet clumped the rocks above and a ray of light probed the recess and lifted without touching them. German voices lifted.

"Nothing in this direction. Post guards on every road and track. With daylight, we'll turn them up. These accursed Italians! Keep an eye out for the woman, too—she'll do to amuse the men at the airfield."

The boots drew away.

For a long time, a long shivering time, the two remained motionless among the rocks. Two o'clock! An eternity away, thought Pietro. He had a shabby little watch; none of the fine Soligene creations that the blackshirts wore, but good enough. He held Nella in his arms, warmed her with his own warmth, felt her shivers die down.

"You can't go back now," he murmured at her ear.

"I've nowhere else," she said. "Nowhere. You should have gone and left me."

"Like hell!" said Pietro in English. Pietro? No, not a bit of it. He was Pete Dominick once more, and glad of it. Such a wealth of time and planning and effort, to serve a few short hours! The thought awed him. Everything, from New York on, for this one little day ashore here—and for what was hidden in his artificial hand, and in his head.

"You'll come. They'll have to take you," he said. "To Malta, maybe to New York. They must if I tell 'em! I'm the big boy right now—what I've got in my head, they must have. The whole British Navy will have to lick my boots if I say so. Understand? You're going!"

"I can't," she faltered. "My goats—my two goats—who'll take care of them?"

Pete broke into laughter at this.

But, later, as the cold night progressed, a sweat of fright took hold on him. What if any of a thousand things kept that destroyer away tonight? He and she were both lost, if they were here at daybreak.

Twice, under the huddle of his coat, he lit a vesta to see the time. Midnight passed. One o'clock passed. Two o'clock drew on.

He rose, stiffly. His hurt rib smarted like the devil, his hurt head ached dully. Nella held the coat open, but not too far. The moment had come. He struck one of the tiny slivers of wax and held it so the light would show to seaward. It burned out and fell.

"Nothing to do now but wait and watch," he muttered.

They watched the heaving waters with agonized intentness. Nothing happened. Nothing showed seaward, as far as they could tell. The moments passed, and his heart dropped.

"Pietro! I can't go, I can't!" she exclaimed abruptly, decisively.

"Damn it, you will!" he said, clutching her against him. "Listen, fiorella—sweet little madonna--think of New York! More of our own people there than in all Sicily!

"And people from here, from this very place, too. My father, Pietro—he won't stick a knife into you! And there's me. I'll make you happy there—"

Her hands caught hold of him suddenly.

"Look—is that it—there by the rocks?"

He strained to see. A dark shadow under the stars, a creeping thing stealing into the heaving water of the niche—his heart leaped.

"Are you there, Dominick?" came a cautious voice.

"You bet!" he rejoined. "Me and a passenger—for New York!"

He held her in his arms as he scrambled down the dark wet rocks; helping hands hauled them aboard—

The errand was done.

X

RED SEA BOAT RIDE

Loot of Murdered Men—the American
Decided He Wanted None of It.

S T E W A R T   H A D   not the slightest intention of desert-ing. Early in the morning Lucca took him aside with a wise wink. "Ha! Leesten, my friend! The plane goes down to load at nine o'clock!"

"Swell," said Stewart. "I'll stow away and have a swim."

"But I am go, also!" Lucca was an Italian prisoner who had remained to interpret. He was a smart man and knew his way around Eritrea. "I meet a fellair. He has some ver' fine Fascist badges and daggers and pistols, yes? Maybe watches, too."

"You're damned tooting!" said Stewart, clapping him on the back. "It's a go!"

Everybody wanted souvenirs. Those blackshirt daggers and watches made swell ones; a bit expensive, but who cared? Stewart had promised his girl, back home, to bring her a Fascist officer's watch, and he meant to do it.

Stewart was down on the books as a worker, a construction expert. He was one of that high-stepping gang who had been moved in to the highlands of Eritrea to construct a whacking big air base and shops—a lend-lease terminal for the Red Sea end of the route.

This was before Rommel got kicked out of Africa, long before. The British had cleaned the Eyeties out of Eritrea and Abyssinia, a big show and a satisfactory one; and just now the word was work rather than fight. Construction gangs were at work up in the Persian Gulf and beyond, in Iran, and here in the Red Sea.

It was hot as blazes, even here in the uplands, a mile high. Manual labor was plentiful, with oceans of blacks to draw on, and there were Italians of all kinds. Poor devils who had brought their families from Italy to colonize the Mussolini empire. Well, they were making the best of things—making big money, too, some of them.

They knew where everything had been cached away when the British smashed the Fascist power. Military equipment of all kinds, but private stuff as well; and even the Eyeties hated the blackshirts and loved to loot them. Anything from a wrist-watch to a ten-ton truck would be produced on demand—for a reward. Those colonists did pretty well by the war, around that time.

Still, up here around the camp all such pay dirt was long ago worked out. Stewart had got in just too late. There was plenty left down at Massowa, though. This was the huge Red Sea port that the Eyeties had made into a first-chop naval base and harbor, only to lose it to better men. It was the big port of Eritrea.

Outside Massowa, the sea was all littered up with islands, a perfect maze of them. The Eyeties had blocked the channel and obstructed the port with sunken wrecks, so for the present certain of the islands were being used as unloading bases by the ships that came pouring in from America. Planes went down from the working camp, taking along a gang of men and bring-ing back full loads of supplies; and on such trips to the islands Stewart was in the habit of stowing away.

It could be easily done; discipline was loose, and nobody ever looked in the toilet of the plane. The gang of loaders, of course, knew about it and winked at it. Stewart was not the only one. Down at the island landing field, it was easy to make for the shore and enjoy a delicious swim while the loading was in progress, then hop back into the plane. That camp in the high-lands had a scarcity of water and a bath was a rare luxury.

A young lieutenant of Engineers, blueprints in hand, came to where the shops were going up and questioned Stewart about the forms he was having built. That was all eyewash.

"They tell me," said the lieutenant, "that you might know where a chap could get one of those Eyetie officers' watches. You know, the kind with a sweep hand and diagrams all over the face, to tell how far away lightning is or an explosion, and so forth."

"Yeah, I know the kind," said Stewart. He was bronzed, fit, and had grown a mustache to lend him authority. His clipped blond hair was sun-bleached. He shoved back his helmet and accepted a proffered cigarette. "I been trying to get one for my

girl. But they don't come cheap, Lieutenant, and they're worth a lot back home. Airmen use 'em."

The officer slipped him an envelope containing Italian folding money.

"There's a wad of nothing," he said. "And twenty bucks on top of that. Says what?"

Stewart grinned. "Looks good," he replied. "If I have any luck, I'll get you one. I'm hoping to have some luck today, so if you're passing around quitting time, look me up."

Lucca came along. He was a spare, trim man in his forties, with a steel-trap mouth and a quick, smiling eye; back in Italy he had been somebody of note. Here he was just another Italian, but a person worth while just the same, being an interpreter and knowing the native dialects. He was on parole and not regarded as a prisoner at all. He was well liked.

"How come you're going to the island?" Stewart asked with curiosity. "You're not a worker."

"I have permission," said Lucca. "A man sent me word maybe he find news of my son. In Massowa. My son Andrea, he was captain in the Sicasteen Calabrian. So I am permit. I go by the plane, go to Massowa, come back by truck. You go swim, I fetch my friend."

"Okay," said Stewart.

The plane went down once every few days, depending on when supplies or ships came in. As it would take a couple of hours to load, Stewart had ample time to go down the island and have a swim. There was a good spot, too shallow for sharks, over there.

When he saw the plane being warmed up, Stewart headed for it. This was an old transport plane; not a large one, but able to carry a dozen workers with ease. The loaders were standing around, the pilot was talking with the ground officer. Stewart just walked up the steps, went in, slid into the toilet, and stayed there. After a while, the plane started, and he came out of hiding.

He was in dungarees like the other men and no one paid him any attention. He crowded to a window, hungry to see. He could never get enough of the amazing sight; he would have stolen the ride for this view alone. The wild flight thrilled him. The start, from over a mile high near Asmara, the capital, down above the mountain passes to Massowa and over the city and farflung port and naval establishment and the Red Sea, two hundred miles across to Arabia. The Red Sea! They told some queer tales of it, seamen and pilots did.

Stewart gaped down eagerly, excitedly. Ships in the distance, tiny dots against the sea; the white-foaming coasts, and, out ahead, the maze of islands offshore. He knew they were headed for the airfield on Dahalak, largest of the islands. This was close to the anchorage in Soghra Bay, being used just now; supplies for the construction gang would be carried over to the airfield.

He lit a cigarette. A "worker"—that's what he was. The hell with it! He had tried for the Air Corps; he had longed to be a pilot. But they were snooty about it in those early days of the war. He did not have the proper amount of education, they said. This, right or wrong, made him furious. He got in on the construction job easily enough but he was sore at everybody in general. Another month or two of this and they were going to Egypt. Once there, he could go over the hill, join up with a British outfit, and really get into the war.

THEY WERE over Dahalak Island and circling; he craned to see. Lucca came and joined him. No ships here. Several were lying out in the anchorage, though. Lighters were plying for Massowa in the main channel, and numbers of Arab dhows were about—queer little craft not unlike a civilized Chinese junk or overgrown fishboat.

The transport banked, came into the wind, and gently settled. The field was not far from one of the native towns on the island—a collection of huts and a mosque. Dahalak was thirty miles long, mostly coral rock and sand, and messroom rumor said it was clocked as the hottest place on earth.

Stewart went back into hiding and waited five minutes. The pilot was gone, the loaders were gone; now was his time to skip. The heat smote him like a blast in the face. He glanced at his watch; two hours. Just right for a fine swim and back in time for noon mess!

He grinned as he strode away, making for the path that led to the bay-shore, down from the town. Thought of the water felt good to his parched body. Arabs from the town had once used that place to dry their nets, until swimmers began to come; then they had moved. Queer thing about an Arab; to him, nakedness was the height of shame. Sooner would a filthy Arab die than bathe as these soldiers and workers did! And then these dames—they would let the wind blow their skirts around their waists, rather than show an inch of their faces!

"Well, I guess it's all in the point of view," said Stewart, lighting a cigarette. He wore only shoes, denim shirt and shorts, and sun-helmet, and was drenched with sweat at that. A sigh of relief broke from him, as the little bay opened out ahead. Plenty of sun and sand, plenty of water, too!

He kicked off his shoes and waded in just as he was. He had brought a cake of soap; he left that with his money and watch in one of his shoes, until he got back. It was salt-water soap, too. Returning to shore, he stripped, laid his garments out to dry in the sun, took the soap, and went back into the water. When he was clean, he went for a swim, and kept inside the reef where there was little or no risk of sharks. Then he stretched out on the sand luxuriously and smoked. He was already too sunburned to worry about a little sun.

He saw Lucca and another man coming, and lazily got into his clothes, rightly judging there might be no time to waste. Lucca introduced his friend as one Swajicoomi, a merchant of the town up the shore, a British subject—some sort of an Indian, thought Stewart. He was an oily dark man who spoke excellent English.

"So'or Lucca tells me," he said, "that you are interested in the watches of Italian officers, like this one."

He extended a beautiful specimen. It was of polished steel, with a black dial on which the numerals and intricate calculating pattern were pricked out in gold. He named a moderate price indeed.

"It's a bargain," said Stewart, reaching for his money. "Got any more?"

"One here," said Swajicoomi, "and quite a number at a spot on one of the outer islands where my company has huts for turtle fishing and curing. We could get there by boat in a couple of hours."

"Hm! How many there?"

"Oh, a dozen, maybe more; very fine ones," said the Indian, showing his white teeth in a smile. "Many Italian officers were drowned in a wreck when a transport sank near there. Our people secured many watches. These, you see, are all waterproof."

"Let's see the other one you have here," said Stewart, thoughtfully, while Lucca watched them with a beaming smile. Swajicoomi, who wore voluminous whites, reached into a pocket and produced a smaller watch of the same make as that favored by the Fascist officers.

THIS ONE was a handsome and expensive specimen with a silver case, which was rare, and a dial of blue and silver. The minute Stewart saw it, he knew it was the one for his girl friend. But, as he examined it, Lucca uttered a sharp exclamation and broke in upon him, apparently in surprise and dismay.

"That watch—strange! You permit, my friend?"

His hand was extended. Stewart relinquished the watch to him; he saw the face of the Italian become dark, dark and passionate with a rush of blood. With an obvious effort, Lucca turned and spoke in Italian. The merchant shrugged and made careless reply. Lucca raised his head and looked at Stewart, in his eyes such a look of chill, despairing anguish that the American was startled.

"Maybe," said Lucca, "we better go with this gentleman and buy up all those watches, what you say? He say 'Mericans got plenty money, sure. He has a boat. I like to buy this watch, maybe I help you buy all."

Stewart turned to Swajicoomi. By the look in Lucca's eyes he suspected some game afoot, but the offer to help with the purchase was really something. He knew he had struck a bonanza, if he could get the watches at a decent price.

He must miss the plane back. This meant a long and arduous journey up to Asmara by truck, and a wigging from headquarters for being absent a day or two. Well, the hell with headquarters! A boat ride on the Red Sea and a fat deal in Italian loot was something not to be passed up.

"What sort of a price do you want for the lot?" he asked. "If you ask too much, no use wasting my time."

"I will not ask too much," said the merchant. "I cannot bring them to my bazaar; the British are very stringent about loot. If we can go out to the turtle-station and I can turn a fair profit, well and good."

HE NAMED a price, a high one. Lucca, who was avidly examining the silver watch, got behind the Indian and made Stewart a gesture of assent, so imperative, so savagely commanding, that Stewart was again astonished.

"Well," he said cautiously, "we can take a chance at looking at the watches, anyhow. Where's your boat? Are you a boatman?"

Swajicoomi laughed. "On such an errand, I must be the boatman. The boat has a good engine and I can steer; I know the channels. Perhaps you will come first to my bazaar in the town yonder, for tiffin?"

"No," snapped Lucca. "No. We have no time. We will take along something to eat."

Stewart shrugged. "All right, let's go."

THE INDIAN stepped out; he and Lucca fell in behind. Stewart knew that the Italian had a good supply of funds. Still, this investment would take quite a lot. As they came to the miserable huts of the town, with its few bazaars and mosque, Lucca suggested that Swajicoomi fetch some food and drink from his bazaar, and meet them at the wharf. To this the Indian agreed, and separated from them. They held on for the wharves, new docks recently installed for the use of ships that had to unload and turn around in a hurry. Stewart kicked a yapping cur out of his way and gave Lucca a curious look. The man had not been the same; he had changed all in a moment.

"Thought you were going to Massowa to look up your son?" he said.

"Not now," replied Lucca. He looked confused, uncertain; lines had appeared in his usually smooth features, lending him age.

"What's wrong?" Stewart demanded.

"Everything. This man Swajicoomi is a rascal."

"A rat, sure. He loots corpses. He's got a bad eye. Sure you've got money enough to go into this thing? I'll have to pay up my half later, when we get back to camp."

"Oh!" Lucca uttered a low, harsh, mirthless laugh. "We not need money, you bet."

They came to the waterfront. Lucca spoke to natives squatting in the shade and was shown Swajicoomi's boat. This was a squat, roomy launch of very scant draft, such as would be needed in working about the islands; she stank abominably, but little Stewart cared for that. A Red Sea boat-ride!

"Hell, I've earned a day's vacation!" he told himself. "And what can they do to me, anyhow? I just missed the plane back—stowed away for a swim! This watch business may be a good thing. There's something cockeyed about it, but who cares?"

Swajicoomi appeared, with a servant who carried a basket. Whether he were a Hindu, a Babu, or what, Stewart had no idea; he was having a hard enough time to get Africans straightened out, without tackling Indian complexities. Certainly he was an oily beggar out for the coin.

The servant put the basket into the launch, helped to raise a canvas that fitted over short poles to make a sun-shade over half the boat, and then went away. The three got in and Swajicoomi started the engine. A few bearded Arabs watched them without interest. Other boats, mostly fishing craft, were drawn up on the sand, but launches were rare.

The mooring was cast off. With Swajicoomi at the tiller, they chugged out into the channel and swept on around the end of the large island, sighting two other towns and then heading outward, apparently for the open sea. At first, Swajicoomi talked. He told about these naked, bleak coasts that harbored Danakil and other tribes of fishermen; he told how the life of all these people was adjusted to the monsoons, that blew up the Red Sea half the year and down the other half. He told about the khamsin, the north wind that blows off Aden and fills the heavens with red sand. He told about the queer currents, and about the queer lights in the sea at night, and the still queerer tricks of refraction and mirage in this strange sea. By and by his droning voice fell silent. He opened his basket, offering food and drink to the others. Lucca refused curtly. Stewart decided to wait a bit.

He smoked and stared out at the horizon. It was playing tricks already; he saw islands which Swajicoomi said were thirty miles away and beyond sight; he lifted a mirage of a mosque and palm-trees which showed a town down the coast fifty miles.

"Cockeyed!" he muttered. "Everything's cockeyed here. The whole place is screwy. And Lucca acts like he's off his nut, too. By damn, I'm beginning to wish I was back up in the highlands! You can have your blasted Red Sea."

Why he was thus uneasy, why his nerves were wriggling, he could not tell, except that it had something to do with Lucca and the silver watch; this was only a guess, of course. He had the horrible feeling that something was going to happen quick and sharp and bloody—why, he could not say. Just vague and indefinite, like a feeling caught out of the queer Red Sea air, which was like no other air on earth.

What did Lucca mean by saying they would not need money to put over the watch deal? That was more screwy than anything else. This Swajicoomi was after money and hot after it, too.

Stewart ate some fruit from the basket, and a bit of rice all oily with ghee, or Hindu butter. He tried to talk with Lucca about his son, but Lucca would not talk. This was queer, too. Lucca always loved to talk about that son of his and was proud of the boy, whom he had not seen or heard from since the Italian surrender.

THE BOAT was making for islands ahead. The Indian pointed to one of them; that was where the turtle hut was, he said.

"Most likely those watches are spoiled," said Stewart, "if they've been kept there."

"Oh, no! They are in a box, and buried," Swajicoomi replied, with a wink and a grin. Hidden loot, buried loot, of course. Corpses from a sunken transport.

The group of islets drew nearer. They were little more than reefs of naked sand and coral rock. Swajicoomi made for the largest of the group; on this appeared a hut close to shore—a long, shelving beach of sand such as turtles love for spawning. The boat chugged along at slow speed, for the approach was dangerous, with reefs and coral heads on all sides.

The heat was terrific. The breeze that blew across the islets and sparkling waters was like a breath from a furnace. Swajicoomi pointed to a pile of something inside the hut. Tarpaulins, said he. Stretched from the hut to poles, like an Arab tent-flap, and wet down with a bit of water, they would make cool sweet shelter. The idea was grateful.

There were almost no tides in this sea, said the Indian; but the water ran out of it during the southwest monsoon, and was blown in during the northeast monsoon. And in here among the islets were currents of all sorts, some of them rotary—and there was never any heavy surf on the reefs. Truly a strange sort of ocean, like no other!

"Where was the wreck you mentioned?" asked Stewart.

"The wreck? Oh, off this next island." The Indian waved his hand vaguely toward the reefs, reached forward and shut off the engine, and they ran in at the shore. "We must pull her up well," he added. "It would be terrible if she floated away."

S H E T O O K the sand gently. They jumped out and pulled her up, then turned to the hut.

Better lose no time with the shade, said Lucca, so they went at it. The tarpaulin was in two big strips. They got it down to the water, wet it, lugged it back, stretched it out, mounted the poles in deep holes cut in the coral rock, and got the tarp up at last, a wet canvas roof and side, with the air blowing through.

This took quite a bit of time but was well worth the labor. Stewart was astonished by the resulting coolness. He stretched out luxuriously in the sand and lit a cigarette, nor did he move when Swajicoomi departed to get the watches.

"Y'know," he said dreamily, looking out seaward at the glare and sun-shimmer, "I've had a notion ever since coming to these parts that I'd like to wander along the shore of the Red Sea and pick up shells and so forth—like a silly kid."

"My son," said Lucca, "he used to do that. On the shore near Reggio, long time back. You got plenty time now."

"Yeah, this is the trip, I guess." Stewart puffed, exhaled and laughed shortly. "Just to say I did it. I reckon I will. Pretty damned hot for a stroll, though. I'll wait a bit. What you think, any sharks along here?"

"Not this side where the reefs are. Swim, huh? Sure, all right."

Hello, here comes the Indian! Stewart flipped the cigarette stub away and sat up. Swajicoomi was holding a small box; he had been digging, inside the hut, and was puffing as he approached. He joined them, sat down, cross-legged, set the box in the sand before them, and got out a round tin of English cigarettes. He jerked one out with the little cardboard squill, and lit it.

"All right, look away," he said, with a wave of his hand.

Stewart reached out; the box was of cardboard, and he lifted away the cover to disclose a jumble of wrist-watches stowed in newspaper. He lifted some out, removed some of the paper, and found more stowed below the top layer.

Lucca, who was holding the small silver watch and looking at it again, caught at one of the bits of paper and smoothed it out. It was from an Italian newspaper published in Massowa.

"Well!" said Lucca, turning to the merchant. "This transport, she sink a long while ago, eh? Maybe sicca month?"

"Oh, yes; about six months," said Swajicoomi.

"And those watch, they have blood on them?"

"Blood?" The Indian gave him a puzzled look. "No. Why?"

"This have blood." Lucca held up the silver watch, then put his thumb to the back and pried until the rear of the case came away. He held it out. "Here, You read. You haven't see it before now."

Swajicoomi took the round bit of silver and looked at it. He tossed away his cigarette. His face changed; a startled sound escaped him. He started to speak—

He never got out the words, for Lucca was at his throat. Stewart did not realize what was happening, so swiftly was it done, so furiously was the stiletto wielded in Lucca's hand. Then he saw the spurt of red deluging the Indian's white clothes; the stiletto had driven to throat and heart in half a dozen rapid lunges.

Lucca pushed the dead man over on his face, then rose and dragged him out and away from the hut, down to the water. He kicked sand over him and came back, kicking sand up over the bloody trail.

"I think maybe you swim. I don't throw him in yet," he said.

"My God!" gasped Stewart. "You gone out of your head, Lucca?"

For reply, Lucca bent over and retrieved the flat back of the silver watch. He put it in Stewart's hand. Stewart looked at it

and saw engraving. Even in Italian, the words made sense to
him—a gift to Andrea Lucca from his father.

"And blood around the edge, in the cracks," Lucca said grimly
and sat down. He lit a cigarette and with his finger stirred the
watches in the box. "No transport sunk," he said. "All lie. Why
you think these watch kept here? Because loot, sure. When
Italiana begin to lose and crack up, some get murdered, killed,
looted. Who know, who care? Nobody. But I care about Andrea
when he disappear. You 'Merican, you help me fine. This bloody
Swajicoomi, he not suspect because you here. He not suspect
I been on trail long time."

The light began to break upon Stewart. He saw that, after
all, it was no accident, no chance matter, but the climax of a
careful campaign.

"Loot of murdered men—poor devils!" he said. "Look here,
I don't want any of it. Be damned if I do!" He rose. "Let's get
out of here! Let's go back."

"You wait," said Lucca calmly. "This merchant, big man of
gang; top sergeant, see? Maybe eight, ten more, maybe others.
Ecco! They kill, he sell. But these watch, they can be traced or
found again. Maybe all the gang Indians like him; many East
Indians here. So the watch from many murders kept here until
he getta chance to sell to somebody safe, like a 'Merican. Now
I can eat. Not with him, but he's dead now."

Lucca dipped into the basket and produced wine and bottled
water, fruit and bread and cheese. Stewart stared at him frown-
ingly.

Plain enough—a gang had been at work, murdering Italians,
chiefly officers or Fascist troops. Catching them one by one, up
dark alleys, around dark corners. Murdering, robbing, looting.
After the surrender, they picked on prisoner officers. The
watches were highly valuable but unsafe—yes, it was all clear
now.

"And you've been running down the gang quite a while, eh?"
said Stewart. "Well, why stick around here?"

Lucca smiled a seraphic—or diabolic—smile, and tapped his nose significantly.

"You not speak Hindustani. I do. I study to have place in customs service here, to deal with Hindu merchants," he said blandly. "Swajicoomi speak to servant who bring the basket, in Hindustani. He say: Tell my sons not to come before sunset. Now you get it? He have two sons, dark young men. He think maybe kill you and me too, have these watch and our money and everything so nice. His sons come, you see, nice young men, two young men in a boat. Very easy done, all okay and safe."

"By damn!" said Stewart. Lucca nodded smilingly.

"Sure. They kill my son Andrea. I wait; his two sons get killed like Andrea. Now you go, get fine swim before I bury him in water. We wait."

"And when do we go home?" demanded Stewart.

"Oh, early morning sunrise, back to Massowa, hitch-hike to camp, you and me!"

Stewart, somewhat dazedly, shed his garments and went for a swim, Lucca promising to keep a lookout for sharks.

THE WATER within the reefs was lovely and clear and sunlit and warm. He swam slowly and enjoyably; by degrees his overheated and excited senses came back to normal. It was very odd, he reflected, how he had felt a foreboding of some such horror as had happened—it had been in the air, right enough. Nice old Lucca, all this while, scheming and planning to play a killer's part! Small blame to him, either.

There must have been a lot of dirty work going on about the time of the Italian collapse, he reflected. The blackshirts were bitterly hated by the Italian soldiery, and factional strife was common. The Galla and other Ethiopian tribes murdered them ruthlessly wherever met—the fallen conquerors paid the penalty of despotic rule in these days of defeat. Even in the towns there was no safety for them; they had become pariahs on whom all could prey with impunity, and the unhappy colonists had no refuge except in the camps of their British foes. No, Lucca could scarcely be blamed, with a son to avenge!

Stewart came ashore at last, glanced down the beach for the body of Swajicoomi, and saw it not. He came up to the hut, where Lucca sat.

"What become of him?"

"I put him out of sight," said Lucca.

"Did it give you any satisfaction to kill him?"

"No," said the Italian gravely. "To kill a man, however bad, hurts the soul. Someone must do this, must act for justice. Toward sunset, his sons will come. Then—this. I took from him."

He displayed a pistol. Stewart sat down, ate some fruit from the basket, took a gulp of the wine, and lit a cigarette. There was nothing to be said, nothing to be done. It was not his affair, he felt. Lucca wanted no help and needed none.

A long time after, Stewart waked from a doze. The sun was low in the west, riding on the Ethiopian mountain-peaks. Lucca's voice had wakened him; now Lucca spoke once more.

"They're coming. There is the boat."

Stewart sprang up, only to sink back again. A boat, a dot, yes—far away against the horizon, lifted into sight long before its time by the infernal refraction of the Red Sea.

"A long way off."

"Currents, bad currents maybe," Lucca observed in his gentle voice. "I put those watch in the boat. They bring much money back at camp. You take this one, you like it."

He extended the small silver watch that had belonged to his son.

"No, not me," said Stewart, shaking his head. "I'll keep the one I bought off him, for the lieutenant. I don't want any part of the rest; damn it, there's blood on 'em like you said!"

Lucca wrapped the silver watch in a bit of newspaper and pushed it into the breast pocket of his tunic, with a shrug.

"That are foolish, I think," he declared. "Those watch make very bada luck for those murderers, yes, but not for hones' men like us. Maybe you change your mind. It is not good sense to throw money away. We better finish this grub before they come."

Stewart, nothing loath, joined him in a final attack upon the provisions. They discovered in the bottom of the basket a small bottle of *mastika*, a colorless Greek brandy on the order of vodka. Lucca seized on it with delight, bat Stewart shook his head.

"Not me, thanks. There's only about one good drink there; keep it. I don't like that stuff. Tastes like resin and hellfire mixed."

Lucca laughed heartily, and put the tiny bottle aside.

"Okay," he said. "We celebrate with that—later on. I will, sure."

"Where'd you bury Swajicoomi?"

Lucca jerked a finger at the reefs. "While you were swimming. Can you run the boat engine?"

"Sure," said Stewart. "No trick to that. I can con the way to Massowa, too."

The basket was emptied. They smoked, lazily, and watched the approaching boat. It was a small craft with a tiny engine, making very slow way, two figures aboard. Two men, men coming to be killed; this thought irked Stewart.

"I don't like it."

"Me too," said Lucca. He was not smiling; his dark eyes were brooding. "Don't matter. Even if they want to loot us. It don't like me. My son Andrea, he be paid for already."

"Then lay off. You're no murderer," said Stewart quickly. "Besides, we don't know it's a plan to murder us; that's guesswork."

"We see," said Lucca, dubiously. Evidently he did not like the thought of more killing, either. "Maybe, maybe no."

The small boat with the two figures was approaching, inside the reefs. Two slim brown men, young, wearing European whites like their sire. They waved and called. Lucca waved back. The sun was at the horizon, a ball of molten gold.

The young men called again, repeatedly. Lucca grinned; they were calling Swajicoomi, he said. The small boat was only a few hundred feet out. One of them stopped its motor, and they shouted anew. Lucca shouted back. Stewart sat and listened to the thin voices so flat on the calm water. Suddenly one of the two stooped and started his engine.

Their boat spun around and started back whence it had come. Both men crouched low in the boat, trying to hide along the gunnel. Lucca cursed, then laughed.

"Look! Scared. Not see him, guess the game is up—think we shoot! You see? Very bad conscience make him run."

"I expect you're right," said Stewart. He felt vastly relieved. "We could catch 'em with the launch, but no use. Well, that's that."

He noted that Lucca made no move to use the pistol. The small boat chugged away and disappeared in a channel among the islets. The sun went down and violet mists climbed along the sea. Stewart, who had been tinkering with the compass from the boat, spoke up.

"Look here, I've been getting ranges on the mountain peaks back of Port Smyth. You don't want to stick around here till daylight, do you? I don't."

"Not me," agreed Lucca. "But you can't run the channels at night."

"Don't intend to," Stewart said. "We're south of Dahalak Island; it's open water due west of here, toward the coast and the South Massowa Channel. Why not clear out of here when the starlight gets strong and work over that way? I'd feel safer to be gone from here. We could anchor at one of the islets near the Massowa Channel and sleep safe till daylight, then work up to the town and harbor."

"Okay," assented Lucca. "Okay. We go slow, maybe hit no reef."

"The reefs show at night anyhow," Stewart added.

"Sure," said Lucca, and laughed.

They smoked and talked as the night gathered. They could make out the Shab Shaks light and one or two other beacons; all enemies having been cleared out of these seas, the beacons had been restored for the sake of the convoys arriving.

There would be no moon. When the stars blazed out strong and bright, the two stirred themselves. All was stowed in the boat, the tarpaulins folded and tossed in amidships, the compass replaced. Inside the hut was nothing at all but bare sand and evil smells. Ready at last, they shoved out the heavy boat.

"Hello!" cried Lucca. "Look what I found—the *mastika!* You have a drink?"

"Nope," said Stewart, fiddling with the engine as the boat slowly floated offshore. "Not me. Not that hellfire—good gosh! Looky there—looky there!"

The water below them had suddenly become illuminated as though on fire.

STEWART DID not need his companion's explanation; he had heard stories enough about this peculiar habit of the Red Sea. Without warning or known cause, whether in calm or storm, in depths or shallows, a patch of water will dart all alive with luminous brilliancy, like a flood of phosphorescence breaking upon rocks. He paused to stare, then caught a cry from Lucca, who was at the rail amidships.

"*Ecco! Ecco!* There he is, drifting! I did not put enough stones in his pockets—"

Stewart looked over the rail, and swallowed hard. There, by heavens, was the dead Swajicoomi himself—there, deep down but lit by the ghostly radiance! He was looking up at them with a ghastly grin, his arms outspread as though swimming; a rock tied to his feet held them down. From Lucca burst a laugh.

"I drink to you, my friend! Give my love to my son Andrea if you see him, among the dead! *Eviva!*"

He drained the little bottle of Greek brandy at a gulp, and flung the vial out to fall with a splash. The ghostly light disappeared as suddenly as it had come.

"Give me some water," said Lucca, reaching for the bottle. "Thanks. *Per Bacco!* That stuff is strong, like fire! Swajicoomi, he laugh at me, you see?"

He gulped some water, replaced the bottle, and sat on the thwart amidship.

Stewart got the engine going, throttled it down to low speed, took the wheel and conned the water in the starlight. He had the shaded light going over the compass; his course was not important, as long as he cleared the south end of Dahalak Island.

He lit a cigarette, grunting to himself. That incident had shaken him, although it was in no way supernatural. The glimpse of Swajicoomi looking up at them and laughing did have a horrible jolt in it. However, it was all gone and behind them now, the island was gone from sight, the cool night breeze was fanning them, everything was jake.

"Any time you want to turn in, say so," he observed. Lucca made no answer. Asleep, thought Stewart.

"If I'd been in his boots," ran on his musings, "the sight of that grinning Swajicoomi would have given me a bad turn. He laugh at me, says you; and damned if it didn't look like it, too!"

Stewart's jangled nerves eased down. The slow, steady motion of the boat, the calm peace of the starry night, the coolness, all soothed him. Lucca stirred not nor spoke. An hour must have passed, thought Stewart, when he discerned a faintly luminous patch off to starboard. An island or reef.

"Hey, want to throw the hook over?" he called. Lucca did not respond. With a grunt, he shifted the engine into neutral and went to where the Italian sat, and caught his arm. "Hey! Wake up—"

His voice died. Convulsively, he caught hold of Lucca; the latter was leaning on the gunnel but slid sideways. He was stiff—not only cold, but stiff. He had been dead a long time, dead without a wound of any kind.

Stewart sank down on the thwart. His mind flew back to the little bottle of *mastika*. Strong like fire, Lucca had said. Then a drink of water—and nothing more. Not a movement or a word. Lucca must have died swiftly, all in an instant.

"No wonder Swajicoomi laughed at him!" muttered Stewart, and wiped sweat from his cheeks. "Poisoned, by thunder! The stuff was poisoned. He had meant to do us in, sure enough! Then his sons would come and help loot us. When they came and saw their old man gone, they knew the game was up—that's why they skipped in a hurry! So Lucca was right about it after all."

Another smoke, and he shut the engine off and thought. Lucca was gone; damned hard luck, for he had been a good guy. Well, what about himself? He could ease into Massowa in the morning easy enough, tell that he had stolen a ride and missed the plane back, so had borrowed a launch and come into the harbor. That was all jake. But he must get rid of Lucca, and do it now.

Then, the watches. Questions would sure be asked if he brought those watches in. He reached for the box, and with an oath slung them all over the side.

"Blood on them—the hell with 'em anyhow!" he said. A thought struck him. He reached to the breast pocket of Lucca's tunic and took out the little silver watch in its wad of paper. He hesitated, then thrust this into his own pocket.

"You gave it to me, so that's all right," he said. "And the girl friend will like it. Well, pal—so long! I'll say a prayer over you."

He did, too; and anyone who knew him would have said this was the queerest thing about the whole business—Stewart praying!

Maybe it was, too; both the queerest and the best.

XI

ONE DAY IN TRINIDAD

They Stepped from a Train in
Trinidad and Were in India!

O NE OF the most wonderful places in the whole world—

The phrase dinned in Cregar's memory as he shaved and dressed, in his thirty-cent room in the Salvation Army Men's Hostel on Edward Street. Beds cost only eighteen cents, but he was willing to pay for privacy. He had reasons.

He breakfasted in the restaurant, then sought the street. His whites were soiled and dingy. Under his seaman's cap his bright, hard features, his quick eyes, challenged this marvellous environment. Trinidad was, without doubt, one of the most wonderful places on earth—for a millionaire tourist. For anyone else, it was just an Arabian Nights' dream jazzed up with jeeps and airplanes.

Cregar had been here two very full weeks and knew his way around the island as no tourist ever did. It was, basically, a British island upon a Spanish foundation; but now it was something that made the senses and the imagination reel. This island off the coast of Venezuela had become a roaring, bustling fantasy of the Orient all out for war.

Stopping in at a chemist's shop, a very British chemist's shop, Cregar got the use of the telephone.

"Four seven six one," he called. "Hello—American Consulate? This is Mr. James Cregar. I'd like to speak with the Consul, please."

Almost at once came the voice he knew. "Hello, Cregar!"

239

"Anything new, sir?"

"Yes. A man named Blythe has turned up with definite information. An Englishman; he speaks Hindustani. He's waiting
for you now at the Canadian Bank of Commerce."

"Thank you, sir."

IN THE street again, Cregar headed for the broad, dusty
thoroughfare known as Marine Square, the crosstown heart of
the lower city. The stolid, substantial English buildings were
transformed by gay awnings and strange Oriental names and
lively advertisements; the busy throngs jamming the streets
would have put Hollywood to shame.

Englishmen on bicycles, Hindus with brass and silver orna-
ments for sale, Chinese by wholesale, East Indian women
swathed in shawls, barefoot Negro men and women with heads
crowned by tremendous bundles, Venezuelans and Indios,
British officers and soldiers, coolies jabbering like mad—and
Americans. Seamen, soldiers, Ferry Command pilots and me-
chanics, Navy airmen, Army flyers, engineers, oil field workers,

Pan-American pilots just down from Miami, others heading back. Every day the Miami plane dropped in.

It was a wild, fantastic jumble of races and colors and creeds; but an orderly jumble. They worked together, they melted together, they were as one—for Trinidad, most strategic of the West Indies, had become the crossroads of the world at war, quite literally, with her air and navy bases from which Lend-lease flowed by sea and air to Africa and Europe. The roar of planes was almost constant in the sky.

In this island, where hosts of Chinese, Bengalese and Hindu coolies had been settled in bygone years until these orientals now numbered a third of the teeming population, it was an easy place for a man to lose himself—particularly if he had a touch of the Orient in him. So Cregar knew to his cost.

He turned into the imposing portals of the Canadian bank, and stood looking around. A man approached, with inquiring eye. A man in sun-helmet and whites.

"Not Mr. Cregar, by any chance? Yes? Delighted! Blythe is my name. I say, we can't talk here very well."

"No." Cregar shook hands and turned. "Let's go down the way to Lo Wing's chop-suey joint. It's cool there, we can get a drink, and it's quite safe."

"Right," said Blythe, swinging into step at once.

An odd man, Blythe. All of fifty, thought Cregar, with a lined, weary face and tired eyes; pretty well burned out. Wiry, tough, lean as an old tiger, with a hard jaw.

They settled in a private booth at Lo Wing's place. Blythe got out a pipe and it seemed to inspire him. He went right to work.

"I was in San Francisco," he said. "Retired. Spend a goodish while in India. I saw in a newspaper that the gov'ment—I'm a U. S. citizen now, y'know—was anxious to find John Traynor. I knew where he was, or had been a few months ago. I knew him in India; we were pals there. When I came to the States, he took a bit in the importing business I started; it did well and I've been remitting money to him ever since. So I knew, y'see."

"And you know why Washington, and London as well," Cregar asked, "are so keen on finding him?"

Blythe nodded. "I also know what nobody else does—why he doesn't want to be found. That's why they sent me here. Won't do you chaps the least good if you do dig him up, y'see. But I might talk him into it."

CREGAR SURVEYED the man with a swirl of incredulity and impatience.

"Sounds screwy. Look! Let's get down to cases. A couple of years before the war, this Traynor was living in Bombay. He offered first London, then Washington, a new, cheap and absolutely topping type of gas mask, conceived on new and quite different principles; it would nullify the effect of any known gas. He was turned down in both capitals, and bobbed out of sight."

"Right," said Blythe. "He was a first-class chemist. And now our precious brass-hats are frightened. Japan is preparing to use gas against us as well as in China; we've actually captured some of the apparatus and the gas cylinders. Germany is getting ready to use gas against us, manufacturing immense quantities of it at Mannheim and storing it at Minsk, away from the bombing area. We know what's coming—and we want Traynor's invention. We want it damned bad."

"And you can't get it or him."

"Exactly," assented Cregar. "The War Department was tipped off that he was here on Trinidad, that he had become an opium user or something of the sort and gone to the bad. No effort to find him has been overlooked; we've not turned up the least trace. I was sent as a forlorn hope. I've been pottering around the dives and low-life spots in Coolie Town and elsewhere. Not a glimmer."

Drinks, long cool ones, were brought.

"Well," Blythe said, more cheerfully, "I don't have name,

address and so forth; but I can find him, through the process of finding someone else. I'm trying to be quite frank with you, but I have a certain moral responsibility."

"To whom?" Cregar demanded sharply. "Yourself? Your country? Or the world?"

"Just at present, to John Traynor," said Blythe. "Remember, I'm in the dark, too."

"Hm! You might tell me what you know, and let me investigate."

"I've refused to do that; I want to be in on the investigation. Why? Because anyone else might blunder and lose what we're after. I want to secure Traynor's gas-mask for our cause, just as much as you do. I think I can do it. I don't think you can."

Cregar relaxed. "I see. How!" He lifted his glass and drank. "You may have the right angle. Well, where do we start?"

"We may need a car. I don't know Trinidad."

"I do. Cars are no trouble to get; plenty of rent cars going begging."

"Good. The man to find, then, is Amir Ali Chand. He used to be a jute merchant in Bombay. He came to Trinidad some years ago. He's a pukka Hindu and I think quite wealthy. The Consulate could get no line on him right away, but is trying at Government House; they are rather slow there, however."

"I'll say they are," said Cregar fervently. "Good Johnnies, but slow and stately. I can locate the guy while they are making up their minds. Any address?"

"Oh, yes," Blythe replied. "At least, he used to be located in Coolie Town. I think he's gone somewhere else in the island. Sorry to be so vague, but there it is."

"Vague? Why, man, after what I've been up against the past two weeks, you're a regular walking machine-gun!" said Cregar, smiling. "Let's go. We'll do Coolie Town first, and get the car if we need one. What's the relation between this man and Traynor?"

"Traynor, in India, placed him under deep obligations—saved

some of his family during a famine or inundation or something. So that, if Traynor came here intending to hide out, this Amir Ali Chand would take care of him faithfully."

"Hide out I don't get it. You don't know why, either? All right; let's go."

They sallied forth and caught a tram, which took them off parallel with the shore. Cregar waved a hand toward the upper city on their right.

"Too bad you can't see that; Government House, you know, and Queen's Park, and all the cricket clubs and so forth. If you're around at four in the afternoon, join the rush. The town shuts up shop and off we go for the cricket field! You're still English enough for it."

"Oh, yes," said Blythe. "And the Indian bazars—why, it's astonishing! I've already seen things I never expected to see outside of India!"

"Well, there's Coolie Town ahead, and you'd better brace yourself against beggars and smells. I'll take you around to some of the chief bazars and you can ask after your man. Better say you owe him money, as an excuse for wanting to find him."

And so, to the utter amazement of Blythe, they got off the tram and were in India. The buildings, from the bazar fronts to the Mosque and the Hindu temple down the street; the merchants of Bombay or Madras, the artificers hard at work on every hand—this was the incredible thing about it. Everyone was in a rush of work. All Trinidad was producing for war, from the pitch lake to the silver bazars. One might expect to see an elephant come swinging down the street at any moment; but if there were no elephants, there were all sorts of caste marks, and every manner of Hindu, lordly or pariah.

"Better still," said Blythe suddenly, "you do the asking. They'll not dream that I understand what they say. Be American, very American—they're used to American tourists."

"Good!" exclaimed Cregar.

Turbaned Madrassies, fierce-eyed Rajputs, fat polite Babus—

he questioned them all alike about Amir Ali Chand, to whom he had owed money since he made a trip to India, long years ago. Had not the merchant owned a bazar here? He was from Poona, prompted Blythe.

They regarded him with pity and swore by their gods they had never heard of such a man. Some joked about it. Others argued—there were dozens by such a name, but not from Poona. Others remained quite blank. But, nonetheless, tongues buzzed ahead and behind, and in the silent shadowed bazars.

"Come on," said Blythe suddenly. "Let's go."

Cregar complied. They hopped a tram back to the city. Once aboard, Blythe chuckled.

"It worked—my hat, it worked!" he said, admiringly. "Twice, they knew of him and spoke to one another in Hindustani. One said he had gone to San Fernando—where's that?"

"Another city, down the island. Did they say where?"

"Somewhere near there. The name sounded like Usine St. Lucie—mean anything to you?"

"Lord, yes! Usine—sugar factory—St. Lucie is one of the big sugar plantations down in the plains near San Fernando!" Triumph thrilled through Cregar's veins. "Boy, we've got it! We can rent a car; it'll cost us about twenty-five bucks."

IN TWENTY minutes they had bargained for a car—without a driver. Cregar was quite competent; he had been over the roads and knew them well—and there was no chance of getting lost. A guarantee by the American Consul, because of his disreputable looks, ended all protests, and they were off, with the morning not yet half over.

"I see why you came, now," said Cregar, as they struck out for St. Joseph, the former Spanish capital, along roads lined with hibiscus hedges and bougainvillea, past picturesque natives, dodging carts and no end of peeps and jeeps from the air bases up north. "Teamwork is what does it, sure!"

"But I must warn you," said Blythe. He squirmed a little, as at some uncomfortable thought. "Anything is possible if we find our man. He's a queer sort. And, to be honest about it, he labors under the delusion that he was—well, that he was not treated fairly in our relations."

"Yes?" prompted Cregar. There was more to all this than appeared on the surface, he suddenly perceived. But Blythe shifted.

"THAT'S WHY it's necessary for me to speak with him and convince him," he said, and let the subject die there.

From St. Joseph they turned south, crossing a number of rivers, leaving the mountains far behind and heading into the rich plains. Army camps made their presence felt; aviation training, military establishments and bases—war was on all sides, even as the planes swarmed across the blue skies.

Cregar stepped on it. They passed Dabadie and Marabella Junction, where the road forked for Princes' Town and the mud volcanoes, and after a quick thirty-five-mile trip eased into San Fernando, shipping point for the sugar district.

Over the hill with its fine residences they swept, and on to the business district and port, to draw up on the Harris Promenade and seek a somewhat belated luncheon, also directions for the St. Lucie plantation.

Half an hour served for both objectives, and they were moving again—only six miles to their destination. As they drove, Cregar chatted of the oil fields and pitch lake on ahead to the south; he probed, now and again, but Blythe remained silent about anything that was troubling him. Something was, thought Cregar; he could not get at it, though.

St. Lucie came into sight ahead, an avenue of coco-palms leading to the house, the other buildings being off to themselves. Somewhere, Cregar guessed, would be a village of coolies working on the estate; their man would be there. He was right and wrong, as a foreman at the house informed them.

"There's a village between here and Boca Grande, the next plantation," he said. "The coolies for both places live there. Your man has a bazar of some kind, I believe."

"Ever hear of any whites there?" asked Blythe.

The foreman laughed. "Lord, no! We'd not permit it. You're not thinking of St. Peter?"

"Who's that?"

The other tapped his forehead. "A dippy half-caste hermit, down the shore road past the village. He wanders about at times in breech-clout and sandals. He's harmless; one of these religious fanatics lookin' for the end of the world any time. St. Peter, they call him."

They got directions for the village, a mile distant, and drove off.

"St. Peter, eh? That doesn't sound like a top chemist," said Cregar. "Or does it?"

"Traynor always had a soft streak about religion," Blythe replied, squirming again. He mopped sweat from his chops. "Anything's possible."

Cregar began to be distinctly annoyed. The man knew something and would not talk; he had admitted as much. From his actions, it was something pretty bad, too. He was afraid. Then why was he going on this errand?

"Do you want to pull out?" he demanded bluntly. "You can stay with the car; we have to leave it this side of the village. I'll go on, if you like. No use your protesting about it; you're in a funk."

Blythe went to pieces. "I know it, I know it," he babbled. "God, I know it! But I've got to go ahead. It means too much; it's a big thing, this gas mask of his. Means a lot to your people and mine, to everybody! That's why I've come. Got to do it in spite of myself. No, I can't tell you more about it. Carry on, and I'll hold up my end, no matter what turns up! Without me you can't wangle a thing out of him. I've got to do it at all costs."

"Well, what in the devil's name are you scared of? You've got the wind up; why?"

"None of your business," snapped Blythe, with an effort at pulling himself together. "I'm doing it for—for our people, our boys in the service. I've been a coward long enough. I've got two boys in the service myself. That's why, damn you!"

Cregar was puzzled, but asked no further. The man's agitation was upsetting. All the way from San Francisco, fighting fear— of what? Because he had two boys in the service and must do this for them and for others like them. It did not make sense.

"It's all screwy," Cregar told himself. "This St. Peter isn't the only nut around here, if I'm any judge. Well, here we are."

They were approaching the village, where the road ended. It was a jumble of huts and hovels near a creek, with enormous thickets of bamboo higher than the buildings, and the usual wealth of tropic blooms everywhere. They left the car at the edge of town and walked down the single street, assailed by swarms of begging coppery children. There was one bazar or store in evidence. Blythe pointed to its sign in Hindustani scrawls.

"That's our man's name," he said. "Come on."

A few men were beating copper or working at leather; women muffled in shawls and veiled to the eyes went their ways. The bazar was a ramshackle structure, half drowned under gorgeous masses of royal purple bougainvillea. Cregar tossed a handful of coppers into the dust, and as the screeching children battled for them, the two men turned into the bazar.

Amir Ali Chand? An old man in purest white robe, his face a calm, unlined mask behind horn-rimmed spectacles; he sat absolutely motionless, like a graven image, his eyes darkly luminous. Cregar could feel the mere presence of him—a strange sense of poise, of utter composure.

Blythe did all the talking; at first quietly, then with growing agitation. The Hindu, whose forehead bore a blue caste-mark, made brief responses. Cregar would have given a good deal to understand that conversation; it grew sharper on Blythe's part, touched with excitement but also with deep earnest. At last Amir Ali Chand spoke in flawless English.

"My friend, I am sorry for you," he said, his words slow and calm and unemotional. "Your desire does you credit; I can admire your fortitude in coming here. But I must warn you that the man whom you seek, and whom I have helped and protected and shielded this long time, has not attained to the heights. He is bitter and resentful. You are here because you conquered yourself; he has not conquered himself. You are ready to make reparation; he has not risen to the point of forgiveness."

"That does not matter," said Blythe, forgetful of Cregar's presence. "I must do what I must. For the sake of those whom I love, and for my people."

"Yes, you say truly. I have seen this coming; I have seen that sooner or later the paths of Karma must come together in the eight-fold way," said the Hindu musingly. "For all debts, whether good or ill, must be paid, and it is far better to pay them here than in the next life. You realize this; I respect your wisdom, and you. Since you know where to find him, go your way and leave your friend here with me. I salute you, and send my . blessing with you, Sahib Blythe."

He gestured with his hand. Blythe turned and looked at Cregar, and smiled.

"Wait here, till I try my luck," he said, and walked out.

Cregar was so astonished by that smile that he could make no reply. It changed the whole look of Blythe's face; it lent him an air of sweetness, of peace and happiness, of joyous resolution. The whole man was altered, and for the better. Cregar shoved back his cap, stared after Blythe, then looked at the motionless Hindu.

"What's it all about?" he demanded. "I don't get it."

There was no response. Amir Ali Chand was smiling faintly. Cregar went on, a bit angry.

"It's all cockeyed! He doesn't want to come, but he comes. He says no one else can make our man do what we want; how does he know he can? And you, with your queer words—"

He broke off, suddenly realizing that he was speaking like a querulous child. But Amir Ali Chand, as though replying to a child, broke into soft, appeasing words.

"Stand back and look at yourself, and you will understand; for you, too, have a part to play, sahib. Your friend, in the past, did a great wrong to Traynor Sahib; and now, in order to obtain what you and your people desire, has come to pay his debt. He has conquered himself for the sake of his two sons in the service, and other men's sons. He is willing to perish, in order to obtain for them the thing you seek."

"You seem to know what it is," said Cregar.

"I know all about it," was the quiet response. "Here among these flowers comes to an end an old trail, an ancient trail. For, sahib, there is no such thing as chance; the action you do today, may have been caused a thousand years ago. Destiny is Karma, and Karma is the love of God—the love that God bears to all men. This is so simple a thing that you cannot comprehend it. What your friend does today, no matter how it ends, will gain him great merit in the world to come. That is why I respect him, admire him, and salute him."

"I think you're nuts," said Cregar irreverently.

"One part of you says that. The other part pays me homage," said the Hindu. "The real self, the real you, is one with me and comprehends the truth of what I say. Stop and think, sahib; stop and listen to yourself. You are witnessing here something in which you have no part except as a witness; you were brought to look on, and to play an after-part, a role not concerned with the past. You carry on this action into the future, while others close the paths of the past."

Cregar felt his brain whirling. The devil of it was that somewhere deep inside he was impressed by the truth of what this man said; but he rebelled against admitting it.

"Absurd!" he heard himself saying. "1 don't know what it's all about. I'm going to see about Blythe; if Traynor's here, there's something queer going on."

"You would think it queer," said Amir Ali Chand. "But it is

not. However, nothing stops you; go ahead, for you cannot avert the will of the gods. The path leads from the village on down beside the creek; you cannot miss it. And what you seek lies within the metal box on the shelf. Go in peace."

Cregar turned and walked out of the place, driven by anger and fear and a vague perplexity; he could not straighten it all out. He felt tossed about by queer unseen forces, as though he were dealing with madmen.

Yet, as he walked on through the village and found the path beyond, he was alone; no shrieking children pursued him, no one seemed aware of him. And slowly, as the giant bamboos closed in to right and left, as lush flowers and tropic growths shut out the world, his mind found a certain ordered sanity in what had so perplexed him.

Yes, he was playing a part in some old drama unknown to him. Blythe had feared to come here and push through the errand, because it meant facing Traynor, whom he had somehow wronged deeply in the past. How? This did not matter a jot. Blythe was sacrificing himself and facing restitution, in order to give the world what it now needed—in order to save his sons and their comrades from the savage onslaught of evil. For love of them, Blythe was indeed acting a great and noble part.

"I don't savvy it—and it doesn't matter," Cregar told himself desperately. "We'll see what the end is. A metal box on the shelf! Now, why did that old humbug tell me?"

From somewhere ahead, muffled by the greenery, he heard the thudding explosion of a shot—the short, sharp bark of a pistol.

This quickened him, hastened his steps. St. Peter—a half dotty maniac—could that be Traynor? Traynor, taking vengeance for some old grudge, some ancient wrong? He broke into a stumbling run, cursing the moist dank heat here among the trees.

A compound opened ahead, a clearing on a ledge beside the creek. In the compound was a little thatched house, with huge-leaved banana trees leaning across the front. No sound came, there was no sight of Blythe. At the compound fence, Cregar paused, calling Blythe's name, and had no response. The stillness was that of death.

He leaped the low fence and went straight on to the little house, whose door hung open and sagging. No one spoke. Nothing moved, except lizards flashing across the veranda. He stepped into a room and paused, momentarily blinded by the change from intense sunlight to cool shadow.

His vision slowly returned. The room was not large; at the far end, closing off another room, were curtains of eucalyptus buds strung together. There was a table in the room, and a chair before it; in the chair sat Blythe. Otherwise the room was empty, even of furnishings. Cregar relaxed.

"Hello!" he said. "Thought something had happened to you."

Something had, sure enough. Blythe was dead. He had been shot through the heart.

The shock of this finding put Cregar in a whirl. He stared around; nothing moved, but he had the sensation of eyes watching him. As he tried to pull himself together, a voice spoke.

"Who are you?"

The voice came from the curtains; the eucalyptus buds moved slightly. Cregar froze.

"Well, answer me!" came the voice. "Who are you? Why did you come with him?"

"I—we came to find you, Traynor," he answered hoarsely. "Your invention—the gas mask—"

His words died out. After all, he was helpless, without a weapon; and this maniac was watching him, no doubt had a gun trained on him.

"That's what he said. Then he told the truth, for once." The voice was controlled, it was sane. Cregar's spasmodic horror began to pass. Blythe was dead, no doubt of that; it was real.

"Yes, it was the truth," he said with an effort. "No need to murder him, or me."

"You're in no danger. He had it coming, and he knew it. He was a scoundrel. He had cheated me," said the voice. "Blythe was a clever fellow. He knew the truth about me; he knew that if I killed him, there could be no more evasion and hiding. There's British law here. Now there'll be a magistrate and an inquiry and no end of red tape; I'm done for. He knew that I'd be finished if I killed him. He let me do it, he taunted me, he made me do it, d'ye hear? That was his purpose."

Perhaps it had been, Cregar thought desperately.

"I don't know anything about that," he began. The voice cut in on him.

"D'ye know what he did? He turned me over to the police, in India; he handed me over to a living death, to live out the rest of my life in hell! Well, I got away. I came here; I could be free here. Nobody knew the truth about me except Amir Ali Chand, and he protected me. He made it possible for me to exist in freedom, instead of in hell."

Cregar got out a cigarette and lit it. The tobacco eased his nerves.

"You and your story aren't important," he said. "Blythe seems to have deliberately sacrificed himself; he isn't important, either. Nor am I. The great thing is to get this invention of yours to the proper hands. The world needs it now, your country needs it, all civilization needs it—"

A laugh, curt and sharp and unassumed, rang out.

"Civilization? Be damned to it!" said the voice bitterly. "My country? Be damned to it! Civilization forced me here, to play the part of an imbecile if I wanted to be free—a halfwit, protected against civilization, against my country, by one loyal Hindu friend! And now you've tracked me out, followed me, discovered everything!"

What was this man Traynor—a criminal of some kind? Cregar's brain probed desperately but could not uncover the secret. Certainly the man was sane; his words proved it. And he thought Cregar knew everything. Careful, now! It was no time for idle words.

So Traynor was not going to hand over his invention.

"The Army needs that gas-mask of yours," Cregar said crisply. "That's all that I'm after. I've no interest in your personal affairs. I'm empowered to meet your terms, Traynor. I want to take back—"

"You won't take it back," snapped the invisible voice. "You've left me only one way out, and my invention goes with me. I offered it to the government and was ridiculed. To hell with them all, and you, too!"

His meaning, his intention, his resolution—all was perfectly clear. The man meant to destroy himself and his invention.

Cregar's eyes flitted about, while his brain tried to cope with the problem but with scanty success. That Traynor was some sort of criminal, that Blythe had in the past turned him in, that he had escaped and found a haven here—this seemed to be the explanation, yet it did not fit. It was nothing so simple as this.

Suddenly, unexpectedly, he saw it. Except for that tip from Amir Ali Chand, he would have missed it.

To the right of that curtained doorway, shoulder-high, a bamboo shelf stood out against the rattan partition. On the shelf was a small box, of the type that used to be sold to farmers for the protection of valuable papers against fire. It was painted a dingy yellow, and so merged with the bamboo and rattan as to be almost invisible. But this must be it.

And, quite clearly, to reach it was utterly impossible. Cregar weighed his chances; he had none. That pistol behind the curtain held him absolutely helpless. He began to argue with the unseen voice. He pointed out the bitter necessity facing the Allied armies, the death and suffering that would be entailed—and the voice only mocked him.

"All that is nothing to me. If my blasted country could get its hands on me, even now, even if I handed over my invention, I'd be jerked back into the hell of a living death! Sure, that's the law. They'd regret it, but they'd do it. The British would do it. Any of them would. Well, it goes with me! John Traynor will be remembered, all right, for what he might have done for the world—had not the world hounded him!"

Cregar tried to argue again, and was shut up.

"Get out of here! What's your game? To keep me occupied while police and soldiers close in?"

"No. I came here alone with Blythe—"

"Then get out, or stay here with Blythe and burn with him and me!" snapped the voice. "I don't want to kill you, but your time's short. Clear out! Vamose! I've got to finish it and I will—get back to the door and walk out or I'll drill you!"

The shrill emphasis of the voice spoke determination. Cregar would have risked a bullet, but the result was too certain altogether; there was no risk. Even did he reach that box, he could not get away with it, which was the important thing.

He sniffed. The penetrating odor of gasoline reached him. Traynor meant to fire the ramshackle structure and kill himself.

"For heaven's sake don't be a fool!" he exclaimed sharply. "There's no need of suicide, Traynor!"

"If you got a good look at me you'd know better," said the voice grimly. "Get out or go along. At the count of three—one, two—"

Cregar turned and walked to the door, fearing a bullet in the back. None came.

"Out and off, damn you!" shrilled the voice. "And you can take back word to Washington that John Traynor was smarter than them all. Get out!"

The pistol roared. The bullet went high—deliberately high. Cregar jumped, instinctively. As he dodged out the doorway, he heard the high, shrill laugh of Traynor.

But he knew what was coming, now. And dodging out of sight, he flung himself down on the veranda, at one side of the doorway. As in the erratic aisles of a nightmare, he could guess precisely what this maddened, hopeless creature meant to do—

fire the place and put a bullet through his brain. The back room was already drenched with gasoline....

And knowing, Cregar made swift preparations. He jammed the cap over his head, wriggled out of his jacket and held it ready, and waited, tense. The seconds seemed interminable; time stopped; the sunlight drenching the rattans seemed to burn and smoke and dance. A lizard, off at one side, poised on front legs akimbo and lifted himself up and down, up and down, as a lizard does—

CREGAR JUMPED. From inside came a *"whoosh!"* of gushing flame, then a swift mounting crackle as fire rushed through flimsy rattan—a crackle and a roar. Upon this exploded a shot—a second shot. It was done.

Muscles suddenly released, Cregar was on his feet, darting in at the doorway. He shrank back, appalled—there was a solid sheet of roaring flame, bursting through a wall of black smoke, where the curtains and partition had been.

He flung jacket over his head and face and hurled himself forward, desperately holding his breath; the danger came quickest if flame were breathed in. He went into it, slap into it, reaching out as a man reaches out in a dark room for something he knows. He found the burning partition, found something solid, and caught it. The box! Then around and a dash out, skirting the table and the dead thing before it.

Time had stopped again. The horror of it! Flame was surging across the roof, flakes were dropping on him, hands and arms and body were jumping and twitching as the fire-teeth bit. Then the door, fresh air, and he was tearing the burning jacket from about his face as he darted out. He fell at the steps, plunged to the ground, and went rolling over and over, the box safe under his arm.

That roll probably saved him. When he got to his feet and slapped out the burning patches on his trousers, he had left the fire behind, he broke into a run to get away from the consuming heat of the roaring structure.

That was all he remembered, until he found voices around him, was given a drink, and realized that Amir Ali Chand was holding his arm. He came to himself at once.

"The box—"

"Here it is, my friend—pardon, sahib," said the gentle controlled tones.

Cregar stared into the quiet, placid features.

"What's it mean?" he demanded. "What's back of it all—why did he do it? Why had Blythe turned him in to the police? Was he a criminal?"

"Oh, no," said Amir Ali Chand. "He was something which the authorities regard as much more terrible. He was a leper. He had caught leprosy somewhere in India. Poor man! He could never resign himself to it, or accept the inevitable—"

That was all Cregar cared about—there was no more mystery about anything. And in the metal box, sure enough, were all the plans and specifications that Blythe had died to win for his two boys in the service—as you probably know if you have received your own Traynor Anti-gas Mask from the G. I. authorities.

XII

BOMBS AND OLIVE OIL

Tony Gorman Was Good at Two Things—
Making Friends and Plane Spotting.

TONY GORMAN was down to his dog-tag and a pair of shorts. This might have discouraged anyone else; but not a screwball like Gorman. It only put a new and more reckless glint in his dancing dark eyes, and brought a new twist to his cheerful grin.

How he got into an open boat in the Strait of Otranto was a yarn all by itself. He was part of that unlucky former National Guard regiment that got walked over by the Nazis at the Faid battle. Gorman was started for Italy with a lot more Iowa boys, and the Italians made a wild scramble to get them there, in order to have something to show the home folks.

The ship carrying his crowd made a frantic push to get away from Allied planes and British patrols, and instead of making Sicily, got away over eastward and took shelter at Brindisi. About the same time, some cruising Mosquito bombers took a swipe at Brindisi in passing, with the result that there was hell to pay in that harbor.

Gorman took advantage of the occasion to slip overboard. Not so crazy as it looked, for he had seen a drifting boat close by. He made it, and hauled himself in. The boat was empty except for some clothes up forward; there was a stiff offshore wind blowing, which caught the high bow of the boat and sent it slapping along. Also, the sun was going down, and by the time it went and twilight came, Gorman stuck up his head to see land far away and nothing in sight.

So he curled up and went to sleep. He had got away from the Eyeties, he was free, and tomorrow could take care of itself.

Tony Gorman was one of those people to whom things happened. If a grain elevator anywhere in the Middle West blew up, he was there. If a train was wrecked, he was there. Same way in the army, ending up in Tunisia. He was at Faid and get caught. And, as just described, he got away. This, although he did not know it, was only the start of his story.

There were two things at which Tony Gorman was extra-good. One was making friends. He had a way of capturing anybody; even a motor cop at home would get to talking with Gorman and end up by telling him to run along. People liked his friendly grin and his dancing eyes, and back of these he had something on the ball. Something hard and defiant and reckless.

His second accomplishment was plane spotting. This was a knack, too. He had cultivated it since reaching Tunisia, and air crews marveled at it; they lost money at it, too, because the Iowa boys would put him up against anybody and he would take the bets easily. He had learned the English and Nazi and Italian planes like nobody's business. Not that this promised to do him any good, naked and afloat in an open boat somewhere between Italy and the Albanian-Greek coast. It just went to show that there was something corny about Gorman, and he seemed to enjoy it too. He could about get away with anything when he really turned on the heat.

He wakened in the gray dawn, stiff and cold, the boat rocking to the sea-swells. He could see nothing, so he got under the pile of clothes forward and went to sleep again, to really wake up when the first rays of the sun touched him. He sat up and looked around, and found something to look at.

What with the wind and currents, the boat was moving right along and was approaching a rocky, hilly island, with mountains towering behind it. He had not the least idea where he was, and supposed it to be Italy. Just offshore was a beat with a sail, a low lateen canvas, and it was headed for him; he saw two men in her, watching him.

He waved, and they waved in response and headed down at him. When they got close, they hailed, but their words meant nothing to him. The sail fluttered, and the other boat drifted down. One of the men was old and stooped, the other was old and erect, with gray hair and mustache and a hard brown face. Again they hailed him.

"No use," rejoined Gorman, "I don't savvy your talk. No speak English?"

"Sure thing, fellers!" Gray-mustached man. "You English?"

"No, American."

"Hurray!" came the response in evident delight. "Me too! Where you from?"

"Gosh!" exclaimed Gorman in amazement. "You, an American?"

"Sure thing feller!" Gray Mustache flung him a line. "Clark Street, Chicago —that's me! You know Chicago, Dearborn Street, Old Hellas restaurant? Cristoff, that's my name; I was a waiter there. Get in, we'll tow your boat; a good boat's worth money."

DAZEDLY, GORMAN managed to scramble into the other craft. The two men grinned, shook hands, and poured a torrent of language at him; meanwhile they were heading in for the island shore as soon as the sail filled and began to draw.

"You're Greeks!" he exclaimed, and pointed at the mountains. "Is that Greece?"

"Hellas? No, that's Albania," said Cristoff, and pointed to the craggy island. "This is Corfu."

To Gorman, that meant nothing. The mountainous island was beautiful, in contrast with the barren peaks of Albania, eastward.

Valleys and slopes were of vivid green, now bright and alive in the vineyard stretches, now dusky and grayish along the olive groves. The shore was uneven and broken and ragged; he perceived that the two boatmen were keenly intent upon the waters ahead, Cristoff studying them with a pair of binoculars. There was a good load of fish in the boat, and Gorman, slowly getting adjusted, wondered at it all.

"What you watching for?" he demanded.

"Wops! Dagoes! Eyeties! Italiani," said Cristoff. "It is not allowed to fish, because of mines and war. If they catch us, good night! You can't see the city from here—hey, who's winning the war?"

"We are," said Gorman, "or were when I got captured. By this time I expect the Nazis are all out of Africa. Sorry I missed the big last show; it was on the way, all right."

"You hungry?"

"I could about eat one o' those fish raw."

"Don't. Stick around. You go home with me, see?"

The telltale canvas was lowered, two big sweeps put out, and the boat was rowed for the last quarter-mile. It rounded a rocky promontory unexpectedly and dived into a tiny cove among the rocks. Olive groves appeared, and a few snowy houses; a dozen men and women were waiting on the shore.

These seized the boat and helped pull it up, broke into a wildly astonished babble at sight of Gorman and the boat in tow, then fell furiously upon the fish. It was easy to comprehend that Cristoff and his companion had acted for the sake of all. The nets were carried off. The fish were grabbed and divided and carried away, leaving a good share for Cristoff. Then all had vanished, even Cristoff's companion.

"Hi! You come with me, Mister," said Cristoff, shouldering his share of the fish in a tub. "What's your name?"

"Gorman. Tony Gorman."

"Tony? Antonio? Tonio, eh! That's a good Italian name. We don't love these Eyeties, but we get on. They grab Corfu—well, never mind. Come along."

So began the very, very queer story of Tony Gorman and what happened in the island of Corfu, of which so many different versions have been told.

He knew nothing about this beauty-spot of the Ionian Sea, where in peaceful days more than one crowned head had sought repose from the world's cares, and where through four centuries the arms of Venice had formed a bulwark against the Turk. All that it meant to him, at the moment, was the rambling old house above the shore where Cristoff ruled supreme among a dozen gabbling relatives of all kinds—Cristoff, who had spent ten years in Chicago and now had two sons in America. Cristoff had sought peace in Corfu, too, but had been caught here by the war.

These people, living on frugal rations, found the fresh fish a rare banquet, and Gorman was welcomed at it. Cristoff gave him some ragged garments and a clean shirt. While they ate, talking loudly over excellent mavrodaphne wine, planes droned far overhead. That was nothing new, said Cristoff. Planes were frequently overhead, but yesterday they had begun to make trouble and the first bombs had fallen; two damaged Italian destroyers lay in the harbor and evidently the Allies had discovered them.

"So our lovely island must get bombed," Cristoff said mournfully. "Our young men are forced into the Italian army or have fled to Greece, where the Germans kill them—ah! This is my niece Helena. If she is here you will soon find Capitano Luigi Trucco coming around, eh?" Cristoff roared at his own joke, and the girl, remarkably pretty in her peasant costume, blushed. She spoke no English but names were names.

"Who's Trucco?" asked Gorman, dipping bread in the olive oil that had helped cook the fish, and wolfing it.

"A friend of mine," said Cristoff calmly. "A good feller. He has been in America, too. Now he is a big shot here."

A big shot indeed—Trucco was an army captain and also the head of the Fascisti organization in Corfu, which made him more important even than the governor of the island. Further, he was in command of the artillery and ack-ack defenses, such as they were. The Greek islanders were in great fettle and the Italians were close to panic over events in Africa, with feverish preparations being made—for the Allies were coming. There were no Germans here, Corfu being an unimportant island with only a small air base, for flying boats.

Gorman found himself the center of attention, with Cristoff translating his reports of the African fighting, which was all news to these people. After the glorious meal was over, he went down to the little cove and had a dip in the sea, and asked Cristoff what would happen if the Italians learned of his presence.

"Pouf!" Cristoff waved his hand grandly and stroked his big gray mustaches. "I will say you are my son from America—I will make up a story how you came here from Alexandria to see me, and sailed by boat from Albania. The strait is only a couple of miles wide. I am a good liar, Tonio. You see!"

H E   H A D   his doubts whether such a yarn would be swallowed, but did not argue the point. He did not care much about anything, right now. He was too happy to be alive, to be free, to be among friends. It was like being in another world here.

In mid-afternoon he wakened from a delicious sleep under the olive-trees, to find a blaze of excitement at the house. He joined the assembled relations on a terrace behind the building, overlooking the sea. The reason of the excitement was not far to seek; planes were coming down the sky—American planes! They were too high to be seen, however.

"They don't sound American to me," said Gorman to Cristoff. "Let's have those binoculars of yours."

He got the glasses. A lone plane was diving at the island.

"Biplane," he said. "A British reconnaissance and torpedo-spotter; an Albacore, sure! That fin and rudder are distinctive. And—hello! Look at that formation up above, five of 'em! Long-range Beaufighters, they are—the new type with marked dihedral tailplanes! Oh, boy, look at 'em go! They're not coming here, either. The Albacore is probably getting some pictures of the harbor—there, she's heading off. Doesn't like the flack."

A curious dead silence had fallen all around, but Gorman was unaware of it. He was intent on the sky. A few bursts of flack, evidently from Corfu batteries, followed the reconnaissance plane. The heavy drones lessened in the blue heavens and were gone.

"Well! Where d'you reckon they came from?" Gorman lowered the glasses and looked around. "That Albacore was sure—"

His words died. He was conscious now of the silence, and of a new figure added to the group—a figure standing staring at him and listening. He jumped, at sight of it. A tall, dark-faced man, fairly young, clad in all the stagey outfit of a Fascist—tasseled cap, dangling silver-hilted dagger, black shirt and trousers and shiny boots, with medals and ribbons covering half his chest.

Cristoff turned quickly, greeted the newcomer, shook hands with him, and there was an outburst of eager talk in Greek and Italian. The new arrival strode toward Gorman, eyeing him attentively, and addressed him:

"You speak English?"

"Don't speak anything else but," said Gorman, grinning. His impudent friendliness brought a smile to the dark face. Cristoff intervened. This was Captain Trucco—he had driven out from town for a visit among his friends. And this was Tonio, my son from far-off America—followed by a lengthy explanation.

"So you are a Greek!" said Trucco.

Gorman shook his head. "Nope. American."

"You know airplanes. It was wonderful to hear you."

"Just a gift," Gorman said carelessly. "I know 'em all. I made a study of it."

"Oh!" said Trucco. "You know Detroit? I was there three years, working in the Ford plant. Ah, that is a grand place! Well, it is odd to find a stranger here."

He became friendly, affable, intimate; one liked him almost at sight. He was on the best of terms with everybody here, though it was evident that his chief interest lay in the girl Helena. He had come to stay for supper, and as his contribution had brought two tins of army beef—a real treasure to these people. With such a gift, the devil himself would have been a very welcome caller; and Luigi Trucco was far from that.

Gorman sized him up, shrewdly and without haste, between now and supper time; he had an idea that his life and liberty might depend on just how well he could savvy this Fascist big shot. Trucco was good company. Everyone here, including Helena, liked him.

"He's no angel," decided Gorman. "I'd say he's out for number one, fairly able, quite unprincipled, honestly in love with Helena—and doesn't give a tinker's damn for Il Duce, the grand Fascist party, or Italia. He's an opportunist. In other words, he's on the make, but not a bad guy in his way. And I don't like the way he looks at me."

Twice, indeed, Trucco reverted to the subject of planes, asking "Tonio" whether he knew as much about all planes as he did about the British types—which he did—and whether he knew anything about ack-ack fire—which he promptly disclaimed.

It was a pleasant, even hilarious sunset meal beside the sea, with plenty of wine to keep it company. But Captain Trucco wanted to be back before dark and the blackout. So, seizing an opportunity, he took Gorman up to have a look at his car, which was on the road some distance from the house.

"Never mind the car," he said, when they were alone. "Friend Tonio, you would not like me to ask a lot of unpleasant questions; and it would be very sad for our friends if I did. This is war, you know. It would be much better to accent Cristoff's story of how you got here, eh?"

"Might be a good idea," said Gorman cautiously. Trucco beamed and produced cigarettes.

"Now, I heard you talk about those planes. You are wonderful; you are the very man I need in town. You see, we have warships lying in the harbor. That reconnaissance plane was not here for any good. More bombings are coming. There are British, American and Italian planes, and quite a few German. They come from everywhere—and until their bombs drop, we don't know who they are. We have shot down one German plane by mistake, and one of our own."

He seemed to think this was a good joke, and Gorman quite agreed.

"So," he said, "you shall ride back to the city with me and make yourself useful to me there."

"Not as a soldier," said Gorman quickly.

"Oh, no! As a friend. A man just come from Albania, a Greek.

There is nothing to prevent you giving me wrong information about the planes that come, but you would find the results quite unpleasant, I fear. What do you say? Shall we be good friends?"

Gorman swiftly considered the astonishing offer. Trucco, of course, was working for his own hand; he needed help acutely. He strongly suspected the truth about this Tonio, but if he got the help he needed, nothing else mattered to him. And, decided Gorman, except in the case of American planes coming, which was most unlikely, there was no reason why he should not play the game. He might throw a monkey-wrench into the Italian machinery, too. Tell the Eyeties how to shoot down British planes? Not much. By double-crossing these birds he might really accomplish something worthwhile.

"Okay," he said amiably. "But why do you get so many different planes over here?"

"Why? Look where we are! Planes from Alexandria and Syria bound for Italy, pass us; those from North Africa reach us sometimes; those from Italy or from Greece or Crete, Nazi or Fascist planes bound for Africa, pass us—and so on. It did not matter much until we got those destroyers in the harbor. Now we are getting bombed, to sink them."

It was rather an outrage, having those destroyers here, he inferred.

So this was how Tony Gorman came to be riding into town in the last of the daylight, beside Captain Trucco, whose car was little and old but still a car. The island roads were splendid, having been built by the English during a long-past occupation.

AS FOR the city itself, tightly squeezed on a low plateau surrounded by water on three sides, Gorman saw little of it. Darkness was already descending when they got there. The blackout was a by-guess-and-by-gosh sort of thing, to which Captain Trucco's headlights paid no attention whatever; nor, apparently, was there much danger from night bombers.

"Tonight we will talk," said Captain Trucco, halting the car, "and find you some better clothes. This is my house; I rent it from a patriot. A Greek patriot; he is dead, so the rental can wait. You shall have a room with friend Bellini, my assistant party chief. He speaks no English. He is a lieutenant in the artillery like me. If you have the other bed in that room it will be good; he can bring no more friends here to sleep. He is a fine man but he has too many friends."

A blackshirt sentry was at the house entrance. It was a high and narrow house; and past the saluting sentry, Gorman was astonished by the luxury of it. The furnishings were rich, the tiles and decorations gorgeous. Candles and lamps were alight, and a staff of servants were in evidence. Trucco laughed at his guest's expression.

"The family servants remained," he said. "A good thing for them. All the houses here are like this, built in the Venetian style, narrow and high; Venetians were master here during four hundred years. Yes, a nice house, very comfortable. Of course, party members get the best of everything. I did a good thing for myself when I joined the party and became a prominent man, eh? This is your room. My office is downstairs. Come down there later and we'll be comfortable. I'll send you a razor at once."

Gorman received toilet articles from the hands of a Greek servant, made himself presentable, was given some better garments, and descended without a guide or guard to a large room on the ground floor—a combination of office and living-room comfortably furnished. A radio was going full tilt, and Trucco presented him to several Fascist officers, none of whom spoke English. Thick Turkish coffee was served, the tobacco was excellent, and although he gathered that the radio was giving the news of the final clean-up in Tunisia, everybody seemed at ease.

Luxury, rampant luxury. Fresh from the suffering and khamsin wind and sirocco, blowing now north, now south, fresh from the bitter hard, the incredibly hard African warfare, where men fought hourly on the intolerable edge of exhaustion, Gorman was slow to find it real here. The divans, the conversation, the liqueurs, the air of ease and comfort and soft living, the utter appalling selfishness—these men were like Trucco himself. Looking out for number one, that was it. The dry rot of Italian life, far different from those sturdy peasants who had fought and died in Tunisia.

And later, in the soft bed, upstairs, lulled to sleep by breezes from the starry bay, he wondered how far, if at all, he could trust these Fascist gangsters who ruled and plundered in the name of Italy.

He woke to blustery day, wind on the sea and a windy sky. His room-mate was gone. He dressed, noticed a balcony outside the window, and stepped out on it. Instantly he was enthralled by the scene, near and far, stretching before him.

Here was the town crammed together with narrow, twisting little streets, and the white houses all pricked out with pale green shutters; it centered about the oval Esplanade, a spacious parked expanse bordered by collonaded structures, with the crumbling old Fortezza Vecchia on the south side, its high rocky pile shutting off the sea view, and a crumbling palace opposite. Everything was crumbling, dingy with age, yet sparkling with life.

The two destroyers lay lined up by the docks, and beyond showed yet another ship, evidently just in; a two-thousand-ton freighter. The Esplanade was filled with soldiers and townfolk; batteries were emplaced on the ruinous old fortress and about the harbor, and above the island peaks hung cumulus clouds shifting in the wind, casting sharp contrasts of light and shade along the slopes.

Captain Trucco appeared, brisk and smiling. Breakfast was ready, and work waiting; the wireless had brought word of fleets in the air, a ship had put in for shelter, bombs were a certainty; the sirens, indeed, started to wail while Gorman was swallowing his fruit and coffee. There was no attempt here at bomb shelters. When Gorman and Trucco went out to the waiting car, long lines of frightened people were being evacuated by soldiery, and the roads leading out of town were jammed.

They crossed the wide moat to the old fortress, left the car and climbed to a battery on the rock, and here was Trucco's headquarters. The island governor appeared with his glittering staff, talking nervously with Trucco, then scattered. Gorman was given a magnificent pair of Zeiss binoculars and settled down in the gun emplacement with the captain; telephones connected them with the other batteries.

Almost at once, dots began to roam the skies; they seemed to come from any and all directions. Officers and soldiers alike were jittery in the extreme. In wild excitement they were getting ready to open fire on a flight of five ships winging overhead, when Gorman halted them; these were Stukas with Italian markings, as tokened by the long nose, square rudder and large underslung radiator. They vanished to the south.

Out of nowhere a single bomber came streaking across the sky, shrieking down in a long dip over the end of the island. Again the gun-crews leaped into action, an officer shouting that it was a Bristol Beaufighter. Again Gorman called a halt.

"Messerschmitt 210!" he told Trucco. "It looks like a Beaufighter—but the conical engines show the difference, and the greenhouse on top—"

A radio report came from the ship, at this moment; a Messerschmitt indeed, giving warning that a fleet of Allied planes from Africa were sweeping the seas, apparently headed for German air bases in Greece.

Almost before the Messerschmitt had vanished in its frantic flight for safety, down from midheaven pierced the deeper note of bombers flying high and invisible; and upon this grew the aerodynamic vibrations of escorting Spitfires far below, but hidden by cloud. Barely had Gorman determined on what they were, when out of the west suddenly grew a single plane heading slap across the fleet's course. At first glance, it was a Lightning, to judge by the twin booms, and it was going like a bat out of hell.

Suddenly it perceived its danger, altered course, and dipped.

Not a Lightning at all, but a Focke Wulf 189—the projecting rear tip of the fuselage and the distinctive greenhouse showed it for what it was. Out of the clouds came three Spitfires, and the hapless Focke Wulf never had a chance. It fled hurriedly northward with the Spitfires on its tail, and a black smoke-plume went up from the northern sea horizon to mark its end.

Not that anyone noticed; for out of the clouds broke five bombers detached from the stratosphere fleet—they looked almost like Junkers 88s, until Gorman sighted the distinctive Blenheim tail unit, and the British markings. He did not need to proclaim it—others were aware of the danger. The guns began to pump and bark, flack bursts starred the sky, but the five paid no heed. They came, they passed, they drew into the distance—and stick after stick of bombs hurtled and shrieked to the mark. As though in contempt, the Blenheims did not return or pause. Their work was done and they knew it.

Gorman dived like the others as a bomb hit squarely on the old castle above, filling the air with dust and flinders. The others fell on the docks and harbor, straddling the destroyers, scoring twice on the freighter with direct hits, and sending up a lone plume of spouting water from the sea beyond, as though the last bomb had been tossed away in disdain.

That mighty sweep of fleets unseen had swept the skies clear; gods and men were satisfied, and peace fell once more upon the little island nook. Gorman saw himself forgotten, as Trucco and his companions rushed away for the harbor, and forgotten he was glad to be; he calmly made his way back into town and to the Fascist headquarters.

He found the house without trouble. The blackshirt sentry was gone from the entrance. Instead a young lieutenant with one arm in a sling stood looking about hesitantly. He was hand-some, in the lean dark wolfish way of many an Italian, and a certain set look in his face spoke of resolve and suffering. He stopped Gorman with a question.

"Sorry," said Gorman. "*No parlo Italiano,* nix ferstany, nothing doing."

"Oh! You speak English!" exclaimed the other, and his face lit up. "I'm looking for Captain Trucco."

"Better come on in and wait, then," Gorman rejoined. "Did you get hit in this raid?"

"No, no; I just came ashore from the freighter that came in last night. She got away from Bizerte two nights ago, but her captain was killed and one of the officers fetched us here, after landing everyone else at Catania. Mostly Nazis."

The house seemed deserted. Gorman led the way into the ground floor office. The young officer looked at the imposing picture of Mussolini and the gaudy Fascist emblems on the wall with a growl that told he was no party member.

"Make yourself comfortable," said Gorman. "Have a drink? I need one. Smoke. The house is yours, as far as I'm concerned. I'm known as Tonio around here."

The lieutenant frowned at him, puzzled. "I am Lieutenant Colonna," he said. It was one of the most ancient and historic names of Rome, but meant nothing to Gorman. "Who are you? You talk like an American. Not a prisoner? I do not understand."

A well-stocked tantalus stood near the radio. Gorman poured drinks, handed one to Colonna, and lifted his own glass.

"How!" he said. "And be damned to Il Duce!"

"Same here," said Colonna, and smiled.

Gorman lit a cigarette. Impulse told him to plunge. He liked this officer, who had a rare air of poise, of resolute balance.

"Okay," he said, and grinned. "I'm from Africa, like you. Not a prisoner, but I was. Right now it's a queer layout. I don't know just where I stand. You know Trucco, do you?"

"Know him? I've known him for years. I came here to Corfu to find him; we are such old friends," said Colonna, but his eyes held a wolfish light. "You are surprised that I speak English? Many Romans speak it well. I went to school in England. But tell me about yourself."

Gorman did, quite frankly. Any such fishy yarn as Trucco had accepted would not hold water for an instant with a man like this; so he told the simple truth. His infectious mirth, his dancing, defiant eyes, his whimsical screwball air, captivated the Italian; in no time the two men were laughing together, each admitting to a strong liking for the other.

"You got off that freighter just in time," Gorman concluded. "She got blown to hell by those bombs—looked to be sinking, last I saw of her. Did you know Trucco before he went to America?"

"Yes, and after he returned," said Colonna. He glanced about the room, his face darkening. "They are scavangers, these Fascisti! Looters, thieves, rascals!"

"Well, what else do you expect of gangsters? But Trucco's not a bad sort."

"No. He's a pleasant fellow," Colonna said, with a snarl. "He will be very much surprised to see me. When my regiment went to Africa he should have gone with it; instead, his influence got him detailed here. A nice place, Corfu! There are good pickings to be had. Trust Luigi for that! So he's in love with a girl here, eh?"

"Head over heels," said Gorman. He had told about Cristoff. "She's a fine girl, too."

Colonna nodded. "If I were you," he said, "I'd get out of here and go back to your friend Cristoff. You could stay with him and nobody will care. Nobody is going to care about anything, now. Italy is beaten; the Axis is beaten. So far as we're concerned the war is over. Nobody cares. It is these Fascist dogs who have ruined Italy!"

"You don't think it will be safe for me to stay here?"

"Do you know that my people hate these swaggering rascals second only to the Nazis? The break-up is at hand. Soon a blackshirt will be safe in Italy only if he is protected by Nazi bayonets—perhaps not then! Those accursed Germans shot us down, betrayed us, in Tunisia; they sacrificed us that they might escape! You should know that."

Gorman nodded.

"Sure. And you think that in Italy, they'll do something now about the blackshirts?"

"If you had been ruled by Chicago gangsters and gunmen for a generation, and they lost their grip—what would you do about it in America?"

"I get you," said Gorman. He waved his cigarette. "This is a soft spot, all right, for the blackshirts. Your soldiers—they're a different stripe. Fine men!"

The officer's hard, tense features softened. "Ah, you say that! Yes, they're fine. They've suffered, bled, done their best—our people weren't cut out for ferocity. But the peasant boys did their best, and the damned Fascists betrayed them. Remember, many of us have personal wrongs, deep and bitter, to avenge as well. Shall we have another drop to drink?"

"Second the motion," said Gorman. "Haven't had lunch yet, but I don't mind saying when that bomb hit just back of us, my heart skipped three beats. Hm! Perhaps I should push off but look here! Trucco needs me. He'll come looking me up; and he already knows darned well that I'm no native son of the island."

Lieutenant Colonna, left arm in sling, held the glass in his right hand, swished it about, and tasted the drink.

"Ah! Better than the first," said he. "Well, my friend, let me tell you something. Luigi Trucco will not come looking you up. I can promise that! Go back to Cristoff and you'll not be bothered. What will happen here, I don't know. The Nazis may throw in a force to defend the island; the Allies may jump in from Cyprus; anything may happen, anything, you understand? There is only one certainty, one thing of which you may be sure: Luigi Trucco will not look you up. For this, you have the word of a Colonna."

Meeting those dark, intent eyes, Gorman wanted to ask why; but he held his peace. In this man's air was something tense and ominous and terrible—something so impressive that it brought a shiver to his spine.

"Let me tell you something that I discovered in Africa," Colonna went on. He took a fresh cigarette; Gorman held the light for him. "Before El Alamein, when Rommel had driven the English back into Egypt, we thought all was won. Perhaps that may be the excuse for what took place; I do not know. But after El Alamein, when Montgomery shattered the Afrika Korps and our Italian legions—it was different. One of our Fascist leaders was killed. I was with him when he died. Cirro, his name was."

He paused, puffed at his cigarette, and shrugged lightly.

"Before dying, Cirro told us about a deal in ammunition and in olive oil—the cargoes of six ships, taking ammunition to us in Africa, and olive oil back to feed our families at home. There was neither ammunition nor olive oil, but dummy casks. Graft! And Cirro was at the head of the blackshirt ring which pocketed the money. This old friend of mine, Luigi Trucco, was another in on the game, as you Americans say."

H E   B R O K E off abruptly, lifting his head; a startled look shot through his eyes. Gorman came to his feet, then paused. Too late, too late; the open windows permitted voices to drift in from the street, the sound of a car coming to a halt, boots ringing on the cobbles, steps and laughing voices at the door.

Captain Trucco had returned.

The door swung open. Into the room burst the worthy captain, with two of his chief aides, all three exuberant and filled with mirth. Trucco did not see Colonna at once, for the door opened back against him, but he saw Gorman and hailed him eagerly.

"Ha, my friend Tonio! You did very well this morning. There will be no more bombing; there are no more ships. Maybe we go out to Cristoff's farm for supper—"

A movement caught his eye and he saw Colonna, and froze. All three Fascists stood staring at the lieutenant; but Trucco seemed absolutely incapable of movement. His words died out. His very breath seemed to stop.

Colonna nodded pleasantly to the three, and turned to Gorman.

"Will you leave us, if you please. I have private business with these gentlemen. It is a pleasure to have met you."

"Colonna! Giovanni Colonna—it is you, in the flesh, alive!" burst out Trucco. "A thousand welcomes!"

Gorman stepped out of the room and closed the door. He heard Colonna's voice saying something in Italian. Something about Cirro and Africa and olive oil. Then he walked out of the house. A sentry was at the entrance now, and saluted him.

He felt as though in a dream. He knew what was going to happen inside that house—felt, rather than knew. That narrow white house with green shutters was a miniature Italy; what was taking place there was, on a tiny scale, what was taking place all over Italy, or soon would be. It was not his affair.

It came to him, as he stepped into the street, why Colonna had so positively assured him that Luigi Trucco would not look him up. But he could not escape the wild turmoil that suddenly welled up behind him; the staccato explosion of pistol shots, the clamor of shouts, the pound of booted feet echoing among the houses as a crowd swirled.

He strode rapidly along; he could not miss his way, the street brought him into the road and the open country. He thought of Cristoff, of the gentle face of the girl Helena, of the pleasant farmhouse and the little cove beside the sea. These beckoned him on; the town melted away behind. The dream faded, the unreality passed.

"No, I guess Trucco won't come this way again," Gorman muttered to himself. "I hope Colonna will come looking me up, though—but I don't expect he will. Poor devil! I don't blame him a bit."

He squared his shoulders and strode on down the long road, to what awaited him.

BEDFORD - JONES IS a Canadian by birth, but not by profession, having removed to the United States at the age of one year. For over twenty years he has been more or less profitably engaged in writing and traveling. As he has seldom resided in one place longer than a year or so and is a person of retiring habits, he is somewhat a man of mystery; more than once he has suffered from unscrupulous gentlemen who impersonated him—one of whom murdered a wife and was subsequently shot by the police, luckily after losing his alias.

The real Bedford-Jones is an elderly man, whose gray hair and precise attire give him rather the appearance of a retired foreign diplomat. His hobby is stamp collecting, and his collection of Japan is said to be one of the finest in existence. At present writing he is en route to Morocco, and when this appears in print he will probably be somewhere on the Mojave Desert in company with Erle Stanley Gardner.

Questioned as to the main facts in his life, he declared there was only one main fact, but it was not for publication; that his life had been uneventful except for numerous financial losses, and that his only adventures lay in evading adventurers. In his younger years he was something of an athlete, but the encroachments of age preclude any active pursuits except that of motoring. He is usually to be found poring over his stamps, working at his typewriter, or laboring in his California rose garden, which is one of the sights of Cathedral Cañon, near Palm Springs.

Bedford-Jones has written stories laid in many corners of the earth, but among his most popular tales were the John Solomon stories which started many years ago in the *Argosy*.